The Hundred Days

Also by Joseph Roth

THE
HUNDRED
DAYS

Joseph Roth

Translated by Richard Panchyk

A NEW DIRECTIONS BOOK

Originally published in German as *Die Hundert Tage* by Verlag Allert
de Lange in 1935.

First published in cloth by New Directions in 2014
Manufactured in the United States of America
New Directions Books are printed on acid-free paper.
Design by Erik Rieselbach

Library of Congress Cataloging-in-Publication Data
Roth, Joseph, 1894–1939.
[Hundert tage. English]
The hundred days / Joseph Roth ; translated from the German
by Richard Panchyk.
pages cm
This edition previously published: London ; Chicago : Peter Owen, 2011.
ISBN 978-0-8112-2278-5 (alk. paper)
1. Napoleon I, Emperor of the French, 1769–1821—Fiction.
I. Panchyk, Richard, translator. II. Title.
PT2635.O84H813 2014
833'.912—dc23   2014015141

10 9 8 7 6 5 4 3 2 1

New Directions Books are published for James Laughlin
by New Directions Publishing Corporation
80 Eighth Avenue, New York 10011

Contents

The Hundred Days

BOOK ONE

The Return of the Great Emperor

I

THE SUN EMERGED FROM THE CLOUDS, BLOODY-RED, tiny, and irritable, but was quickly swallowed up again into the cold gray of the morning. A sullen day was breaking. It was March 20, a mere day before the start of spring. One could see no sign of this. It rained and stormed across the whole land, and the people shivered.

The weather in Paris had been stormy since the previous night. The birds fell silent after a quick morning greeting. Cold and spiteful wisps of mist rose insidiously from the cracks between the cobbles, moistening anew the stones that had just been blown dry by the morning wind. The mist lingered about the willows and chestnuts in the parks and hovered along the edges of the avenues, causing the nascent tree buds to tremble, chasing clearly visible shivers along the damp backs of the patient livery horses and forcing down to ground level the industrious morning smoke that was here and there attempting to rise from chimneys. The streets smelled of fire, mist, and rain, of damp clothes, of lurking snow clouds and temporarily averted hail, of unfriendly winds, soaked leather, and foul sewers.

Despite this, the citizens of Paris did not remain in their homes. They began to gather in the streets at an early hour. They assembled themselves before the walls onto which broadsides had been affixed. These papers carried the farewell message of the King of France. Barely legible, they looked tear-soaked, for the night's rain had smeared the freshly inked letters and in places also dissolved the glue with which they were adhered to the stone. From time to time, a stormy gust of wind would blow a sheet completely off the wall and deposit it into the black mud of the street. These farewell words of the King of France met an ignoble fate, being ground into the muck of the road under the wheels of wagons, under the hooves of horses, and under the indifferent feet of pedestrians.

Many of the loyalists regarded these sheets with a wistful devotion. The heavens themselves seemed unfavorably disposed to him. Gales and rains zealously endeavored to obliterate his farewell message. Amid wind and rain, he had departed his palace and residence on the previous evening. "Do not make my heart heavy, my children!" he had said when they got on their knees and begged him to stay. He could not stay; the heavens were against him ... everyone could see this.

He was a good king. Few loved him, but many in the country liked him. He did not have a kind heart, but he was royal. He was old, portly, slow, peaceable, and proud. He had known the misfortune of homelessness, for he had grown old in exile. Like every unfortunate, he did not trust anyone. He loved moderation, peace, and quiet. He was lonely and aloof—for true kings are all lonely and aloof. He was poor and old, portly and slow, dignified, deliberate, and unhappy. Few loved him, but there were many in the land who liked him.

The old King was fleeing a menacing shadow—the shadow of the mighty Emperor Napoleon, who had for the last twenty days been on the march toward the capital. The Emperor cast his shadow before him, and it was a ponderous one. He cast it over France and over practically the entire world. He was known throughout France and the entire earth. His majesty was not derived through birth. Power was his majesty. His crown was a conquest and a capture, not an inheritance. He came from an unknown family. He even brought glory to his nameless ancestors. He had conferred splendor upon them instead of gaining it through them, as was the case for those who were born emperors and kings. Thus he was equally related to all the nameless masses as he was to old-fashioned majesty. By exalting himself he ennobled, crowned, and exalted each and every one of the nameless masses, and they loved him for that. For many years he had terrorized, besieged, and reined in the great ones of this earth, and that was the reason the commoners saw him as their avenger and accepted him as their lord. They loved him because he seemed to be one of them—and because he was nonetheless greater than them. He was an encouraging example to them.

The Emperor's name was known across the world—but few actually knew anything about him. For, like a true king, he was also lonely. He was loved and hated, feared and venerated, but seldom understood. People could only hate him or love him; fear him or worship him as a god. He was human.

He knew hate, love, fear, and veneration. He was strong and weak, daring and despondent, loyal and treacherous, passionate and cold, arrogant and simple, proud and humble, powerful and pitiable, trusting and suspicious.

He promised the people liberty and dignity—but whoever entered into his service surrendered their freedom and gave themselves completely to him. He held the people and the nations in low regard, yet nonetheless he courted their favor. He despised those who were born kings but desired their friendship and recognition. He believed in God yet did not fear Him. He was familiar with death but did not want to die. He placed little value upon life yet wished to enjoy it. He had no use for love but wanted to have women. He did not believe in loyalty and friendship yet searched tirelessly for friends. He scorned the world but wanted to conquer it anyway. He placed no trust in men until they were prepared to die for him—thus he made them into soldiers. So that he might be certain of their affection, he taught them to obey him. In order for him to be certain of them, they had to die. He wished to bring happiness to the world, and he became its plague. Yet he was loved even for his weak ways. For when he showed himself to be weak, the people realized he was one of their own kind, and they loved him because they felt a connection to him. And when he showed himself to be strong, they also loved him for that very reason, because he seemed not to be one of them. Those who did not love him hated him or feared him. He was both firm and fickle, true and treacherous, bold and shy, exalted and modest.

And now he was standing at the gates of Paris.

The orders that the King had introduced were discarded, in some instances out of fear and in others out of elation.

The colors of the King and his royal house had been white. Those who had acknowledged him wore white bows on their jackets.

But, as if by accident, hundreds had suddenly lost their white bows. Now they lay, rejected and disgraced butterflies, in the black muck of the streets.

The flower of the King and his royal house had been the virginally pure lily. Now, hundreds of lilies, of silk and cloth, lay discarded, disowned, and disgraced in the black muck of the streets.

The colors of the approaching Emperor, however, were blue, white, and red; blue as the sky and the distant future; white as the snow and death; and red as blood and freedom.

Suddenly, thousands of people appeared in the streets of the city wearing blue-white-red bows in their buttonholes and on their hats.

And instead of the proud, virginal lily, they wore the most unassuming of all flowers, the violet.

The violet is a humble and sturdy flower. It embodies the virtues of the anonymous masses. Nearly unrecognized, it blooms in the shadows of imposing trees, and with a modest yet dignified precocity it is the first of all the flowers to greet the spring. And its dark-blue sheen is equally reminiscent of the morning mist before daybreak and the evening mist before nightfall. It was the Emperor's flower. He was known as the "Father of the Violet."

Thousands of people could be seen streaming from the outskirts of Paris toward the center of the city, toward the palace, all of them adorned with violets. It was one day before the start of spring, an unfriendly day, a sullen welcome for spring. The violet, however, the bravest of all flowers, was already blooming in the woods outside the gates of Paris. It was as though these people from the suburbs were carrying the spirit of spring into the city of stone, toward the palace of stone. The freshly plucked bouquets of violets shone a radiant blue at the ends of the sticks held aloft by the men, between the warm and swelling breasts of the women, on the hats and caps that were being waved high in the air, in the joyful hands of the workers and craftsmen, on the swords of the officers, on the drums of the old percussionists and the silver cornets of the old trumpeters. At the front of some of the groups marched the drummers of the old Imperial Army. They rapped out old battle melodies on their old calfskin drums, let their drumsticks fly through the air and caught them again, like slender homing pigeons, in fatherly hands held open in welcome. Heading up other groups, or contained within their midst, marched the ancient trumpeters of the old army, who from time to time set their instruments upon their lips and blew the old battle calls of the Emperor, the simple, melancholy calls to death and triumph, each of which reminded a soldier of his own pledge to die for the Emperor and also of the last sigh of a beloved wife before he left her to lay down for the Emperor. In the midst of all the people, raised upon shoulders, were the Emperor's old officers. They swayed, or rather were swayed, above the surging heads of the crowd like living, human banners. They had their swords drawn. On the sword tips fluttered their hats, like little black flags decorated with the tricolored cockades of the Emperor and the people of France. And from time to time, as if compelled to release the oppressive longing that had quickly built up in their hearts once again, the men and women cried out: "Long live France! Long live the Emperor! Long live the people! Long live the Father of the Violet! Long live liberty! Long live the Emperor!" And once more: "Long live the Emperor!" Often, some enthusiast from within the center of the crowd would begin to sing. He sang the old songs of the old soldiers, from battles of days past, the songs that celebrate man's farewell to life, his prayer before death, the sung confession of the soldier lacking the time for final exoneration. They were songs proclaiming love of both life and death. They were tunes in which one could hear undertones of marching regiments and clattering muskets. Suddenly someone struck up a song that had not been heard for a long time, the "Marseillaise"—and all the many thousands joined in singing it. It was the song of the French people. It was the song of liberty and duty. It was the song of the motherland and of the whole world. It was the song of the Emperor just as the violet was his flower, as the eagle was his bird, as white, blue, and red were his colors. It glorified victory and even cast its sheen upon lost battles. It gave voice to the spirit of triumph and its brother death. Within it was both despair and reassurance. Anyone who sang the "Marseillaise" to himself joined the powerful community and fellowship of the many whose song it was. And anyone who sang it in the company of many others could feel his own loneliness in spite of the crowd. For the "Marseillaise" proclaimed both victory and defeat, communion with the world and the isolation of spirit, man's deceptive might and actual powerlessness. It was the song of life and the song of death. It was the song of the French people.

They sang it on the day that the Emperor Napoleon returned home.

II

MANY OF HIS OLD FRIENDS HURRIED TO MEET HIM EVEN
as he was still on his way home. Others prepared to greet him
in the city. The King's white banners had been hastily removed
from the tower of the city hall, already replaced by the fluttering
blue, white, and red of the Emperor. On the walls, which even
that same morning had still carried the King's farewell message,
there were now posted new broadsides, no longer rain-soaked
and tear-stained, but clear, legible, clean, and dry. At their tops,
mighty and steadfast, soared the Imperial eagle, spreading its
strong, black wings in protection of the neat black type, as if he
himself had dropped them, letter by letter, from his threatening
yet eloquent beak. It was the Emperor's manifesto. Once again
the Parisians gathered at these same walls, and in each group
read, in a loud voice, the Emperor's words. They had a different
tone from the King's wistful farewell. The Emperor's words were
polished and powerful and carried the roll of drums, the clarion
call of trumpets, and the stormy melody of the "Marseillaise."
And it seemed as if the voice of each reader of the Emperor's
words was transformed into the voice of the Emperor himself.
Yes, he who had not yet arrived was already speaking to the people of Paris through ten thousand heralds sent on ahead. Soon,
the very broadsides themselves seemed to be speaking from the
walls. The printed words had voices, the letters trumpeted their
message, and above them the mighty yet peacefully hovering
eagle, seemed to stir his wings. The Emperor was coming. His
voice was already speaking from all the walls.

His old friends, the old dignitaries and their wives, hurried to the
palace. The generals and ministers put on their old uniforms,
pinned on their Imperial decorations, and viewed themselves
in the mirror before leaving their homes, feeling that they had
only recently been revived. Even more elated were the ladies of
the Imperial court, as they once more donned their old clothes.

They were accustomed to viewing their youth as a thing of the past, their beauty as faded, their glory as lost. Now, however, as they put on their clothes, the symbols of their youth and their triumphant glory, they could actually believe that time had stood still since the Emperor's departure. Time, woman's enemy, had been halted in its track; the rolling hours, the creeping weeks, the murderously slow and boring months, had been only a bad dream. Their mirrors lied no more. Once again, they revealed the true images of youth. And with victorious steps, on feet more joyously winged than those of youth—for their feet were revived and had awakened to a second youth—the ladies entered their carriages and headed toward the palace amid cheers from the thronging, waiting crowds.

They waited in the gardens before the palace, clamoring at the gates. In every arriving minister and general they saw another of the Emperor's emissaries. Besides these exalted persons, there came also the lesser staff of the Emperor—the old cooks and coachmen and bakers and laundresses, grooms and riding-masters, tailors and cobblers, masons and upholsterers, lackeys and maids. And they began to prepare the palace for the Emperor so he would find it just as he had left it, with no reminders of the King who had fled. The exalted ladies and gentlemen joined the lowly servants in this work. In fact, the ladies of the Imperial court worked even more zealously than the servants. Disregarding their dignity and the damage to their delicate clothing or their carefully cultivated fingernails, they scratched, clawed, and peeled from the walls the tapestries and the white lilies of the King with vindictiveness, fury, impatience, and enthusiasm. Under the King's tapestries were the old and familiar symbols of the Emperor—countless golden bees with widespread, glassy, and delicately veined little wings and black-striped hind ends, Imperial insects, industrious manufacturers of sweetness. Soldiers carried in the Imperial eagles of shiny, golden brass and placed them in every corner, so that at the very moment of his arrival, the Emperor would know that his soldiers were awaiting him—even those who had not been able to be at his side upon his entrance.

In the meantime, night was falling, and the Emperor had still not arrived. The lanterns in front of the palace were lit. Streetlamps at every corner flared. They battled against fog, dampness, and the wind.

The people waited and waited. Finally, they heard the orderly trot of military horses' hooves. They knew it was the Thirteenth Dragoons. At the head of the squadron rode the Colonel, sabre shining a narrow flash in the gloom of the night. The Colonel cried: "Make way for the Emperor!" As he sat high upon his chestnut steed, which was barely visible in the darkness, his wide, pale face with its great black mustache over the heads of the thronging crowd, unsheathed weapon in his raised hand, repeating from time to time his cry "Make way for the Emperor!" and occasionally lit by the yellowish glint of the flickering streetlamps, he reminded the crowd of the militant and supposedly cruel guardian angel that was alleged to personally accompany the Emperor, for it seemed to the people that the Emperor, at this hour, was issuing orders even to his own guardian angel ...

Soon his dragoon-escorted coach came into view, the rumble of its hurried wheels inaudible over the trampling of the horses' hooves.

It stopped at the palace.

As the Emperor left the carriage, many pale, open hands reached for him. At that moment, entranced by the imploring hands, he lost his will and consciousness. These loving white hands that stretched toward him seemed to him more terrible than if they had belonged to armed enemies. Each hand was like a loving, yearning pale face. The love that streamed toward the Emperor from these bright, outstretched hands was like an intense and dangerous plea. What were the hands demanding? What did they want from him? These hands were praying, demanding, and compelling all at once; hands raised as if to the gods.

He shut his eyes and could feel the hands lifting him and carrying him along on unsteady shoulders up the palace steps. He heard the familiar voice of his friend General Lavalette: "It is you! It's you! It's you—my Emperor!" From the voice and the breath on his face he realized that his friend was in front of him, climbing the steps backward. The Emperor opened his eyes—and saw the open arms of his friend Lavalette and the white silhouette of his face.

This startled him, so he closed his eyes again. As if sleeping or unconscious, he was carried, led and supported along to his old room. Both frightened and happy, he seated himself at his writing table with a fearful joy in his heart.

He saw some of his old friends in the room as if through a fog. From the direction of the street, on the other side of the shut windows, he heard the boisterous shouts of the people, the whinnying of horses, the clinking of weapons, the high-pitched ring of spurs, and, from the hall behind the high white door opposite his seat, the murmuring and whispering of many voices; from time to time he seemed to recognize one of them. He was aware of everything that was going on; it seemed clear and immediate yet vague and distant, and all of it instilled in him both happiness and a feeling of awe. He felt that he was finally home and was at the same time being rescued from some kind of storm. Slowly he forced himself to pay attention; he commanded his eyes to notice and his ears to listen. He sat, perfectly still, at the writing table. The cries from just outside the windows were intended for him alone. It was for his sake that so many voices were murmuring and whispering in the hall beyond the closed door. Suddenly it seemed to him that he was looking at all of his countless thousands of friends throughout the entire great land of France, who were standing and waiting for him. Throughout the whole country millions cried, as hundreds were doing here: "Long live the Emperor!" In all the rooms of the palace they were whispering, chattering, and talking about him. He would have enjoyed allowing himself some leisure to think about himself from a stranger's perspective. But, behind his back, he could hear the ruthlessly steady ticking of the clock on the mantel. Time was passing; the clock began to strike the hour in a thin and sorrowful tone. It was eleven, one hour before midnight. The Emperor stood up.

He approached the window. From all the towers of the city

the bells chimed the eleventh hour. He loved the bells. He had loved them since childhood. He had little regard for churches and stood at a loss and sometimes even timidly before the Cross, but he loved the bells. They stirred his heart. Their chiming voices made him solemn. They seemed to be announcing more than just the hour and celebration of worship. They were the tongues of Heaven. What inhabitant of earth could comprehend their golden language? Every hour they rang out devoutly, and they alone knew which was the decisive hour. He remained at the window and listened eagerly to the fading echoes. Then he turned abruptly. He went to the door and yanked it open. He stood at the threshold and allowed his gaze to sweep across the faces of those who had assembled. They were all present; he recognized every last one, never having forgotten, since he himself created them. There were Régis de Cambacérès, Duke of Parma; the Dukes of Bassano, Rovigno and Gaeta, Thibaudeau, Decrès, Daru, and Davout. He glanced back into the room— there were his friends Caulaincourt and Exelmans and the naive young Fleury de Chaboulon. Yes, he still had friends. Some had betrayed him on occasion. Was he a god, who should scorn and punish? He was but a man. They, however, took him for a god. As from a god they demanded anger and revenge; as from a god they also expected forgiveness. But he had no time left to act like a god and become angry, punish, and forgive. He had no time. More clearly than the shouts of the crowd outside his windows and the racket made by his dragoons in the gardens and house, he could hear the soft but ruthless ticking of the clock on the mantel behind him. He had no time left to punish. He only had time to forgive and allow himself to be loved, to bestow and to give: favors, titles, and posts, all the pathetic presents an Emperor may give. Generosity requires less time than ire. He was generous.

III

THE BELLS STRUCK MIDNIGHT. TIME WAS FLYING, TIME was running out. The cabinet! The government! The Emperor needed a government! Can one govern without ministers and without friends? The ministers whom one appoints to oversee others must themselves be overseen! The friends one trusts, they themselves become distrustful and awaken distrust! Those who today cheer before the windows and turn night into day are fickle! The God in whom one puts one's trust is unknown and unseen. The Emperor has now assembled his cabinet. Names! Names! Decrès will be in charge of the Navy and Caulaincourt the Ministry of Foreign Affairs; Mollieu in charge of the Treasury and Gaudin overseeing Finances; Carnot will, he hopes, be the Minister of the Interior; Cambacérès the Lord Chancellor. Names! Names! From the towers strikes one, then two, and before long it will be daybreak ... Who will oversee the police?

The Emperor needed police and not just a guardian angel. The Emperor remembered his old Police Minister. His name was Fouché. The Emperor could easily order the arrest of this hated man, even his death. Fouché had betrayed him. He knew all the secrets in the land and all the Emperor's friends and enemies. He could betray and protect—and both at the same time. Yes, all of the Emperor's trusted friends had mentioned this man's name. He was clever, they said, and loyal to the powerful. Was the Emperor not mighty? Could anyone dare doubt his power or be allowed to see his anxiety? Was there a man in the country whom the Emperor should fear?

"Get me Fouché!" ordered the Emperor. "And leave me alone!"

IV

HE LOOKED AROUND THE ROOM FOR THE FIRST TIME
since he had entered. He stood before the mirror. He observed
the reflection of his upper body. He furrowed his brows, tried
to smile, pursed his lips, opened his mouth, and regarded his
healthy white teeth. He smoothed his black hair down onto his
forehead with his finger and smiled at his reflection, the great
Emperor grinning at the great Emperor. He was pleased with
himself. He took a few steps back and examined himself anew.
He was alone but he was strong, young, and vibrant. He feared
no treachery.

He walked about the room, looked at the tattered lilies of the
recently ripped-down tapestries, smirked, lifted one of the brass
eagles that stood in the corner, and finally stopped before a small
altar. It was a smooth piece made of black wood. A forlorn, faint
odor of incense escaped from the closed drawer, and on the altar stood, spectral white, a small ivory crucifix. The bony, angu-
lar, and bearded face of the Crucified One stood out, unmoving,
unchanging, and eternal, in the room lit only by flickering candlelight. They had forgotten to dismantle the altar, thought the
Emperor. Here had the King kneeled every morning. But Christ
had not heard him! "I don't need it!" the Emperor suddenly cried
out. "Away with it!" He raised his hand. And it was at that moment that he felt he should kneel. But at the very same instant he
brushed the cross to the ground with the back of his hand, which
he had opened as if to smack someone across the head. It fell with
a hard, dull thud to the narrow swath of uncarpeted flooring. The
Emperor bent down. The cross was broken. The Savior lay on the
narrow strip of pale, bare floor, His thin ivory arms outstretched,
no longer torturously constrained by the Cross. His white beard
and narrow nose faced the ceiling, with only His crossed legs and
feet still attached to what was left of the little crucifix.

At that moment someone knocked on the door and announced the Minister of Police.

V

THE EMPEROR REMAINED WHERE HE WAS STANDING. HIS left boot covered the whitish crucifix fragments. He folded his arms, as was his custom when he was waiting, when he was pondering or when he wished to create the impression he was thinking. He held himself such that he could feel his body and count and regulate his heartbeat with his right hand. People knew and loved this stance of his. He had rehearsed it hundreds of times before the mirror. He had been painted and drawn in this pose thousands of times. These pictures hung in thousands of rooms in France and all over the world, even in Russia and Egypt. Yes, he knew his Police Minister—dangerous, skeptical, old, and unchanging, a man who had never been young and had never believed in anything. A scrawny, brilliant spider who had woven webs and destroyed them; tenacious, patient, and without passion. This most doubtful of men, this faithless priest, was received by the Emperor in the stance in which millions of his followers were used to seeing him. As he stood there, arms crossed, he not only felt it himself but also made this hated man feel the faith of the millions of followers who revered and loved the Emperor with his folded arms. The Emperor waited for the Minister like a statue of himself.

The Minister was now standing before him in the room, head bowed. The Emperor did not move. It was as if the Minister had not bowed his head as one does before the great ones but rather as one does when one is hiding one's face or searching for something on the ground. The Emperor thought of the broken crucifix, which he was covering with his left boot and would certainly have hidden from anyone, not only the glare of this policeman. It seemed to the Emperor undignified to move from his place yet also undignified to be concealing something.

"Look at me!" he ordered, injecting his voice with its old, victorious ring. The Minister lifted his head. He had a wizened face and eyes of indeterminable color, somewhere between pale and dark, which endeavored in vain to stay wide open, to counter the compulsion of the eyelids, which kept drooping on their own, although he seemed constantly to be trying to keep them up. His Imperial uniform was immaculate and proper, but, as though to indicate the unusual hour of night at which its wearer found himself requested, it was not completely closed. As if by accident, a button on his vest had been left undone. The Emperor was to notice this defect, and he did. "Finish dressing!" he said. The Minister smiled and closed the button.

"Your Majesty," began the Minister, "I am your servant!"

"A faithful servant!" said the Emperor.

"One of your truest!" replied the Minister.

"That has not been particularly noticeable," said the Emperor softly, "in the last ten months."

"But in the last two," answered the Minister, "I have been preparing myself for the joy of seeing Your Majesty here now. For the last two months."

The Minister spoke slowly and faintly. He neither raised nor lowered his voice. The words crept out of his small mouth like plump, well-fed shadows, robust enough to be audible but mindful not to seem as vigorous as the Emperor's words. He kept his long, slightly bent hands calmly and respectfully at his sides. It was as if he were also paying homage with his hands.

"I've decided," said the Emperor, "to bury the past. Do you hear, Fouché? The past! It is not very pleasant."

"It is not pleasant, Your Majesty."

He grows trusting, thought the Emperor.

"There will be much to do, Fouché," he said. "These people mustn't be given time. We must anticipate them. Incidentally, is there any news from Vienna?"

"Bad news, Majesty," said the Minister. "The Imperial Minister for Foreign Affairs, Monsieur Talleyrand, has spoiled everything. He serves the enemies of Your Majesty better than he has ever served Your Majesty. I have never—as Your Majesty will recall—taken him for sincere. There will be much to do, truly! A steady hand will be required to carry out all the tasks ..."

Fouché kept his hands at his sides, half closed, as if hiding something in them. The rather lengthy gold-embroidered palms on his sleeves seemed to purposely conceal his wrists. Only the long, eager fingers were visible. Traitor's fingers, thought the Emperor. Fingers made for spinning malicious little tales at a writing-table. These hands have no muscles. I will not make him my Foreign Minister!

While he was pondering, the Emperor had unintentionally lifted his foot off the crucifix fragments. He wanted to go to the window. He thought he saw Fouché stealing a glimpse at the cross from under his sagging eyelids, and he felt embarrassed. He took a quick step forward, lifted his chin and said in a loud and commanding voice, so as to bring the meeting to a rapid end: "I appoint you my Minister!"

The Minister did not budge. Only the lid of his right eye rose a bit above the pupil, as though he were just waking. It seemed his eye was listening but not his ear.

In a voice that seemed to the Minister rather casually unceremonious, the Emperor continued: "You will head the Ministry of Police, which you have previously overseen in such a meritorious fashion."

At that moment, the interested eyelid fell back over the pupil. It veiled a slight green gleam.

The Minister did not move. He is pondering, thought the Emperor, and he is pondering too long.

Finally Fouché bowed. From a rather dry throat came his words: "It gives me sincere pleasure to be permitted to serve Your Majesty once again."

"*Au revoir*, Duke of Otranto," said the Emperor.

Fouché rose up from his bow. He stood rigidly for a little while, gazing wide-eyed with astonishment in the direction of the Emperor's boots, between which lay the shimmering bits of the crucifix.

Then he left.

He strode through the hall, occasionally offering a half-hearted greeting to an acquaintance without lifting his head. His steps were silent. He walked gently in light shoes, as though in stockinged feet, down the stone steps, past the crouching, lying, and snoring dragoons, into the garden, past the whinnying and pawing horses, past the half-lit rooms and not yet fully closed doors. He moved carefully among the strewn harnesses and leather gear. When he stood before the gate he whistled softly. His secretary appeared. "Good morning, Gaillard," he said. "We're policemen again. He can only make war and not politics! In three months I will be more than him!" He indicated with his finger backward over his shoulder toward the palace.

"It already looks like an army camp," said Gaillard.

"It already looks like war," replied the Minister.

"Yes," said Gaillard. "But a lost one."

Side by side, like brothers, they went down the street into the late-night mist, completely at home in it, and soon completely enveloped by it.

VI

TIME WAS INEXORABLE, APPEARING TO THE EMPEROR TO pass more rapidly than ever before in his life. Sometimes he had the humiliating feeling that it no longer obeyed him as it had years ago. Years ago! he said to himself and started to calculate, then caught himself at it, thinking and counting like an old man. Previously he alone had ordained and directed the course of the hours. It was he who shaped and filled them, it was his might and name that they proclaimed in many corners of the world. These days, perhaps the people still obeyed him, but time was fleeing from him, melting away and vanishing whenever he attempted to grasp it. Or maybe the people no longer obeyed him either! To think, he had only left them on their own for a brief while. For a few short months they had ceased to feel his taming, alluring glance, the firm yet flattering touch of his hand, the threatening and tender, the harsh and seductive tones of his voice. No, they certainly had not forgotten him—could anyone forget a man of his kind?—but they had lost touch with him. They had lived without him, many of them even turning against him and falling into league with his royal enemies. They had grown accustomed to living without him.

He sat there, alone amid a frequently changing selection of acquaintances and friends. Soon his brothers, sisters, and mother came. Time passed. It grew brighter and warmer, and the spring of Paris became vigorous and magnificent. It seemed practically like summer. The blackbirds warbled in the Tuileries gardens, and the lilacs had already begun to emit their deliberate, strong fragrance. On many an evening the Emperor could hear the nightingale's song as he walked alone through the garden, hands behind his back, gaze lowered toward the gravel pathway. Spring had arrived. At such times he realized that all his life he had been aware of the ever-changing seasons in the same way that he had been used to taking notice of favorable or unfavorable opportunities, of precisely followed or completely misunderstood orders, of agreeable or objectionable situations, of Nature's benevolent or malevolent moods. The earth was a terrain, the sky a friend or enemy, the hill an observation point, the valley a trap, the brook an obstacle, the mountain a shelter, the forest an ambush, the night a respite, the morning an offensive, daytime a battle, and evening a victory or a defeat. It had been that simple. Years ago! thought the Emperor.

He returned home. He wanted to see the painting of his son. In gloomy times he longed for his child more than his own mother. Abnormal as he was, the product of a caprice of Nature, it was as if he had perverted its laws, and he was no longer the child of his race, but had in truth become the father of his forefathers. His ancestors lived through his name. And Nature was vengeful—he knew that! Since it had allowed him to endow his forefathers with glory, it was bound to keep him apart from his own offspring. My child! thought the Emperor. He thought of his son with the tenderness of a father, of a mother, and also that of a child. My unhappy child! he thought. He is my son— is he also my heir? Is Nature so benevolent that she will bring forth my mirror image? I have fathered him; he was born to me. I want to see him.

He looked upon the picture, at the chubby-cheeked face of the King of Rome. He was a good, round child, like thousands of others, healthy and innocent. His soft eyes gazed out with devotion into the still unknown, terrible, beautiful, and dangerous world. He is my blood! thought the Emperor. There will be nothing left to conquer, but he will be able to preserve what he has. I have good advice for him ... yet I cannot see him!

The Emperor took a couple of steps back. It was late afternoon, and the twilight seeped through the open window and crept slowly up the walls. The dark clothes of the Imperial son merged with it imperceptibly. Only his sweet and distant face continued to shine with a pale luminosity.

VII

ON THE TABLE WAS AN HOURGLASS OF POLISHED BERYL. Through its narrow neck, filling the bottom bulb, flowed a relentless stream of soft yellowish sand. It seemed only to be a slow trickle, yet the bottom appeared to fill quickly. Thus the Emperor had his enemy, Time, constantly before his eyes. He often amused himself with the childish game of tipping the glass before the sand had finished its journey. He believed in the mysterious significance of dates, days, and hours. He had returned on March 20. His son had been born on March 20. And it was on March 20 that he had one of his guileless enemies executed— the Duke of Enghien. The Emperor had an excellent memory— but so did the dead. How long until the dead took their revenge?

The Emperor heard the hours passing even when speaking to his ministers, friends, or advisors, and also when outside, before the windows, the frenzied crowd was issuing its shouts. The patient, measured, uniform voice of the clock was stronger than the roaring of the masses. And he loved it more than the voice of the people. The people were fickle friends, but Time was a loyal enemy. Those hateful cries still rang in his ears, the ones he had heard when he departed the country ten months earlier, vanquished and powerless. Every jubilant shout from this crowd was a painful reminder of each of the hateful cries of the other crowd.

Oh! He still had to rally those who were unsteady in their faith, to make the liars believe they were not lying to him and to show love to those he did not love. He envied his enemy, the lethargic old king who had fled with his arrival. The King had ruled in God's name and through the strength of his ancestors alone had kept the peace. He, however, the Emperor, had to make war. He was only the general of his soldiers.

VIII

IT WAS A MILD MORNING IN APRIL. THE EMPEROR LEFT
the palace. He rode through the city on his white horse, wrapped
in his gray military cloak, wearing his martial yet delicate boots
of soft kid leather on which his gallant silver spurs shimmered
menacingly, black hat on lowered head, which from time to time
he unexpectedly lifted as though he were suddenly coming out
of deep meditation. He paced his animal. It drummed with its
hooves softly and evenly upon the stones. As those who watched
the Emperor ride by heard the patter of the horse's hooves, they
had the feeling they were listening to the hypnotic, measured call
of threatening war drums. They remained still, removed their
hats, and shouted "Long live the Emperor!"—moved, unsettled,
and also certainly shocked at the sight of him. They knew this
image from the thousands of portraits that hung in their rooms
and the rooms of their friends, decorated the edges of the plates
from which they ate each day, the cups from which they drank,
and the metallic handles of the knives with which they sliced
their bread. It was an intimate, familiar, yes, quite familiar picture of the great Emperor in his gray cloak and his black hat on
his white horse. That was the reason they were often startled
when they saw it come to life—the living Emperor, the living
horse, the genuine cloak, the actual hat.

He rode considerably ahead of his retinue; the magnificently
uniformed generals and ministers followed at a respectful distance.

The cheery early sunlight was filtering through the fresh,
light-green crowns of the trees along the edges of the avenues
and in the gardens of Paris. The people did not wish to believe
the sinister rumors that came from many corners of the country.
For days now there had been talk of revolts against the Emperor
by those still loyal to the King. It was also said that the powerful ones of the world had decided to destroy the Emperor and
France along with him. Fortified and terrible, the enemy waited
at all the borders of the land. The Empress was in Vienna at the

house of her father, the Austrian Emperor. She did not come home; they would not let her return to France. The Emperor's son was also being held captive in Vienna. Death was lying in wait at all the French frontiers. Yet on this bright day the people were willing to forget about the sinister rumors, the war waiting at the frontiers and lurking death. They preferred to believe the happy news that the papers printed. And when they saw the Emperor riding through the city, looking just as they had always imagined him, mighty and serene, clever and great and bold, the Lord of Battles, riding in the young spring of the Parisian streets, it seemed obvious to them that the heavens were on their side, the Emperor's side, and they released themselves to the comforting melody of this joyous day and their joyful hearts.

The Emperor was riding to Saint-Germain, as it was Parade Day. The Emperor halted. He removed his hat. He saluted the assembled people of Saint-Germain, the workers and soldiers. He knew that the simple folk liked his smooth black hair and the smooth curl that fell over his forehead of its own will and yet obediently. He looked perfectly poor and simple to those poor and simple people when he appeared before them bareheaded. The sun was nearing its zenith and beat hotly upon his uncovered head. He did not move. He forced his horse and himself to uphold that statuesque stillness, the powerful effects of which he had known for years. From the midst of the crowd, in which flamed hundreds of women's red scarves, came the familiar sour and greasy odor of sweat, the unpleasant smell of the poor on holiday, the scent of their jubilant excitement. Emotion gripped the Emperor. He sat, hat in hand. He did not love the people. He distrusted their enthusiasm and their smell. But he smiled anyway from his white horse, the rigid sweetheart of the crowd, an Emperor and a monument.

In rigid squares stood the soldiers, his old soldiers. How alike they looked, the sergeants, the corporals, and the privates, all of whom death had spared and who had been reabsorbed into the harsh poverty of peasant life. One name after another occurred to the Emperor. There were some whom he remembered well and whom he could have called out. His heart was silent. He was ashamed. They loved him, and he was ashamed that they loved him because he could feel only sympathy for them. He sat on his sunlit and doubly luminous white horse, his head uncovered, hemmed and pressed by the jubilation. Inside the squares the old soldiers now began to beat their drums. How well they drummed! Now he waved his hat, and loosening the reins a bit and easing the pressure of his knees so that the horse understood and started to frisk, the Emperor began to speak—and it seemed to the people in the crowd as if the drums that they had just heard at this point were bestowed with a human voice, an Imperial voice. "My comrades," began the Emperor, "connoisseurs of my battles and my victories, witnesses to my fortunes and misfortunes …"

The white horse perked its ears and gently pawed with its front hoof in time with the Emperor's words.

The sun stood at its zenith and glowed, youthful and mild.

The Emperor put on his hat and dismounted.

IX

HE APPROACHED THE CROWD. THEIR ADORATION HIT him with their every breath, it shone from their faces as brightly as the sun from the heavens, and he suddenly felt that he had always been one of them. At that moment the Emperor saw himself as his devotees saw him, on thousands of pictures on plates, knives, and walls; already a legend, yet still living.

During his long months in exile, he had missed these people. They were the people of France; he knew them. They were ready to love or hate in an instant. They were solemn and derisive, easily inspired but difficult to persuade, proud in squalor, generous in good fortune, devout and thoughtless in victory, bitter and vengeful in defeat, playful and childlike in peace, merciless and irresistible in battle, easily disappointed, trusting and distrusting at the same time, forgetful and quickly appeased by the right word, always ready for thrills, yet ever loving of moderation. These were the people of Gaul, the French people, and the Emperor liked them.

He no longer felt mistrust. They surrounded him. They shouted at him "Long live the Emperor!" as he stood in their midst, and it was as if they wished to prove to him that even when he stood among them, they could not forget he was their Emperor. He was their child and their Emperor.

He embraced one of the older non-commissioned officers. The man had a somber, sallow, bold, and bony face, a long, flowing, thick, and neatly combed graying mustache, and he towered a full head above the Emperor. During their embrace it looked as though the Emperor was under the protection of the thin, bony soldier. The man leaned forward clumsily, a bit comically, hindered by his own awkward height and the corpulent shortness of His Majesty, and allowed himself to receive a kiss on the right cheek. The Emperor tasted the smell of his sallow skin, the sharp vinegar that the man had rubbed on his freshly shaved cheeks, the tiny beads of sweat that dripped from his forehead, and also the tobacco on his breath. There was an intimate familiarity to the entire crowd. Yes, this was the odor of the people from whom the soldiers had sprung, the wonderful soldiers of the country of France; this was the very scent of loyalty, the loyalty of the soldiers—sweat, tobacco, blood, and vinegar. When he embraced one of them, he embraced all of them, the whole of his great army, all its dead and all its living descendants. And the people who saw the short, chubby Emperor in the protective arms of the tall, thin soldier felt as if they too were being embraced by the Emperor, as if they themselves held him. Tears filled the spectators' eyes, and with hoarse voices they cried out: "Long live the Emperor!" but the lustful desire to cry stifled their cheering throats. The Emperor relaxed his arms. The man took three steps backward. The old soldier stiffened. Under his bushy, bristling eyebrows his small black eyes lit up with the dangerous yet obedient fire of loyalty.

"Where have you fought?" asked the Emperor.

"At Jena, Austerlitz, Eylau, and Moscow, my Emperor!" replied the sergeant.

"What is your name?"

"Lavernoile, Pierre Antoine!" thundered the soldier.

"I thank you," cried the Emperor loudly enough so that all could hear him. "I thank you, Lieutenant Pierre Antoine Lavernoile!"

The newly minted lieutenant stiffened again. He took another step backward, raised his lean brown hand, waved it like a flag, and cried in a choked-up voice: "Long live the Emperor!" He stepped back into the ranks of his comrades from which the Emperor had summoned him and said softly to all those who gathered around him: "Just think, he recognized me instantly! 'You were,' he said, 'at Jena, Austerlitz, Eylau, and Moscow, my dear Lavernoile! You have no decorations. You will. I promote you to lieutenant.'"

"He knows us all," said one of the non-commissioned officers.

"He hasn't forgotten any of us!" said another.

"He recognized him," whispered dozens. "He knew his name.

He even knew both his first and middle names. 'Pierre Antoine Lavernoile,' he said, 'I know you.'"

Meanwhile, the Emperor mounted his horse again. Lavernoile, he thought, poor gangly Lavernoile! Happy Lavernoile! He raised his hat, stood erect in his stirrups, visible to all, and called out with a voice accustomed to being heard and understood over the noise of cannon: "People of Paris!" he shouted "Long live France!"

He turned his horse. Everyone swarmed him, separating him, his radiant animal and his gray cloak from his retinue. There were hundreds of people around him, men in uniform and civilian clothes and women whose red scarves glinted in the youthful sunshine.

X

HE HEADED HOME, WEARY, SAD, AND ASHAMED. HE WAS
always embracing unknown poor people, giving them titles and
orders, buying their support and winning them over. They loved
him. Yet he was indifferent to them. He was ashamed. If he had
to embrace one more Lavernoile ...! Was that the name? Lavernoile? There were thousands of non-commissioned officers in
the Emperor's great army, hundreds of thousands of soldiers.
He was ashamed, the great Emperor of the little Lavernoiles ...

XI

THE EMPEROR ORDERED THAT IN EACH CITY IN THE land one hundred cannon rounds be fired. This was his language. This was how he proclaimed to the people that he had beaten his rebellious enemies, the friends of the King.

The cannon resounded throughout the land, sending their mighty echoes far and wide. The people had not heard the thunder of cannon for some time. They were startled when the sound came to them again. They recognized once more the mighty voice of the returning Emperor. Even peace was proclaimed with artillery.

The Emperor's brother said: "Why did you fire cannon? It would have been better to ring bells."

"Yes," replied the Emperor. "I love the bells, you know that! I would have liked to hear them. But the bells can wait. I'll let them ring once I've defeated my powerful enemies, my true enemies."

"To whom are you referring?" asked his brother.

The Emperor said slowly and solemnly: "The whole world!"

His brother stood. At that moment he was afraid of the entire world, which was the Emperor's enemy, but he was also afraid of this brother who had the whole world as an enemy. Outside, at the door, before he had entered, he felt pity and anxiety for the Emperor but had decided not to reveal it to his face. But now, as he stood before him, he gave in, as usual, to the Imperial gaze and the Imperial voice. The brother felt as though he were one of the mighty Emperor's anonymous grenadiers.

"Sit down," said the Emperor. "I have something very important to tell you. Only you, and to you alone can I say it. I would have liked to have had the bells rung, but I ordered the cannon to be fired because the bells would have been a lie—a lie—as well as a promise I cannot keep. There is yet no peace, my brother! I must make the people familiar with cannon fire. I want peace, but I am forced toward war. If my postmaster had not deprived them of horses, all the ambassadors of the various countries would have left Paris long ago. They were accredited by the King. They are not guests of the French people or the Emperor. They delay my couriers at the frontiers. The Empress receives none of my letters. Oh, my brother! If one comes from our family, he knows nothing about this great world. That's our mistake, my brother, a peasant mistake. I have humbled the kings, but to be humbled by me, by people like me, by people like us, doesn't make them small. It only makes them more vengeful than they already were. The lowest of my grenadiers is nobler than they. It was an easy matter to defeat the poor rebels in the country. That doesn't merit any bell ringing. There are still more enemies, even in France—the representatives of the people. They are not the people—they are the chosen of the people. The Parliament! I am subservient to them. But I alone can will freedom, I alone, because I am powerful enough to preserve it. I am the Emperor of the French because I am their General."

"So you will wage war," his brother said softly.

"War," answered the Emperor.

XII

HE NEEDED THREE HUNDRED THOUSAND NEW GUNS. HE ordered them. And so there began, in all the factories of the land, a mighty hammering and forging and casting and soldering and welding. He also needed men for the three hundred thousand guns. And so, throughout the country, young men left their sweethearts, their wives, their mothers, and their children. He needed provisions. So all the bakers in the land began with triple zeal to bake loaves that would keep fresh; all the butchers in the land began to salt their meats in order to make them last longer; all the distillers brewed ten times more liquor than usual—liquor, the drink of warriors, making cowards brave and brave men still braver.

He ordered and ordered. The submission of his people filled him with lustful delight, and this lust for power made him place still more new orders.

XIII

IT WAS POURING RAIN WHEN THE EMPEROR MOVED INTO the other palace, the Elysée, outside the city. Nothing could be heard except the powerful, uniform drubbing of the rain on the dense treetops in the park. One could no longer hear the voices of the city or the loyal, dogged cheers of the people: "Long live the Emperor!" It was a good, warm early summer's rain. The fields needed it, the peasants blessed it, and the earth absorbed it willingly, greedily. The Emperor, however, was thinking of rain's negative effects. Rain softens the ground, so that soldiers cannot easily march, and soaks a soldier's uniform. The rain could also make the enemy practically invisible under certain conditions. Rain makes a soldier weak and sick. One needs the sun to plan a campaign. The sun fosters acceptance and serenity. The sun makes soldiers drunk and generals sober. Rain is not useful to the enemy who is attacking, but rather to the one waiting to be attacked. Rain turns day practically into night. When it rains the peasant-soldiers think about their fields back home, then about their children, and then about their wives. Rain was an enemy of the Emperor.

For an hour he stood at the open window and listened to the unrelenting downpour with devoted and weary concentration. He saw the whole land, the entire country, whose Emperor and supreme lord he was, divided into fields, gardens and forests, into villages and towns. He saw thousands of ploughs, heard the deliberate swishing of scythes and the more rapid shorter strokes of whirring sickles. He saw the men in the barns, in the stables, among the sheaves, in the mills, each one devoting himself to a peaceful love of industry, anticipating the evening soup after a full day and then to a night of lustful sleep in his wife's arms. Sun and rain, wind and daylight, night and fog, warm and cold, these were things familiar to the peasant, the pleasant or unpleasant gifts of the heavens. At times an old longing rose up from deep within the Emperor's soul, one that he had not felt during the confused years of his victories and defeats—nostalgia for the earth. Alas! His ancestors had also been peasants!

The Emperor, his face turned to the window, remained alone in the dusk. The bitter fragrance of the earth and the leaves mixed with the sweetness of the chestnut flowers and lilacs, the moist breath of the rain which smelled of decay and faraway seaweed wafted into the room. The rain, the evening, and the trees in the park conversed peacefully with an intimate rustling in the pleasant dusk.

So, as he was, bareheaded, the Emperor left the room. He wanted to go to the park, to feel the soft rain. All around the house, lights were already burning. The Emperor walked quickly, almost angrily. He strode through the harsh brightness of the halls, head lowered as he passed the guards. He entered the park, walked up and down, hands behind his back, to and fro along the same short and wide avenue, listening to the busy conversation between the rain and the leaves.

Suddenly, to his right, from amid the dense darkness of the trees, he heard a strange and suspicious sound. He knew that there were men who wished to kill him. The thought flashed through his mind that it would be a ridiculous end for an Emperor such as he—in a peaceful park, in the midst of this ridiculous rain, a wretched assassination, a wretched death. He walked between the trees across the soaked ground and headed in the direction from which the noise seemed to have come, when to his consternation and amusement he spotted a woman a few steps ahead. Her white bonnet shimmered. "Over here!" called the Emperor. "Over here!" he called again when the woman did not move. Now she approached. She stood face to face with the Emperor, hardly two strides away from him. She was without doubt a servant woman. Probably, thought the Emperor, she has just left a man's company. The same old story! They amused him, these everyday common stories.

"Why are you crying?" asked the Emperor. "And what are you doing here?"

The woman did not reply. She lowered her head.

"Answer!" ordered the Emperor. "Come closer!" The woman stepped close to him. Now he could see her. She was certainly one of his serving maids.

The woman fell to her knees, onto the damp earth. She kept her head lowered. Her hair nearly touched the tops of his boot-legs. He bent down toward her. Finally, she spoke.

"The Emperor," she said. And a few moments later: "Napoleon! My Emperor!"

"Stand up!" ordered the Emperor. "Tell me what's wrong."

She must have detected impatience and menace in his voice. She rose. "Tell me!" ordered the Emperor. He grabbed her arm and led her into the avenue. He stopped, let go of her, and ordered once more: "Tell me!"

Now he saw from the reflection that fell upon the windows along the avenue that the woman was young.

"I'll have you punished!" said the Emperor, at the same time caressing her wet face with his hand. "Who are you?"

"Angelina Pietri," said the woman.

"From Corsica?" asked the Emperor—the name was familiar.

"Ajaccio," whispered the woman.

"Run! Quickly!" ordered the Emperor.

The woman turned, lifted her skirts with both hands, ran across the stones, and vanished around the corner.

He continued onward, slowly. Ajaccio, he thought. Angelina Pietri from Ajaccio.

He changed his clothes. He was going to the opera. He arrived in the middle of the second act. He stood upright in the box, hat on his head. A brilliant strip of his dazzling snow-white riding breeches shimmered above the deep-red velvet of the balustrade. The audience stood and stared at the box where he sat, as the orchestra played the "Marseillaise."

"Long live the Emperor!" called one of the actors from the stage. The whole house echoed this.

He waved and left the box. On the staircase he turned to his adjutant and said: "Note this: Angelina Pietri from Ajaccio."

He forgot the name again instantly. He thought only of Ajaccio.

XIV

HE NEEDED WEAPONS, SOLDIERS, AND A GRAND PARADE.
For the benefit of the representatives of the people, whom he disdained, for his soldiers, whom he loved, for the priests of the faith (in which he did not believe) and for the people of Paris, whose love he feared, he intended to show himself as the protector of the country and of freedom. For a few hours on this day all the workshops in which preparations were being made were idle. The forges and ironworks were shut. However, the millers, bakers, butchers, and distillers were busy preparing for the celebration. For this day the soldiers were to don the new uniforms that had been made for the war.

The master of ceremonies developed a plan for a grandiose and drawn-out display.

The celebration took place on June 1. The day was one of the warmest since the Emperor's return. It was a hot and ripe summer's day. It was a strange heat, unknown this time of year. The year seemed hasty to reach maturity. The lilacs were already past their peak. The cockchafers had quickly disappeared. The great chestnut leaves had reached their full size and achieved their deep-green color. In the woods the strawberries had long since been ripening. Thunderstorms occurred frequently and with midsummer's intensity. The sun blazed; its brilliance was savage. Even on calm, cloudless days the swallows dived very low, practically touching the cobbles in the streets, as they did in other years only before impending rain. Here and there could be heard whispers, both open and hushed, of coming disaster. The newspapers of the land promised peace, but in all the villages and all the towns new recruits were drafted and old soldiers were recalled into the army. And not without dread did the people hear the armorers hammering away busily. They listened with horror as the butchers told of the magnitude of the government's order, and they watched the menacing zeal of the soldiers drilling on the parade ground. And on this festive day they were curious, indeed, but also distrustful.

Soon the celebration began on the great festival ground. Representing each regiment there were officers, both commissioned and non-commissioned, and privates. Two hundred men bore the shining Imperial eagles of brass and gold; here stood the dignitaries of the Légion d'Honneur and the Councillors of State, there the university professors, the city judges, members of the city council, the cardinals, the bishops, the Imperial Guard, and the Garde Nationale. The sabres and bayonets of forty-five thousand troops glinted. Hundreds of cannon thundered. In every direction there were people, a solid wall of people, a vast and anonymous mass, curious, pitiable, and full of zeal. The sun burned ever stronger over the wide, shadeless plaza. From time to time a harsh word of command was heard, a short drum roll, the blare of a trumpet, the clanging rattle of arms, the dull thud of guns on the ground. The people waited. And ever more fierce burned the sun.

Then they heard the Emperor coming. He arrived in a gilded carriage drawn by eight horses, the white plumes on their heads swaying arrogantly, proud silver flames; on both sides rode his marshals. His pages were dressed in green, red, and gold. Dragoons and mounted grenadiers followed behind. The Emperor arrived. He was hardly recognizable in his mother-of-pearl-colored cloak, breeches of white satin, and white-feathered black velour hat. He was barely recognized in the presence of his white-clad brother. He mounted the tribune, a massive, high throne. On either side of him stood his brothers and below him were chancellors, ministers, and marshals. So magnificent were they all that they too were hardly recognizable.

He felt as lonely as ever. Had anyone recognized him? He stood there, alone on his raised throne, under a blue sky, under a hot sun, high above the people and soldiers, between the wide, blue, calm, and enigmatic heavens and his audience, which was equally vast and mysterious.

He began to speak. He was confident of the power of his voice. But today even his own voice seemed strange to him. "We do not want the King," he cried, "as our enemies do. Faced with the choice between war and humiliation, we choose war ..."

A few days earlier, when he had jotted down these words, they had seemed to him very simple and natural. He knew the French. Honor was their god, disgrace their devil. They were the best soldiers in the world, for they served the Goddess of Honor, the warrior's most unrelenting mistress. But as for the Emperor himself, what god did he obey?

This question began to gnaw at him while he recited his manifesto with his alien voice. For the first time he was speaking to his Frenchmen from a great high platform; for the first time he wore a silken mother-of-pearl-colored cloak and on his head a strange hat with strange feathers. For the first time he felt the relentless, desolate emptiness of physical solitude. Alas! It was not the same familiar solitude that he had always known. It was not the loneliness of the mighty, nor the betrayed, nor the exiled, nor the humiliated. Here, upon this great, elevated platform, ruled the solitude of the physically alone. The great Emperor was filled with a sense of hollow prominence. Not a single one of the thousands of faces could he distinguish. He only saw over their heads; over the caps and hats, and far in the background were the unrecognizable faces of the crowd called "the people." And his words seemed to him as hollow as his solitude. There, upon the tribune, he felt as if he were on some bizarre and absurd apparatus, on a throne and stilts at the same time. His cloak was just a disguise, the crowd was an audience, and he and the officials were actors. He was accustomed to speaking in the midst of his soldiers, dressed in his customary uniform, feeling the exhalation of those around him, detecting the beloved smell of sweat and tobacco, of pungent leather and caustic boot polish. But now he stood high above these odors, poor and great, empty and disguised, alone under the blazing sun. Even the weightless plumes on his head were a heavy burden, feeling like useless and ridiculous massive lead feathers. He suddenly removed his hat, practically yanking it off his head. Now, from all directions, the people could see his familiar dark, shiny hair. With a powerful thrust of his shoulders, he shed his cloak. It seemed that his shoulders themselves had done the work of his hands in casting it away. Now everyone could see him in his familiar uniform, just as it was depicted on a hundred thousand walls, on plates, on knives, in all rooms, in all the cottages of many lands. And with a different voice, that is to say, with his old familiar tone, he cried: "And you, soldiers, my brothers in life and in the face of death, comrades of my victories!" It was completely still. The Emperor's voice echoed through the stifling air. The deputies and officials were no longer attentive; they were desperate for some shade. The people and the soldiers, however, were too far from the Emperor. They understood only every third word. But they now saw him as they loved him. And thus they cried: "Long live the Emperor!"

The Emperor quickly ended his speech. He hurried down the steps toward the cheers of the crowd. Ceremony dictated that he descend the steps with a deliberate slowness. But he was overcome with the impatience of a homecomer. He had lingered up there for too long, ungrounded. Ever quicker were his steps. More like a soldier than an Emperor, he practically leaped from the bottom step to the earth.

One could see on the abandoned platform his mother-of-pearl-colored cloak, limp and pitiful, a sorry and gorgeous mistake of the Emperor's. His white-feathered hat had been retrieved by one of the dignitaries. The man held it helplessly, yet solemnly, with both hands. The people and soldiers gathered at the sutlers' tents. Spirits, pudding, and bread were being given away.

Midday had long since passed, but the sun burned, splendid, torrid, insatiable, and very cruel.

XV

THIS WAS HOW THE EMPEROR SOLEMNLY SWORE TO PRO-
tect the liberty of the French. It thus seemed that he was no longer the brutish Emperor of old. Yet the people throughout the
land heard only the clinking of weapons and the singing of soldiers: both the old soldiers, who were returning to their barracks
after long months, and the fresh young recruits. The Emperor
was gathering an army, there was no doubt. The people no longer believed the newspapers, which wrote that all the powers of
the world were eager to make peace with the Emperor as quickly
as possible. Lies fluttered over the towns and villages on false,
colorful little magic wings, rising in droves from the newspapers,
coming from the mouths of the hypocrites, the eavesdroppers,
the gossips, and the omniscient. They even circled above the
heads of the soldiers marching toward the capital from all directions and were marching out of the capital further to the north-
west. So there would be war, and the colorfully winged news
stories were lies. Alas, the people of France knew all the signs
that war was coming. A great terror gripped them overnight, in
all corners of the land. The motley little doves, the lies of peace
no longer swarmed through the air; they had fallen, defeated by
the great fear, by the brutal silence that foretold the truth—the
truth about the impending war. The signal fires of the soldiers
marching to the north-west were visible from their mighty en-
campments. Their drums rumbled throughout the land every
morning. The troops marched along the hot, dry roads, cultivated fields on either side; they saw the grain ripening and asked
themselves whether they would one day be able to eat it. Perhaps
they would be dead before the corn was even ground; perhaps
they would by then have become part of the earth, manure for
the fields—and who even knew which foreign fields? The older
among the soldiers, those who had already waged many battles
for the Emperor, thought of their comrades who lay in foreign
dirt. The older soldiers all knew one another. And one could dis-

tinguish them from the others because they conversed in their own special language, a language that all soldiers only learn in the face of death. They shared a hundred thousand common memories, and they saw heat and storms, evening and full moon, morning and midday, a saint's picture and a well, a haystack and a herd of cattle, with different eyes than the younger men.

"Do you remember," one of them might say to another, "that time in Saxony? That was the well where we from Third Company had to wait for two damned, long, stupid days."

"Yes, yes," the other would reply. "The well, I remember; it was three miles from Dresden."

"And how those sausages at Eylau tasted!" said one.

And the other answered: "Sure, sure—that sausage came from a worthy steed!"

"It was the horse of a colonel!"

"This time it's only a captain's."

"Any idea where that dumb little Desgranges wound up?"

"In the Berezina, I think. An old carp swallowed him, he was so small."

"And Corporal Dupuis?"

"Died at Austerlitz in a thunderstorm. What happened to your memory? Have you forgotten good old Dupuis as well?"

The young recruits understood nothing of this talk. They only knew that they too were heading to their deaths. Perhaps, they mused, it was easy for these old soldiers to go to their deaths, since they did, after all, know the Emperor. To them, however, the Emperor was distant and life was immediate. Why did he want a war? Where were they marching to? What was the point?

Nevertheless, they had to march, and so they marched. And when they marched through Paris they went past the palace where the Emperor lived, and they shouted: "Long live the Emperor!"

But he, the Emperor, was alone. With increasing solitude he sat before his maps, huge, colored, and complicated, his beloved maps. They showed the entire great world. And the entire great world consisted of nothing but battlefields! Oh, how simple it was to conquer the world if one just studied the maps upon which it was represented! Here each river was a hindrance, every mill a stronghold, every forest a blind, every church a target, every stream an ally, and every field, meadow, and steppe across the world a spectacular setting for spectacular battles! Maps were beautiful! They showed the world even more beautifully than paintings! The earth seemed very small if one only examined it properly on maps. It could be traversed very quickly, as quickly as time required it, the relentlessly ticking clock, the incessantly running sand ...

The Emperor thoughtfully drew crosses, stars, and lines on the maps, as thoughtfully as if he were playing a game of chess. In this and that spot he jotted down numbers. Here were the dead, there the living, here the cannon and there the cavalry; there the supply train and here the field hospital. Nothing but horses, flour sacks, barrels of spirits, enemies, men, horses, brandy, sheep, oxen—and men, men, men; men all over the place.

Once in a while he arose, left the table and maps, threw open the window, and looked at the plaza below, the great open square on which once, as a young unknown officer, he had drilled many an unknown soldier. Now, thousands of young soldiers were marching to the north-west. He listened to their songs. He heard their drums. They were still the old drummers. He could hear their quick and steady step. Yes, it was the wonderful, nimble, victorious step of the French, the rhythm of their swift and courageous feet, the feet that had traversed the highways of half the world; brave feet, the feet of the Imperial soldiers, more useful and vital than their hands.

At such moments he listened lustfully and greedily to their cries: "Long live the Emperor!" Cheerfully, he sat down once again at the table before his maps and wrote numbers here and there in red, blood-red ink. They represented brandy, horses, oxen, wagons, cannons, and soldiers—the very same soldiers who had just marched past the palace shouting: "Long live the Emperor!"

XVI

THE EMPEROR HAD NOT SEEN HIS MOTHER IN A LONG
time. He had given very little thought to the old woman. Now
he came to bid her farewell before going off to war. Custom demanded it, as did his heart.

She sat clumsily, ordinary yet dignified, in a wide armchair in
a darkened room. She loved the cool dusk, the thick burgundy
curtains that hung over the shut windows, and the mild protective stillness of the sealed house with its thick walls. She was old;
she could not handle the blinding summer sun.

It was late morning when her son arrived. He seemed to bring
along something of the overpowering, stifling heat that ruled the
city. Amid the soft, dark-red, sun-dampening shade that filled
the room, his skin-tight, snow-white breeches shimmered all
too loudly; they practically blared. He had come on horseback,
and his spurs issued a delicate, but in this room inappropriate
and embarrassing, jingle. He bent forward, kissed his mother's
hand, and received a kiss upon his hair, on the very top of his
bowed head. He stayed like that a while, bent over in a highly
uncomfortable position. The large, soft, and very pale hand of
his mother stroked his hair a few times. They were both silent.

"Sit, child!" said the old woman finally. He straightened himself, remaining standing close to his mother. She was not sure
whether it was out of respect or impatience. She knew him. He
was just as reverent as he was impatient. "Sit, my child!" she repeated. And he obeyed.

He sat to the right of his mother, just opposite the window,
so that the reflection of the burgundy, sun-lit curtain fell upon
his face.

His mother turned to him. She examined him for some time.
The Emperor kept his eyes focused on her while she studied him.
He studied her too, looking upon her old face, her large, pretty
mouth, her smooth forehead (which was still free of wrinkles),
her strong chin and her beautiful straight nose. Yes, there was

no doubt: much had he inherited from her. She looked like the mother of the great Emperor that he was. In studying her face, he saw his own likeness and practically his very destiny. Now, however, he had no patience or time for scrutiny. He shifted his foot forward gently. His mother noticed it.

"I know," she said, her head quivering a bit, her voice soft and melancholy. "I know," she continued, "that you have no time. You never had time, my son. You became great through impatience. Beware that impatience does not lead to your destruction. You returned out of impatience. You should have stayed!"

"I could not," said the Emperor. "They hate me too much, my enemies. They would have exiled me to a remote desert island. I had to be quicker than them. I had to surprise them."

"Yes, surprise!" said his mother. "That is your way. But waiting is also a way."

"I've waited long enough!" the Emperor said loudly. He stood. He was speaking now quite forcefully. His voice sounded as if he were shouting blasphemies. "I can wait no more!" he cried. "They will invade while I wait!"

"Now it is too late for waiting," his mother said gently. "Stay seated, my child. I might have more to say to you."

The Emperor sat down again.

"I am seeing you perhaps for the last time, my poor son," she said. "I pray that you may outlive me. I have never, or at least rarely, worried for your life. But now I am anxious. And I can do nothing to help you, for you are the powerful one. I cannot advise you, for you yourself are so wise. All I can do is pray for you."

Now the Emperor lowered his head. He stared at the dark-red carpet then propped his elbow on his brilliant white breeches and his chin on his closed fist. "Yes, pray for me, Mother!" he said.

"If your father were still living," she went on, "he would certainly know a way out."

"My father would not have understood me!" said the Emperor.

"Silence!" she cried, almost shrieked, her pretty, dark, metallic voice ringing out. "Your father was great, wise, brave, and modest. You have him to thank for everything. You have inherited all his qualities—except modesty. He, he had patience, your father!"

"I have a different destiny, Mother!" answered the Emperor .

"Yes, yes," said the old lady. "You certainly have a different destiny."

They were quiet for a while. Then his mother began again. "You seem to have aged, my son. How do you feel?"

"I sometimes grow tired, Mother," said the Emperor. "I'm sometimes suddenly tired."

"What ails you?"

"I don't consult doctors. If I were to send for them, they would tell me I'm deathly ill."

"Can you bear it?"

"I must, Mother, I must. I will return greater than ever. I will flatten them."

He lifted his head. He looked straight ahead, past his mother, toward a goal that he alone could see ... toward a victorious return.

"God bless you!" said his mother. "I will pray for you."

The Emperor stood. He went to the old woman and bowed. She made the sign of the cross over him and offered her large, old, soft, white hand. He kissed it. She embraced his neck with her left arm. He felt the soft motherly warmth of her thick arm through the black silk of her sleeve. At that moment he was struck with a woeful feeling. I wish I could embrace my own son like this, he thought. Happy is she, my mother. She can embrace her son!

A warm teardrop, then a second and a third fell upon his lowered head. He dared not look up, nor could he, as he was held down by the gentle restraint of the motherly arm. When she finally loosened her grip and he was able to straighten, he saw the tears running furiously down his mother's face. She cried with an unmoving face, without changing a feature. Only the tears flowed freely from her large, wide-open eyes.

"Don't weep, Mother," said the Emperor softly and helplessly.

"I weep with pride," said the old woman in a quite ordinary voice, as if she were not actually crying. Her throat, mouth, and voice were unaffected by her tears.

Once more she made the sign of the cross in the air before the Emperor and murmured something inaudible. Then she said: "Go, my child! God bless you, my child. God bless you, my Emperor!"

He bowed again. Then he left quickly. His spurs jingled, his black boots gleamed in the dark-red room despite the dusk, and his snow-white breeches were loud in their dazzling brightness.

XVII

HALF AN HOUR LATER HE WAS INSPECTING THE TROOPS of the Paris garrison one last time before they marched off to war. Although he could still feel his mother's kisses and tears on his head, it seemed to him that a very long time had elapsed since the moment he had departed from the dark-red room. The soldiers of the Paris garrison were more carefully outfitted for this new campaign than all the other soldiers in the country. Even the recruits had sturdy and well-nourished faces. He gazed happily into the brave, young, obedient eyes of these new recruits and into the experienced, loyal, devoted ones of his hardened old soldiers. Sound were the knapsacks, cloaks, and boots. He examined their boots with extra attention, almost with love. In the campaigns that he typically led, much hinged upon the feet and boots of the troops, nearly as much as on their hands and guns—perhaps more. He was even pleased with the weapons. Their barrels had been freshly greased, and they shimmered gently yet dangerously, dull-blue and reliable. The well-sharpened bayonet points twinkled. The Emperor walked more slowly than usual, almost deliberately, amid the stiffly immobile ranks, here and there tugging at a button to check if it was firmly attached, or pulling on a strap, belt, or cord. He visited the great field kitchen and asked what meat they were preparing. When he was told that they were boiling mutton, he requested a taste. He had not eaten boiled mutton and beans since his last unsuccessful campaign. Borrowing a pewter spoon from a sergeant, putting a bread crust in his mouth with his left hand and a filled spoon with his right, he stood with legs wide apart in full view of his soldiers, who watched with jubilant hearts as he ate. Their eyes gleamed with pride and also with tripled appetite. They were filled with a steadfast veneration of an intensity they had never felt at a field mass or in a church, and a solemn, childlike, and at the same time fatherly affection for their great Emperor. He was mighty but also moving. He had them form a square around him and spoke to them as usual, using once again the same old words that he had so often before put to the test—about the enemies of their country, the allies of the shameful King, about the victories of old, about the eagles and the dead and, lastly, about honor, honor, and more honor. And once again the officers drew their swords. Once again the regiments roared: "Long live the Emperor! Long live freedom! Long live the Emperor!" And once again he held his hat aloft and cried "Long live France!" in a choked-up voice, more sincerely moved than he had been in his mother's dark salon. He wanted to embrace someone before he left his regiments, so he searched for a suitable candidate. How often he had embraced generals, colonels, sergeants, and even ordinary soldiers. Then he noticed a little drummer boy, one of the adolescent lads of whom there were many in his great army, the sturdy children of his regiments, begotten perhaps from many a father just before a battle, born perhaps in a vendor woman's trailer in Germany, Italy, Spain, Russia, or Egypt. "Come, little one!" said the Emperor. The boy stepped forward with his drum, hardly having a chance to place both sticks into their loops, and stood motionless before the Emperor, even stiffer than an old soldier. The Emperor lifted both boy and drum. He held the boy up for a few moments, swung him in the air for all to see, then kissed him on both cheeks.

"What's your name?" he asked.

"Pascal Pietri," said the boy with a ringing voice, as a pupil might answer his teacher at school. The Emperor remembered that he had heard this name some days earlier, but could not recall on which occasion.

"Your father lives?"

"Yes sir, Your Majesty," said the boy. "He's a sergeant-major in the Thirteenth Dragoons."

"Make a note," said the Emperor to his adjutant. "Sergeant-Major Pietri."

"Pardon me, Your Majesty!" said the boy. "My father's name is Levadour, Sergeant-Major Levadour!"

The Emperor smiled, and all the nearby officers and soldiers smiled as well.

"Do you know your mother?"

"My mother, Your Majesty, is a washerwoman at court."

The Emperor suddenly remembered. "Is her name Angelina?"

"Yes sir, Angelina, Your Majesty!"

With that, all the nearby officers and soldiers smiled once again, but quickly grew serious.

"Make a note," said the Emperor to his adjutant. "The laundress Angelina Pietri."

His review had lasted a long time. He had purposely drawn it out, for he had not wished to return home with the memory of his mother's dark room still fresh in his mind. By the time he returned to the palace it was late afternoon and the light was fading; it would be evening in an hour. He was satisfied with the day. It felt to him as if he had seen his mother not that very morning but quite a long time ago. He remembered Angelina Pietri, the little housemaid whom he had seen in the darkness of the park. The memory cheered him, and the name Angelina, her little son who beat the drum in his army, and the brave freshness with which the boy had corrected him about his father's name nearly moved him. Yes, these were his people, these were his soldiers! More confidently than he had in days, he bent over the maps on his table. He had them, his enemies; he had them just where he wanted them. This time, as so often before. Surely, Parliament and the Police Minister were potentially dangerous, but he could conquer generals and armies. It was a good day.

What day of the week was it today? His old superstitious nature overtook him. He went to the door, thrust it open, and called into the anteroom: "What day is it today?"

"Your Majesty, it is Friday," answered Marchand, his servant.

He was frightened for a brief second. He did not like Fridays. One had to compensate for Friday, so to speak, and he knew an infallible method. His wife Josephine had often spoken of it. And he even remembered the name of this infallible woman who had so often before foretold the future for the Empress and him. "Is Véronique Casimir still here?" he asked.

"Yes, sir, Your Majesty," said the servant.

51

"Get her!" ordered the Emperor.

It seemed to be a good sign that she was in the house. The dead Empress Josephine had brought her. Like everything else associated with Josephine, Véronique Casimir was good. He well remembered the portly old woman. He waited with confidence.

XVIII

VÉRONIQUE CASIMIR REMEMBERED HER MAJESTY THE late Empress Josephine, who often appeared in her dreams, gratefully and with reverence. She had once been a mere washer-woman, but since her early youth she had shown an unusual talent for card-reading. When the great Emperor was still consul, Véronique had read in the cards that he was destined to wear a crown. Since then she had received many honors, greater ones (in her mind at least) than had been bestowed upon any of the officials, ministers, or marshals. On occasion, she was permitted to fortune-tell for the Emperor. She was the First Laundress of the Imperial court. Her duty had been to tend to the blue silk blouses and lace handkerchiefs of the first Empress, and the more sturdy white silk blouses and cambric handkerchiefs of the second. She read the future of the Imperial house in the cards and sometimes even in the laundry that was given to her every evening. Thirty-six laundresses and bath attendants were under her strict orders. She loved to enforce military-style discipline, and during the long years of her service she had learned to be taciturn and secretive despite being talkative, even loquacious, by nature.

Before heading to bed every evening, and after parceling out the laundry to the men and women under her, she would seat herself at the large table that was at the time standing, solemn and secluded, in the quiet communal dining room, for she required much space for the several packs of cards with which she worked according to a complex system. Sometimes the servants would gather around her at even that late hour. The long and narrow black ebony table, with its highly polished surface, was somber, eerie, practically a catafalque. Here Véronique Casimir sat and laid out cards. Eventually, midnight struck from various towers. At that point she would stop and wait until the bells were finished ringing. Finally she would sweep all her various packs of cards together, tie them up with a greasy old string, and get up without uttering a word. Nobody ever asked her questions.

She rarely discussed the secrets of the supernatural world with which she was so closely familiar.

Since the Emperor's return, she had been waiting for him to call on her. Now she was no longer consulting the cards about the Emperor's fate, but about her own, that is to say, whether he had forgotten her during his absence. "No!" said the cards.

Nevertheless, she was surprised and practically in a fright when he did send for her. She was standing in the expansive washroom, surrounded by her staff, at the time when she normally gathered her workers around her, awaiting the servants with the laundry baskets, and she held in her hand the list upon which her various commissions, orders, reprimands, and warnings were noted. She left immediately and headed for her room. She had a half-staircase to ascend. Her short, fat legs bounded up two steps at a time. She hurried into her room, to her little oval mirror between the two candlesticks on the table, lit the candles, donned a freshly starched cap, sat down, and began with her strong little fingers to powder her sallow and very fleshy face. She sprinkled a few droplets of lavender upon her breast, from the sacred flask that the first Empress, her lady Josephine, had given her, and rose, content and fragrant and quite splendid, in a delicate white cloud of powder. From her case she removed her card packs with a determined, abrupt, practically warlike grip, like a soldier retrieving his weapon when called to sudden conflict. Now she was ready.

After many long months she stood before her Emperor. He sat at his table with his colorfully dizzying maps, which she had already seen a few times previously, immediately before his great campaigns, when she enjoyed the favor of being summoned and consulted. She attempted to perform a curtsy as ladies did in the presence of the Emperor. Spreading her skirts with both hands, she placed one foot back, stretched the other in front, attempted to glide a step forward in this difficult position, and then bend one knee slightly. After she believed she had accomplished all of this gracefully, she remained still, fat and stiff, eyes lowered modestly. The windows were open. The late summer evening's gold-green dusk filtered into the room and competed with the restless little deep-yellow flames of the three candles. One could hear both the soft breath of the wind and the loud, industrious chirping of the crickets.

"Come here!" the Emperor ordered. She hurried over, waddling quickly to his table, fat, dignified, and servile. How she had longed for this moment! She tingled with reverence in the presence of the Emperor and at the sight of the confusing maps that were scattered across his writing table. She also felt her own importance, a shiver for herself and for the ennobled and exalted significance of her tool, the cards. She trembled at the thought that her cards were no less important, perhaps even more important, than the Emperor's maps. It was satisfying to think that the greatest emperor in the world had as little power to grasp the secret of her cards as she, Véronique, had to read his geographical secrets. At this hour she was called upon perhaps to determine the fate of the world, which was normally the Emperor's domain. And thus she stood there, as much in awe of herself as of the Emperor. She kept her gaze lowered. It fell upon her ample bosom and could not go any lower, although she wished to look at the floor in humble pride, but also embarrassment. Through her sunken eyelids she felt the mocking, smiling stare of the Emperor. She held her arms straight down like a soldier, but her hands could reach no lower than her wide hips. She liked, but also required, smooth tables, with nothing upon them, and she wanted to ask the Emperor to clear off his distracting maps, but she dared not.

"So, let's begin," said the Emperor.

It was noticeably darker in the room. A macabre kind of illumination emanated from the sparse candles and strengthened old Véronique's courage and faith in her prophetic abilities. She now ventured to lift her eyes. Her gaze was met with the waxen face of the Emperor, a frozen smile on his mouth—a ghastly smile. Then she began confidently to lay out her greasy playing cards, disregarding the fact that she was placing them atop the Emperor's maps. She tried to forget that she stood before the mightiest Emperor of all and told herself that she was in the service of the otherworld. She whispered: "Take three please, Your Majesty." The Emperor took three cards. The smooth, dark blue card backs reflected the unsteady candle flames.

"What lies before me," she murmured, "what flies before me; what gives me concern, what things I spurn; what makes me glad, what makes me sad." She shuffled quickly with her short but nimble fingers, the speed of which had often astounded the Emperor. "Take six cards, Your Majesty," she said. And the Emperor took six cards. He thought of his first wife, the dead Josephine, and those evenings when, although she knew little of this art, Josephine had attempted to read her own fate and that of the Emperor, the fate of the country and the world, as she laid out Véronique Casimir's greasy cards with her long and slender, beloved fingers. He thought no more of the cards. He was lost in sweet memories of his dead wife. He smiled. He did not hear as Véronique murmured: "Spades to the right will cause a fright; clubs to the left, of power bereft; diamonds are near, danger is here; hearts are away, love won't stay; the queen of clubs is above, she's past, she's past; eight of clubs, eight of clubs ..." She broke off suddenly. She quickly gathered the cards together. She glanced at the Emperor. He bore a distant look, one that seemed to pierce her massive body and see out into the world beyond, perhaps even into the grave where the body of his Josephine was now withering and decaying. Véronique remained silent, her left hand pressing the cards fervently against her bosom.

The Emperor locked his eyes on her, a mocking smile on his lips. "Well, Véronique," he inquired, "good or bad?"

"Good, good, Your Majesty!" she said hurriedly. "There are many years ahead for Your Majesty, many years!"

The Emperor opened a drawer. Inside were little pillars of gold pieces, neat, shimmering columns of gold. From one of these columns he removed ten coins. They were genuine napoleons. "Here, as a keepsake," said the Emperor.

The door was opened. Madame Véronique left hurriedly, walking backward, frantically trying to restrain her panting. When she sensed the open door at her back, her escape, she again performed her clumsy and comical curtsy. Then she was outside and facing the closed door. She curtsied a third time before the closed door, then she waddled, dignified yet hurriedly, down the stairs. On the penultimate step she had to stop. She felt faint for the first time in her life. The banister that she thought would save her seemed to be receding. She fell down suddenly and heavily with a clumsy thud. Two guards picked her up. They carried her into the park. When she awoke and saw the soldiers, she righted herself and said: "God help us all ... and him especially!"

Then she hurried past them and into the great servants' dining hall. It was late. Dinner was already being served.

XIX

THE NIGHT THAT THE EMPEROR LEFT PARIS TO HEAD FOR battle, the sky over the city was deep blue and star filled. In the street in front of the park were the curious and enthusiastic. The servants had gathered at a respectful distance from the Imperial carriage. The Emperor emerged swiftly from the palace door, earlier than had been planned. His staff was still in the midst of packing papers, maps, and field-glasses into the coach. A lackey sprinted up, burning torch in hand. The night was clear enough, offering a gentle, silvery-blue light, so the smoky, reddish flame of the torch seemed unnecessary, even a bit terrifying. It was only the product of a very strict household routine, a harmless device. At this moment, however, it seemed to be trying to harshly interrupt the night's starry tranquility. The trees whispered amicably. A few bats flitted silently above the people's heads, through the rays of light coming from the windows. It was rather still, despite the bustling of the servants, who spoke in low voices, and the restlessness of the horses. The still of the night was mightier than these noises. But the torch was a loud, even improper, incursion; one could clearly hear the crackle of its flame and smell the burning resin, which was like the scent of danger itself. The Emperor seemed tired. He had been working right up until the very moment of departure. The assembled servants were still as he approached. All turned their eyes to him. In the silvery-blue sheen of the night his face looked rather pale to them. They were also thinking about the collapse of the card-reader Véronique.

The Emperor remained standing for a while on the last step. He cast a lingering glance up at the sky, as if searching among the countless stars for his own. His white breeches shone with a ghastly luminescence. His black hat was reminiscent of a little cloud, the only one visible amid the clear sky. He stood still, as in one of his many portraits, alone in the vast, calm summer's night, although the gentlemen of his retinue were following closely behind him on the steps. He was alone and lonely, and he was searching for his star.

He turned, gestured to his adjutant, and spoke a few words. Then he descended the final step. He walked quickly the few paces to his carriage. The servants cried: "Long live the Emperor!" They waved to him with their hands, their empty hands. The cry surprised him. He turned even as he was about to enter the coach. He took a step forward. The women servants fell to their knees. The men followed hesitantly. This was their routine whenever the King departed! thought the Emperor. They must have kneeled like this when he fled from me.

"Stand up," he ordered, and they all rose. He felt compelled to say something more, to obey the theatrical law that commanded just as he commanded his army. What had he to say to lackeys, servants, and slaves? "Long live Freedom!" he cried. And they all answered: "Long live the Emperor! Victory! Victory!"

He turned away quickly. He got inside the carriage with haste, and the carriage door closed with an unusually loud shudder. The torch flickered at the coachman's side. A soft, practically caressing crack of the whip, and they were racing, flying away from the park, sending a few bluish sparks from under the horses' hooves.

Another carriage rolled up. The Emperor's attendants climbed in. It was all done quickly and with a cool precision.

Once they were all inside, but before the carriage set off on its way, the lackey turned his torch upside down and practically bored the flame into the cold, damp night ground. Then he stamped his foot upon the last smoldering remains of the torch. To all who saw him, it seemed he had extinguished an entirely different flame.

Among the servant women in the park was also the maidservant Angelina Pietri.

BOOK TWO

The Life of Angelina Pietri

I

AT THAT TIME ANGELINA PIETRI WAS LIVING AMONG THE anonymous lower servants of the Imperial court. She came from a respected and honored Corsican family. Angelina's widowed father had been a poor fisherman and had died when she was just fifteen years old. Many young people, both boys and girls, were leaving Corsica in those days; they were going to France, where the greatest of all Corsicans ruled—the Emperor Napoleon.

In Paris lived an aunt of Angelina's, Véronique Casimir. The First Laundress at the Imperial court, she was childless, kind-hearted, and a mistress of the art of fortune-telling with cards. Tales were told back in Ajaccio that she prophesied the outcome of battles for the great Emperor himself.

A friend of her father's, old Benito, brought Angelina to Marseilles in his little sailing vessel. He paid for her trip to Paris and escorted the girl to the mail coach. Gravely and sadly, he took leave of her; and, speaking so loudly that all the other passengers could hear, he said: "You will pass along sincere greetings from old Benito Croce. I knew his late father well. If he asks you why I haven't come to Paris myself, tell him I'm too old. Were I younger, I would have gone long ago to join his fight and conquer the world. My son has enlisted in his army in my stead. They surely know each other; he is serving with the Twenty-Sixth—a magnificent regiment! All right, then. Go with God and don't forget to relay everything I've told you."

This was the personal message that old Croce had for the Emperor.

Angelina was quite unable to deliver this message. The Emperor was unapproachable. But she dreamed of him. His portrait hung in all the rooms, the same portrait she had seen in rooms all across Corsica. It depicted the Emperor after a victorious battle, seated on a snow-white steed while reviewing the decimated ranks. His horse shimmered and his red eyes gleamed. He held his right hand outstretched, pointing somewhere into the inscrutable distance. He looked magnificent: both near and remote, kindly and at the same time terrible.

Angelina was under the command of Véronique Casimir. She thus belonged to the section of thirty-six male and female servants charged with washing the laundry of the ladies and gentlemen of the court and keeping the bathrooms in order.

She washed the sky-blue, pink, and white silk blouses, the cambric handkerchiefs, the collars and cuffs, the delicate linen of the beds in which the ladies and gentlemen slept, and the costly stockings in which they walked. Early mornings, in the gray steam of the laundry room amid tubs and kettles, she scrubbed and wrung out the clothes, forcefully beat the damp, rolled-up bundles with a wooden stave, unrolled them, and draped them over the countless ropes that were strung up densely yet in an orderly fashion across the room, forming a peculiar grid, a second and more delicate ceiling of ropes.

In the afternoon dried masses of wrinkled garments lay on the wide table, awaiting their resurrection. Then, just as she had learned to do at home, Angelina would take a mouthful of water and spray it from her bulging cheeks onto the silk, linen, and cambric. After this, she used her strong arms to brandish the smoothing-iron, hot coals glowing from within. To test its heat, she placed a moistened finger on the iron's surface and listened as it sizzled. She began to press—the coarse linen first, then the delicate silk, next the cambric, and lastly the pleated collars and cuffs. And it seemed to her that the more industriously she worked, the closer she was to the ladies and gentlemen of the court and to the Emperor himself. This very shirt that she was ironing might be worn tomorrow by the Emperor. She rubbed his dazzling white breeches with a special type of greasy, insoluble chalk and through her zealous efforts they shimmered like freshly fallen snow.

There were days when Véronique Casimir appeared suddenly, at an unusual hour and wearing an unusual outfit. When this happened, the young laundresses would fall abruptly silent in the midst of a song, for they knew that Véronique had just read the cards for someone of prominence. She wore her heavy black silk gown and around her neck a present from the Empress Josephine, a massive golden chain bearing a vivid green jade amulet. She would stand there, in the steam of the washroom, before her white-clad young girls—portly, ponderous, and solemn, a true dark priestess of the great Emperor. What ominous events might she have just been prophesying? The fate of what corner of the world had she just foretold?

Twice a week Angelina was obliged to attend to the palace bathrooms. Her first stop was the Emperor's bathroom. She could see the fresh marks of his moist feet upon the floor. She could detect the scent of his body in the damp towels, and she would stay for a long time in that spot, bewildered and forgetful of her task. But sometimes she would gather the nerve to clutch a towel against her heart, pressing a fleeting, stolen kiss upon the linen and blushing even though she was all alone. She adored even the slightest evidence of the Emperor's presence. She was anxious that she might accidentally meet the Emperor. However, when she left the bathroom, she felt bitter disappointment within her heart, as though he himself had broken a promise to meet her there. She was devastated yet at the same time euphoric.

One day a handkerchief fell into her hands, one of the simple soldier's handkerchiefs that the Emperor sometimes used, the same type that everyone in his army used. It was a large square of coarse linen: a wide red border surrounded a sky-blue center that depicted a map; on it were noted in red all the sites of the Emperor's battles. It was the map of the simple Imperial soldier.

Angelina regarded this handkerchief with reverence. It bore the greenish tobacco stains of the Emperor's snuff. She imagined him again on his white horse, as he appeared in his portraits, with his right arm outstretched toward some faraway point.

With all the love of her foolishly impassioned young heart, she began to wash the handkerchief. It seemed to contain a special message from the Emperor. In the evening it lay freshly pressed before her, and she ran her fine, young, red fingers over it affectionately. She hid it under her clothes at her breast, and as she felt the wonderful fabric at her heart, she began to believe that it was hers to keep. It was rare to find things of this type in the Imperial laundry. It had not entered the laundry in the usual way, but had come to Angelina on its own; as a greeting, perhaps a message—who knew? Anyway, it was probably already wrinkled at her breast and in a condition quite unfit to be returned. Maybe she could return it the next day, or the day after, or whenever the opportunity arose—although each article was counted. Little Angelina was quite anxious.

She stood there as always at eight o'clock on the dot and took her place among the militarily precise rows of servant men and women to await the stern Véronique, laundry bundle in her outspread arms just like all the others; there were twenty-six pieces—she carried the twenty-seventh upon her heart.

Véronique Casimir began to count: twenty-one, twenty-two, twenty-three ... She held a long, narrow ledger in one hand and in the other a lorgnette of the type owned by the finer classes.

She raised the glasses. "A piece is missing, Angelina!" she said.

Angelina did not move.

"A piece is missing!" Véronique repeated.

Angelina imagined herself being undressed and searched. Lackeys felt her body with lustful hands. They found the handkerchief. Then they drove her, naked, from the palace, from the city, from the country.

She was still silent.

"Answer, Angelina!" ordered Véronique Casimir.

At this moment, little Angelina Pietri felt great strength, and

she said quietly yet firmly: "There were only twenty-six pieces!"
For the first time in her life, she was lying.

That night, in her bedroom in which two other servant girls also slept, Angelina waited until the candle was extinguished. Then she undressed and laid the Emperor's handkerchief over her pillow. That night, for the first time in her young life, she did not sleep a wink. She gave herself up to a euphoric wakefulness, which was even sweeter and more peaceful than a good night's sleep ...

II

EACH DAY, EACH HOUR MIGHT BRING A MIRACLE: THAT
Angelina would see the Emperor. Upon consideration, though,
it would not really be such a miracle but rather an event destined
to happen—as a matter of course. On Sundays she accompanied her aunt Véronique to visit numerous friends. These were
women of quality, of a special standing. Their husbands were
minor court or state officials: a sergeant-major of the Gendar-
merie, the porter of the Elysée, an Imperial forester, an agent
of the Police Ministry, a clerk at the Town Hall, the provost of
the military prison, a Revenue Office sequestrator. As certain as
all these women were of their own social prominence, there was
not one who would dare dispute the mysterious importance of
Véronique Casimir. Each household she visited believed it was
welcoming an intimate of both earthly and heavenly powers.
With a splendid magnanimity, Véronique doled out advice and
prophecies. The advice was revealed to be valuable and most of
the prophecies came true. For how could it be otherwise? She
even knew the results of the Emperor's battles in advance!

Sometimes she also read the cards for Angelina—not on Sundays, but on Fridays between eleven and twelve o'clock at night.
Angelina would sit across from her aunt at the long table in the
dining hall, her meager elbows resting on the surface. Her embarrassed red hands moved helplessly over her flaming face or
fingered the black corset and white apron that comprised an
Imperial laundress's uniform; curiosity and awe filled her heart.
Along the walls and beneath the ceiling of the spacious hall,
eerie shadows engaged in frenzied undulation. These shadows
were not chased away but rather strengthened and intensified
by two wax candles on the table to the right and left of the outspread cards. It was known that Véronique, following some secret magic formula, had mixed some incense into the wax. The
room was fully transformed; no longer was it the great dining
hall where everyone ate on a daily basis, but rather a cavernous

tomb in which the shadows of those buried along the walls were flitting about.

For the young Angelina, the cards always said the same thing: at her feet lay a handsome bearded man in uniform. A child, a boy, appeared from the already dissipating mists of the near future. But death was waiting in the less transparent background, and, strangely enough, it had something to do with a bloody war. Money—or sudden fortune—was nowhere to be seen; neither was there any indication of illness. An enigmatic glimpse of fame was revealed, but even Véronique's sharp eyes could not focus it. Midnight struck finally, in a thin and hollow voice. The hushed commands of the changing guard and the muffled clatter of arms being presented could be heard outside. Véronique rose, packed up her cards and, with Angelina leading, left holding a flickering candle in each hand. "Good night, child," she said. Angelina curtsied, and her aunt kissed her on the forehead, candlesticks in both outstretched arms.

Little Angelina was bitterly disappointed by the ever-unchanging voice of the cards. Every Friday she awaited a new tone; she suspected what it would be but did not dare admit it. A certain type of gossip often ruled the conversation among the servants, and although Angelina did not fully comprehend she got the gist of it. She often heard the lackeys and servants say: "Congratulations, Pierre! Your Caroline disappeared last night!" Or: "Good morning, dear friend. Are you going to take her back, or are you going to duel the little guy?" And she saw by the shameless and open, yet secret-concealing smiles of the men that they were referring to love affairs, and she guessed that these were the Emperor's love affairs. She knew this Caroline, as well as Babette, Catherine, and Arlette. How arrogantly they now began to bustle about among the rest of the servants, their ordinary uniforms appearing magically transformed! Was the mighty one so petty at times that he lusted for maids? Yet was he not so great that everything in the world was his? The mountains, the valleys, and the rivers belonged to him, as did the Kings and their countries, their crowns, their daughters, their wives, the highest-ranking generals, and the common soldiers. Everything, all of it, belonged to him—the magnificent and the mundane, the great and the simple. Why not the maids too? It would be euphoria to be his maiden, to be humiliated by him, to be worshipped by him! Angelina's little heart fluttered and flitted like a caged bird. Her blood surged restlessly, lustfully. She could no longer resist the wondrous impulse to view herself in each of the many mirrors that were hung in the magnificent bathrooms. This compulsion came over her simply enough. It began with a timid mistrust of her own beauty and an unbridled recognition of the other girls' physical perfection. She learned to compare her throat, her breasts, her hands and feet, with the throats, breasts, hands and feet of the others. She began, during the night, to case a furtive glance at their bodies, first with admiration and then with envy. One day, a day of special significance in the simple life of little Angelina Pietri, one of the ladies of the court left her bath later than usual. Angelina saw her naked. She was startled at this proud, carefree nudity. She even forgot to curtsy. She was paralyzed by a terrifying admiration. It was as if the woman were not really naked, but enveloped in some sort of fully transparent beauty. Although her body was exposed to Angelina's eyes, it was far away and certainly unreachable. And if she had ventured to lay a finger on it, it would probably have felt like stone. The woman smiled pleasantly.

"You may get started, child!" she said.

Angelina blushed and paled in the same moment. She was suddenly incensed as she had never been before. For the first time she felt completely humiliated. This pretty woman had the right to call her "child," but at that moment, Angelina felt that the ordinarily kindly term was disdainful. She felt condemned to permanent insignificance.

The lady-in-waiting came and covered her naked mistress with a blue cloak. Angelina was left alone.

For the first time, she detected lustful and at the same time hateful scents in the bathroom. For the first time she looked with interest at the yellow, emerald-green, and ruby-red flasks of perfume, the soaps, the sponges, the almond milk, and the Indian salves. She slowly scooped the milky water from the bath and began to clean with rage and purpose, exhaling forcefully upon the mirror as though she were flinging some evil incantation against the glass—and then she wiped it vigorously as if to crush it. Her young face shone back at her pleasantly. Yes, for the first time she found herself attractive and after a while even beautiful. She was a red-haired, freckled girl, with a forehead that was too high—one could even say too proud were it not littered with freckles. Her eyes were far too small, of a grayish color. Her full lips formed a delicate downward arc. In her chin nestled a dimple. Too bad, thought Angelina, that it was marred by a freckle and rendered nearly invisible.

A senseless desire to study her body gripped her. She stripped off her apron and dress. Her neck was petite and taut, her helpless young shoulders looked to her to be well proportioned and perfect, her breasts too small. Anyhow, there were ways to get rid of freckles. She was determined to be attractive without realizing that she already was.

Every day after that memorable occasion, she studied her awakening body anew. Standing before the mirror she held adoring, silent conversation with her reflection, with her face, her lips, her eyes, her eyebrows. Someone told her to use a certain salve to combat her freckles, but she thought no more about it; even her minor defects had already won her over. She was devout and pious, and she knew that she was sinning. She even took herself to confession.

One day, however, she finally gave in to the mirror in the Imperial bathroom. She had resisted it for some time, out of a combination of fear and awe. Now, though, it compelled her with double strength. Abruptly, she stepped before it, ripped off her apron and opened her collar. Her long white apron strings dragged along the ground. Suddenly, the door behind her opened. In the mirror, she watched as the Emperor's servant entered. She had no time to fix her apron and dress.

"Where is the box?" asked the servant. "Haven't you seen the snuff box?" His sullen eyes darted about the room. Angelina froze, offering no reply. She stood there, still facing the mirror. In the reflection, she saw the servant nearing. He was already at her back. "Turn around!" he ordered.

She clapped both hands to her uncovered neck and turned toward the man. Her apron strings were still dragging on the ground.

"What have you been doing here? What are you hiding there?" he asked.

"Nothing, nothing!" she panted.

Her eyes darted to the right and left, trying to escape from the servant's large figure and broad face.

Suddenly she spied the box. It lay, elegant and silver, on a small table next to the bath. She stretched out her arm and said: "There, there!"

"You must confess at once what you've done!" said the man in a hushed voice that had a stronger, more threatening tone than if he had shouted. "Confess, confess, confess," repeated his monotonous voice as he came ever closer and closer to Angelina. He was tiptoeing, and his soft steps were even more menacing than his whisper.

Finally, he stood directly before Angelina. "The Emperor is still here," he whispered, his breath hissing. "I'm just now shaving him. Quietly, quietly, don't scream! Speak, quickly!" He reached out toward her. It looked as if he were about to rip off her dress.

Don't scream, she thought. Don't scream! But a shrill, deafening scream nonetheless escaped from her heart. At that moment she sprang in the direction of the curtain at her left, which seemed to promise some means of escape. She did not know not what she was doing and brushed against the toilet table, knocking over glasses and flasks and sending them crashing to the floor, where they shattered loudly.

The servant retreated to the door through which he had entered and disappeared. Through the closed door came the angry ring of a mighty voice. She could not understand the words, but to whom the voice belonged she could well guess. It was the scolding voice of the Emperor. Then all was quiet. She held her breath. Her heart fluttered. She conquered her panic, bent down, and began with quiet, nimble fingers, to retrieve the shards. Then she waited motionless. She heard nothing more. She went to the door that led to the corridor, cautiously pushed down the white handle, and stepped into the hall. At that moment she heard the faint clinking of spurs. She trembled. The Emperor was heading her way! She stood there stiff, paralyzed, her bunched-up apron holding the fragments of bottles and flasks, but did not see the Emperor although her eyes were wide open. She only knew that for one eternal moment there had been a glint of white and a jingling of silver. She could recall nothing else. Her little head was empty and desolate.

She ran, she dashed, lost her way in the corridors, finally found the staircase, bounded down the steps and reached freedom.

III

NOTHING CAME OF HER TRANSGRESSIONS AND SHE CON-
sidered herself lucky. She offered up her fervent prayers that
Heaven might forgive her sins. At night she kissed the crucifix
that hung over her bed, held it against her heart, and lay down
reassured. But before falling asleep, she pulled out the handkerchief that she had hidden between the bolster and coverlet and
pressed it too against her bosom. The cross pacified her, but the
handkerchief made her happy.

One evening at laundry inspection, when all thirty-six of the
laundresses were lined up with military precision, Véronique Casimir said: "Angelina delivers first. Come here, Angelina. Someone awaits you."

Behind the door, in the poorly lit corridor, stood a strange
lackey whom she had never before seen, wearing a blue outfit.
He was slighter and more delicate looking than the other male
servants she knew. He wore a fine gold-lace edging on his collar and lapels on his coat. He looked like a dark blue, delicately
gilded, very solemn shadow.

"I beg that you follow me, Mademoiselle!" he said. It was the
first time anyone had used the word "Mademoiselle" and such
a polite form of address. Her courage evaporated with each step
she took. The alien feeling grew with the corridor's every bend.
They entered the garden and by and by came to an unfamiliar
corner. Barely a couple of minutes had elapsed, but Angelina
felt like she had been following the lackey for hours. They re-
entered the palace, through an unfamiliar door. Angelina had
never seen this entrance or the staircase they next ascended.
With a firm grasp on the banister, she trod upon the narrow strip
of white stone that the dark-red carpet left uncovered. The carpet seemed ominous; she only trusted the narrow stone margin.
They entered a spacious room. A thick green drape fell over the
door in heavy silken pleats. Two armchairs stood near a small
table. On the table were bottles and glasses, and cold meats

and cheese on porcelain dishes bearing the Imperial crest. The lackey pushed up a chair and said: "Sit down, Mademoiselle." He then decanted some golden wine into a crystal glass. After that he disappeared behind the portière, dainty, slight, and dark blue. Heavy yet silent, the green folds came together behind him.

Angelina sat stiffly in the wide, soft fauteuil, the golden wine glass before her. Glassy eyed, she gazed at the large windows, the solemn paintings on the walls (which seemed to her nothing more than colored blotches surrounded by gilt frames), the great crystal chandelier in the middle above the table, and the heavy silver candelabra in all four corners of the room. From the burning candles came the scent of wax and violets. To her left was a broad bed, half hidden by light-brown curtains studded with golden bees. She sat there rigidly erect and tried in vain to think.

All was familiar, yet all was foreign. Maybe she had dreamed all this before; maybe someone was coming to kill her. Or perhaps someone was only seeking to punish her. A dozen bizarre tales, ones she had heard at home as a child, filled her imagination. She grew flushed. The warmth, the scent, the candlelight, and her own fears; all these things dazed her. She wished to get up and open a window. She wanted to go and extinguish the candles. They were so bright, they practically roared. Angelina thought that she would be content to sit there if only it were dark. Quite black, as it now was in her bedroom. But she dared not move.

Gradually she became tired. She leaned back and felt the soft embrace of the arms and back of the chair as a new, even greater danger. She leaned forward again and grabbed for the glass. Her hand trembled. She drank, leaned back again, took another sip, and yet another. It was wine, yet seemed to be more than mere wine. It was sweet and bitter, comforting and dangerous— promising. It was the drink of sin. She tried to straighten up a little more so as to replace the glass on the table. She could not. Too late, she thought, too late, and had more to drink.

She sat there, empty glass in hand. Already, she felt more at home. The room felt less alien now. She ventured, with a bold resolution, to stand up, as she had decided to take at least one walk around the chamber. She stopped before the first painting; it was the Emperor, a huge portrait that reached to the floor. One had to lift one's head to see his face. His boots were the first thing to greet the eyes, then his breeches, next his coat, and finally, as if in the clouds high above, his face.

Little Angelina did not go any further. She fled back to the comfortable danger of the armchair. She was trembling, afraid she would drop the glass she held in her hand, so she replaced it with great care on the table. A powerful and terrifying, yet wonderful, premonition overcame her, a fierce and dangerous foreboding that came from without, seemingly emanating from the wine, streaming from the Emperor's portrait, the bed in the corner, and the overwhelming scent of the candles.

The portière's heavy green ripples caught her eye, and with every passing moment she swore she saw them moving. Now she listened and believed she heard voices. Then it seemed the curtains had parted and the Emperor had appeared, looking like his portrait, his head invisible, just below the ceiling; he was large and growing ever larger. She leaned forward, poured herself a fresh glass and sipped it. Then, timidly and reverently, she replaced it on the table.

She now believed she knew why she had been brought here. A sweet fear filled her, and she lustfully surrendered to it—dreamy, childlike, and proud. She drank another sip. She leaned back, clinging desperately to the glass with her reddish young hands. Her gaze swept from the walls to the candles, from the candles to the windows, and always back to the portière. She noticed that one of the candles in the corner was starting to sag from the high heat and she wished to get up and right it, but dared not. With a maid-servant's dutiful ear, she listened in horror to the soft and regular drip of the wax on to the carpet. Her childlike pride died and her lustful fear was overtaken by another, a quite ordinary fear, that of a servant who has neglected her duty. In any case, she was unable to stand. In order to avoid seeing the candle, she closed her eyes.

She fell asleep straight away, holding the glass perfectly upright in her foolish hands, on her still lap. Confusing snippets of dreams floated through her mind. Her lips were slightly open, and her smile was tinged with fear. Her respiration was faint; even in sleep she dared not breathe.

She awoke to the first summer's chirping of the birds. The June morning streamed triumphantly through all the high, wide windows, dampened a bit by the greenery of the trees in the park. Angelina's conscientious eyes immediately sought the drooping candle. A small, bent lump of wax was all that remained of it. On the beautiful carpet, however, was the disastrous rest of the candle—a small dried pond of yellow wax. In the air was a cold blue fog from the long since extinguished candles.

Angelina felt helpless and forlorn. She thought no more of the portière. She wished to be far away, in her house in Ajaccio, amid the beloved nets, the rocky shore, the golden, silver, and steel-blue fish, the scent of the algae and the mussels. She was still holding the wine glass in her hand. She put it on the table and rose.

Suddenly there came the noise of voices and footsteps. A door was flung open, the portière was ripped aside brusquely, and there stood the Emperor. His hair was tousled, a couple of buttons of his vest were open, and in the early morning light he looked ragged, older, and more diminutive than he must actually have been. Angelina jerked ridiculously to her knees with a thud, as though someone had pushed her down. She lowered her head and could see nothing except his Imperial black boots upon the red carpet.

She heard someone enter silently behind the Emperor, spied a blue shoe and a gold buckle, and she guessed it was the blue lackey from yesterday.

"Idiot!" roared the Emperor's voice and then: "Let her out!"

When she raised her head, the Emperor was gone. Before the green curtain stood the slender blue lackey.

"Come, Mademoiselle," he said.

He left her standing in the garden. Somewhere, a tower was

striking six. Work began at six-thirty. Ashamed, confused, and dazed, she ran along the broad avenue. Up ahead glimmered the servants' wing. She was the first of all the maids to report to the laundry.

Since that remarkable night, little Angelina's heart was limp and injured. She tried in vain to convince herself that she had only dreamed the incident. All the particulars lingered in her memory, mercilessly clear, the cruel outline of each one filled in with meticulous details. They stubbornly forbade Angelina from regarding them as dreams and shadows. That night persecuted her doggedly. She could still detect the warm scent of burning wax and violets. She could still taste the cool sharp golden sweetness of the wine. She could yet feel the sudden, painful blow of shame. Her awakening, prescient blood knew that she had been scorned. With a numb hatred little Angelina began to despise the great ladies, those she believed would never have been rejected, even by the Emperor. Her newly aroused vanity faded and died, after briefly flowering, in shame, disgrace, and hatred. She no longer looked at her face; all the mirrors in the world were suddenly reflectionless. At night she prayed only fleetingly and gave the crucifix but a quick glance. The Emperor's handkerchief lay hidden at the bottom of her wooden box.

One Sunday, when she was accompanying her aunt on her round of visits, they came to the Provost's house. There she met his nephew, the magnificent Sergeant-Major Sosthène, whose heart she inflamed from the very first moment.

Nothing distinguished him from most of the other sergeant-majors in the Imperial cavalry. Tall, vibrant, brave, twice wounded and decorated, he was much like the rest of his comrades. When Angelina was only a few steps away from him, she saw him as a world unto himself—a world of sabres, spurs, boots, and woven braid, a world of blue and red. Even his face was a part of his uniform. He was a being composed not of limbs and organs like all other human beings, but rather of colors. Next to him, little Angelina had, in order to converse with him, to cast an upward gaze along his front, as though he were a colorful mountain, and it took quite a while for her to spot the peak, a mighty blue-black mustache with a frightening sheen, and over this two gaping, black, crater-like nostrils.

He left her feeling apathetic—and she only gave the appearance of being interested—when he told tales about his battles and the foreign lands in which he had fought, lived, and loved. Favorably, but not without criticism, he discussed the Emperor's strategies. It would not have taken much for the Emperor to have lost this battle or been killed in that one, or at the very least been taken prisoner. Those people, including the Provost, who had only seen the Imperial Army on parade, had no idea of the importance of chance and luck in battle. Perhaps it was only a coincidence that the Colonel of the Sergeant-Major's regiment had not become Emperor. "Only God can know," said the Provost's wife.

"There's no God!" said the Sergeant-Major firmly. Equally decisively, and with the gallant and noisy bow of an armed beast, he invited Angelina and her aunt to dine with him.

They dined at a fine inn on baked sole, beef with coarse salt, sweet carrots, and tender baby onions—a soldier's meal. The Sergeant-Major rapped on the floor thrice with his sabre, and the waiter brought a sharp Rhineland wine. There too the Sergeant-Major had tamed the Germans, and with every gulp he voiced his recollections. To finish, they drank coffee and several cognacs. At that point Aunt Véronique declared that her work awaited. "One moment," said the Sergeant-Major, "I will escort you, Madame." He hunched over and Aunt Véronique straightened up; thus he could reach her arm with his mighty fist, grab it, and lead her clinking all the way to the door. He offered a military salute and returned, a beaming mountain, to Angelina.

That evening, she learned a good bit about the world—a carriage ride, a fair that was bright as day on account of countless lanterns, another cognac and, finally, a little red-golden room, a bottle of champagne, and love on a cramped sofa no larger than a roomy cradle. Angelina's head hung dazed and confused over the arm, causing painful pressure on her neck. She felt that her body parts were in scattered disarray, much like her clothes were at that moment. A colorful, strange mountain was embracing her with all its might and was about to crush her completely.

She finally emerged from the room to a graying morning sky. In the carriage, as she began to put her hair and clothes in order, she eventually convinced herself that none of her body parts were missing. The Sergeant-Major's whiskers brushed against her face and neck a few more times as they stood before the palace. He let go of her and ordered her to wave. She obeyed and she watched him wave back. She scurried up the familiar staircase to her room. Her roommates were still asleep. She did not pray before bed, for the first time in her life.

With a dark awareness that life was very difficult and quite unintelligible, a dangerous and extraordinary burden, she sank into a deep slumber.

IV

SO IT CAME TO PASS THAT VÉRONIQUE CASIMIR'S PROPH-
ecy was fulfilled—a bearded man in uniform lay at Angelina's
feet. He waited for her every morning at the servants' entrance
after her work was done. He stood there, ever punctual, large,
and colorful. Long before she reached him, Angelina could see
him, gloriously gaudy, through the park fence and the green
of the trees. The first silvery stars were already glimmering in
the clear sky, and the shining dragoon's helmet with its mighty
curved rib and black horsetail seemed almost to reach them. It
was not out of longing that Angelina ran toward him—but fear
and anxious impatience. He waited motionless, like a multicolored rock, until she reached him. She was not bold enough to
look up to his top, to his towering, dazzling zenith. Her sky-blue
bonnet reached only up to the pommel of his sabre and his lowest vest button. With a powerful arm, and without needing to
bend at all, he lifted her up to his face level and, as her legs dangled helplessly in mid-air, his mustache rubbed against her forehead, her closed eyes, and her freckled cheeks, like a soft brush.
She floated breathlessly between heaven and earth for what felt
like an eternity. At last he let her slip dizzily back to the ground
again. She staggered along at his right hip, while his sabre rattled
at his left. His spurs jingled menacingly and his boots crunched
lightly but sharply. Thus they headed off to the evening's leisure.

His leave seemed never to end; apparently he had much in-
fluence in his regiment. Equally evident was the fact that his
need for Angelina's love was a long way from being satiated. He
could, as he had hinted a few times, get himself transferred to a
cavalry regiment in Paris. The mere thought of it filled Angelina
with genuine terror. She dared not ask when he would be leaving. When he reiterated that he could serve just as well in Paris
as in Lyons or Grenoble, she realized that he was waiting for her
endorsement and encouragement. She accepted and submitted
to him with the same resignation as one gives in to fate. He fell

upon her regularly every evening at the same time like a colorful, clattering avalanche. Although broken and exhausted, the very fact that she could rise again with her body in one piece seemed to be blessing enough. Clearly, this man had been destined for her from the dawn of time. Even the cards had foretold it.

High over her head, so that she could hardly understand him, he prattled away tirelessly. She heard rumbling noises, little claps of thunder, and when sometimes he sneezed it sounded like a cloudburst. It was only when she sat across from him at the table that she could actually understand what he was saying, although she could not fully comprehend its meaning. Spellbound but not without rancor, as one can sometimes be entranced by something odious and ugly, little Angelina watched the grotesque movements of the mighty masculine mouth that seemed to be chewing while he spoke, the large red lower lip and the mustache that swept continuously through the empty air. The Sergeant-Major spoke lofty words, but to Angelina their ponderous tedium caused them to fall flat. Still, she did not dare look away from his face.

Although she felt that he alone was the cause of her worst sins, it seemed to be an even greater sin to resist and not obey him. She was therefore completely at a loss. She felt that henceforth she was without the power to choose between virtue and sin, condemned to sway back and forth between two kinds of sin. She realized that since this mighty man had forced himself upon her, she had abandoned her old and comforting habit of attending church, out of fear that—helpless and stained as she believed herself to be—she might infuriate God through her presence alone. She longed to return to the forever-vanished days of her childhood purity.

One evening on their way home, when they were already near the palace, the Sergeant-Major raised a finger, pointed toward the palace and said: "He's had much luck. Perhaps more luck than he deserves."

It was already late in the evening and the streets were so still that Angelina could hear his words clearly, although they rumbled quite far over her head. At first she did not understand what the Sergeant-Major meant. However, she felt immediate disgust, and even before she figured out to whom he was referring, she began to hate him—and only on account of this single remark.

"Who's had luck?" she asked in her thin, timid voice.

"Him, naturally, Bonaparte!" It was unusual for someone to refer to the Emperor with this name and Angelina's hatred of the Sergeant-Major increased.

"The Emperor?" she asked.

"Yes, him naturally!" said the Sergeant-Major.

"You serve in his army!" Angelina replied. She managed these words only with great effort. Her voice was trembling.

"In his army," said the Sergeant-Major (and he intoned the word "his" spitefully), "many serve who dislike him. But you wouldn't understand such things, little one!"

They had arrived at the fence, and suspicion was awakened in Angelina—for the first time in her young life, suspicion!—that the Sergeant-Major had stopped speaking of the Emperor only because he feared someone would overhear him.

He lifted her up as he always did at their parting, but not with one arm as at their greeting; for the guards were no longer watching and it was apparently not worth wasting his strength when there were no witnesses. So he raised her with both arms, kissed her noisily on both cheeks, with a sound that echoed into the silent night and set her down to the ground with a jerk, less gently than when they met. When she was safely on earth again, he said: "Tomorrow we will celebrate my departure. The day after tomorrow my leave ends and can't be extended. The day after tomorrow I must report for duty. Will you be sorry?"

"Yes, I'll be sorry," murmured Angelina.

For the first time since her relationship with the Sergeant-Major had begun, she ran cheerfully up the steps and for the first time in weeks she slept gently, without nightmares. The next morning she awoke just as cheerfully as she had fallen asleep. The last day of her agonizing affair had dawned and she felt like a child on the evening before a happy holiday. In the evening, when the Sergeant-Major appeared at the gate punctual and shimmering as always, she ran to meet him almost happily. For the first time she felt sort of thankful toward this colossus and was in fact somewhat ashamed before him. For the first time also she did not shudder at the mustache that brushed gently against her face.

Later, however, when they entered a café named "The Everlasting Joy," her chipper mood evaporated. To celebrate his farewell, Sergeant-Major Sosthène had invited many of his comrades—non-commissioned officers, two provosts, and some officials. By the time he and Angelina entered, most of them were already assembled. They crowded around the metal-topped counter. Behind it bustled the proprietor, in a green apron and white shirt, with a ruddy bloated face and a cheery black mustache that shone with the same gleam as his eyes. All turned to face the newcomers, as if by command, and cried: "Long live Sosthène!" Mighty and magnificent Sosthène remained at the threshold, open door at his back, for he thought given the circumstances it would be inappropriate for him to close it himself. At his right hip, looking far less impressive than the sabre at his left, clung Angelina. He raised his hand, letting Angelina's arm drop as he did so, leaving her feeling that he was completely abandoning her in the hour of his triumph, and he thundered: "I'm here, comrades!"

At the same moment, an accordion in the corner began to play one of the customary military marches.

They all began to eat right away—quickly, intently, and silently. They ate tremendous mouthfuls with great appetite, drank down voluminous glasses full, and watched their plates zealously. Angelina did not wish to look at the others, but something made her keep looking and every time she saw one of the guests devour a large forkful, she took ever smaller and daintier forkfuls. This farewell evening was going to drag on forever, she thought, and the jovial men gathered here were all her fiancés, so it mattered not whether Sergeant-Major Sosthène's leave ended the next morning. She was betrothed to all his friends and was at their mercy.

Once all the beef had been devoured, a Corporal of artillery got to his feet, rapped on his glass, and began a speech.

He spoke of all of Sergeant-Major Sosthène's heroic deeds and made it sound as if the Emperor had Sergeant-Major Sosthène to thank for all his victories.

After the Corporal was done, the Sergeant-Major stood and confirmed, with only minor corrections, the Corporal's words. Everyone applauded him.

When midnight struck most of the participants were drunk and no longer had their wits about them. And they began to talk about the Emperor.

The first to speak was Sergeant-Major Sosthène. "Each of us sitting here," he said, "could have had the same luck." But in reality, he meant that only he, Sergeant-Major Sosthène Levadour, could have had the same luck and no one else.

"Each of us," repeated the Corporal who had given the oratory on the Sergeant-Major.

"He's a lucky guy!" said one of the provosts taking part in the festivities, a gray-haired fellow with a shriveled-up face.

"He's a fox!" said another.

"He's thoughtless and unscrupulous," began a third. "Think about it, my comrades, think how easily he betrayed the people and their freedom."

"The French people!" interjected a fourth.

"He has betrayed the liberty of the people," said Sergeant-Major Sosthène, "yes indeed, that he has! I must say that, even though I'm one of his soldiers, a soldier in our glorious army."

"Certainly, we have abundant glory," the Corporal of the artillery proclaimed. "And it is quite true that without him we wouldn't have seen the world and it wouldn't have trembled before us. Nevertheless, I must say ..."

The Provost finished the Corporal's sentence: "Nevertheless, I must say that we have him to thank for everything, our Little Corporal."

The company did not entirely agree with him. It remained quiet for some time after these words. Sergeant-Major Sosthène alone, being even more intoxicated than the others, spoke with a bitter tone and a tone that was no longer reliable: "As far as I, myself, and fellows of my type are concerned, we should have conquered the world anyhow. Right, my comrades?"

He looked from one to the next, lips still grinning beneath his moist and disheveled mustache, black eyes glowing spitefully from a warm and ruddy face. Nobody answered him. They all occupied themselves with something or another. One lifted his glass to the light and studied it for possible dust. Another polished his fork with the tablecloth. A third wore a vacant smile, as though he had not been listening to the conversation for hours. A fourth drank the rest of his wine with a conspicuous slowness, as if trying to taste each and every drop with his tongue. Despite his drunkenness, Sergeant-Major Sosthène noticed that the whole group had abandoned him. He propped both his giant fists on the table and stood, seeming to be supporting himself on his arms not his legs. And he said, with a glance at Angelina at his side: "Comrades! What's the General without us? What's an Emperor without soldiers? Who's greater: the Emperor or the army? Who's greater, I ask? Who's greater, I ask?"

But no answer came.

"I say this," continued Sosthène. "The army is greater! Long live the army!"

Angelina had been sitting still the entire time. A powerful fear and a great, previously unknown shame had gripped her chest. She felt that the shame and fear had a tight hold on her heart, compressing it from both sides at the same time like a pair of iron clamps. She had no idea from whence this shame and fright came. She felt defiled in this company and also guilty for listening to them without contradiction. Suddenly she was also filled with hatred and fury toward all the men at the table and especially against Sergeant-Major Sosthène. She wanted to call for help. With great effort she lifted her hand from her lap—her small, young, reddish hand—and grabbed her glass. She drank a little and all at once she imagined herself again in the grand chamber, near the heavy, undulating green portière, sitting before the crystal decanter. She could even see the Emperor's portrait on the wall. She suddenly felt free, strong, and bold. A powerful, exhilarating, and intimately familiar force washed over her. She stood up. A joyful hatred hardened her heart. And an unfamiliar, kindly spirit imbued her with brave words.

"You should be ashamed of yourselves," she said, "for slandering the Emperor. You would be nothing—less than nothing, without him. Not only would you not have seen the world—you wouldn't have ventured even a mile out of your villages or towns. Without the Emperor you'd have no swords, no helmets, and no braid; not even the money to buy the wine you're drinking. You only stood with him in battle because he led you. If any one of you has shown bravery you've only Napoleon to thank for that too. He alone gave you courage and then medals for your service, medals you don't deserve. That's why I say you should be ashamed of yourselves!"

She sat down again. She saw as if from a great distance (although he was sitting at her side) Sergeant-Major Sosthène reach for the carafe and refill his glass. She saw the hands that she knew so well, his stubby-fingered, fleshy, hairy, muscular hands—she saw them both although the Sergeant-Major only stretched one toward the decanter—and she remembered with deep horror and profound shame how these shameless, depraved, hairy tools were used to fondling her flesh, her breasts, her arms, and her thighs.

A great anguish seemed suddenly to have spread around the table. It seemed to everyone that the candles were burning away at a more quick and hurried pace, the tallow disappearing more rapidly, the whole room growing much darker. Nobody felt able to converse with anyone else. It was a pathetic and failed celebration—without a doubt. All were silent.

But just when the spirits of the guests were about to become irretrievably squashed by the gloom, the door flew open and together with the fresh evening breeze that caused the candles to flicker, and, as though carried in with it, Véronique Casimir stormed into the room. She came as if riding, wearing unusually festive clothes—in full armor, that is to say, with bare shoulders and heaving bosom, wearing the light-gray silk gown that was rumored to be a personal gift from the Empress Josephine and which she sported only on special occasions. Between her unnaturally white breasts, from which emanated a delicate cloud of flour-colored powder, hung a heavy and solid piece of jade surrounded by glittering diamonds—a gift from the Empress Josephine and doubtless a magical stone of the first degree. The door remained open for some time, and the stream of fresh night air continued to fan the golden candle flames. The proprietor quickly placed another armchair at the head end of the table. Before they could decide what this gleaming vision portended, Véronique sat down. "I see," she began with the certain voice of a professional seer, "that you have been arguing. Peace must prevail among you."

Her pale, fleshy fingers tapped loquaciously upon the white tablecloth, each individual finger a voiceless tongue. A delicate cloud of white powder wafted from her wide face. Behind the cloud the guests could see her black eyes glowing. All were quiet. Véronique was a confidante of the Imperial House. She had prophesied battles, victories and defeats with the cards. She had been a confidante of the Empress and, who knew, perhaps even a confidante of the Emperor himself.

She well knew what the men were thinking. Her primary concern was the prospective marriage of her niece to Sergeant-Major Sosthène. She knew that Angelina, just like all the women in France, loved the Emperor not Sergeant-Major Sosthène—for every woman in the entire land (and perhaps even in the entire world) loved the Emperor at that time and not their own men. When people spoke maliciously about the Emperor, it seemed to Véronique as senseless as if one were to take a stand against some institution of nature. For the moment, her main concern was Angelina's happiness. Even if Sergeant-Major Sosthène did belong to those Jacobins, he still could marry Angelina eventually.

Still, it upset Véronique Casimir to hear the Emperor slandered. This was not such a rare occurrence at the time; it was even common among the Imperial servants, in many regiments, and among unhappy non-commissioned officers. Indeed, long ago, when the Emperor was still known as Bonaparte, even Véronique

Casimir had been tempted, sometimes even while in confidential conversation with the Emperor's own wife, to let slip strong words against the great one. Recalling this only made her more resolute against those who now dared say anything against the Emperor.

She resolved to deal with these blasphemers on a later occasion, but not to let them see this for the time being. Soon she noticed, however, that the men were gesturing to each other by all kinds of silent and impudent signs that they must have thought were secret and undecipherable to her. Only Sergeant-Major Sosthène sat, gigantic and unmoving, next to little Angelina, and seemingly without comprehension of his friends' behavior. He offered Véronique Casimir some wine. She drank delicately, cautiously, stretching her little finger when she raised the glass, so that her rings glittered in the candlelight. She took tiny sips from her glass, setting it down after each one, and watched the men's conspiracy with a spiteful shrewdness. She listened with open and doubly sharpened ears. And suddenly she hear the Corporal whisper to a sergeant-major: "It makes him weak. We are better in bed ..."

Véronique Casimir knew instantly of what they were speaking. Ah! She was familiar with all the hushed rumors and stories about the fleeting and shameless haste of the Emperor's lovemaking. Maid-servants and laundresses had experienced this brand of love-making, as had ladies of the court and the Empress herself. Yet all of these women, the superior and the inferior, were grateful to the Emperor for his hasty, careless, and indifferent embrace. They never forgot that he was a god and that it is in the nature of gods to love quickly. In those days women could speak the Emperor's name only with hatred, fear, or love, as though the women who gave themselves to his embrace felt during that brief minute all the passion of the entire world—hatred, fear, and love. Véronique Casimir knew that for these women there was passion stronger than pleasure and that was ambition. True they were not sated when they emerged from the Emperor's room, but they were uplifted and ennobled. He dismissed them quickly and disappeared just as fast. They left his presence feeling an infinite hunger and a permanent desire to return to him. He possessed all the characteristics of the gods: he was mighty, terrible in his anger, and brief in his grace. The gods are fleeting.

So Véronique raised her glass with a hurried gesture, swallowed down the rest with a single manly gulp, and said with the hard military voice she used to give orders to her staff: "Gentlemen!" This form of address broke up the men's brazen whispers. Everyone looked up. "Gentlemen!" she repeated. She remained seated, but her face projected such superiority she appeared to be standing. "You don't seem," she continued, "used to taking the presence of ladies into consideration. In any event, you should understand that I belong to the Imperial court and so does my niece." She said "court" and not "household." "The commentary that you are so timidly whispering to each other is perhaps suitable to your barracks, although I know that even there they aren't customary. I leave you, gentlemen! I bid you a pleasant evening. And you, Sergeant-Major Sosthène, be sure to bring the little one home punctually. I will be waiting for her. Come speak to me," she said to Angelina. "Good night!" And before they knew it, she galloped out just as suddenly as she had come in—again leaving the door open behind her for a while, as the wind made the ends of the tablecloth dance and caused the candles to flicker.

All was quiet. For a few moments all felt that they had been scolded by a superior. They looked rather pathetic in their colorful uniforms.

Angelina now felt herself poor, abandoned, and betrayed. She longed for those kind native shores, for her father's house in Corsica and her poor but happy childhood. All at once, she realized she had given the strange, multicolored mountain something he did not deserve. It seemed to her that up to that very moment she had been living outside of her own body, as if she had given it away like some ordinary thing. She foresaw the great and strict law Nature had delineated for women and understood she had violated it. Relentless, sublime, and beautiful, it commanded girls to belong to their beloved and repel those they did not love. She thought of the room with the wavy green curtain and the Emperor's portrait on the wall. Suddenly, she was able to shed her shame, and it was as though she had already recovered from her grave sin. She felt now that she could only love the one who was for her—and this love alone, her ability and readiness to love him, was something so great that sin, misdemeanor, error, and shame no longer had any import.

She finally raised her eyes and now, for the first time, they were proud and indifferent. And thus she was able to see that the colorful mountain by her side was so stiff and silent only because he had lost his senses. It was evidently his own special type of inebriation. It was more terrifying than the loud and more common type. The Sergeant-Major sat there unmoving, his small black eyes wide open and gawking. He was more petrified than drunk. Little Angelina nudged his stony-blue sleeve. Sosthène did not budge. She looked at the others. They took no notice of her. Some of them had risen and were playing dice or cards at another table. One of the provosts, the Corporal, and two sergeant-majors were whispering stories to each other and after each one, all four broke into foolish giggles. Angelina rose. She left the table without a word, taking gentle steps. Not even the proprietor noticed her.

She stood outside looking up at the sky. She had forgotten to check the time in the restaurant. It seemed to be far past midnight, and she gazed at the stars in a sudden, fond recollection of those long-gone childhood nights when she had sailed out to sea with her father and the old man had looked to the heavens to determine the time. This night there were only a few stars visible. Between the black clouds, which despite their ponderous heaviness were chasing across the sky at a surprising speed, here and there an occasional silver prick flashed and then disappeared. The wind blew sharply, seeming to come from several different directions at once. The streets were empty and the late lanterns were lonely, flickering unsteadily and unhappily. Now a pale flash of lightning lit up the houses and was followed by the far off rumble of roaming thunder. Little Angelina was frightened. She wrapped her cloak more tightly around her body. Although she did not know in what direction the route she picked would lead her, she decided to push forward without worrying. When she finally reached a corner from which she thought the lamp-light of a nearby main street was visible, the first heavy raindrops were starting to fall, and at the next moment a close and dazzling flash of lightning split the clouds. Angelina walked ever more quickly. By the time she reached a wide and better-lit avenue, the rain was pouring down violently, so she sheltered herself in the doorway of a large house. Light was streaming from its windows and gilding the pouring rain. Fine carriages were waiting in front of the building. Angelina found this doorway to be quite pleasant. She found herself immediately taking pleasure in everything before her: the rain, the lightning, the carriages, the fine house, and the gracious doorway. A great joyfulness filled her and made everything around her seem pleasing, even the lightning, thunder, and rain.

It must have already been quite late. A liveried porter descended the steps, opened both wings of the colossal front door, and cast an imperious glance at Angelina. All the coachmen suddenly awoke, as if they had been called, crept from inside their vehicles, stood at the carriage doors, and let down the steps. Angelina continued merrily along the street, in the direction her heart led her. She took measured steps, neither slow nor quick, even though her coat, her dress, and her shoes were wet.

By the time she spied the palace, the rain had eased and the morning was growing noticeably stronger. The sentry was asleep in his guardhouse and did not see her. For the first time since she began working in Paris, she passed without apprehension through the narrow gateway that opened smoothly, silently, and practically hospitably. She climbed the steps. All was calm and peaceful. The misty morning was beaming through the high narrow windows at the staircase landings, and out of the distance came the tentative first song of the awakening birds.

Angelina took from her box the Emperor's handkerchief, which she had not looked at in a long time, pressed it against her heart and then her cheek, undressed herself, and slept quickly and easily, with the colorful handkerchief under her nightgown, near her happy heart ...

V

ALL ACROSS THE LAND AND THE WORLD, WOMEN LOVED the Emperor. But to Angelina it seemed that to love the Emperor was a special and mysterious art; she felt betrothed to him, the most exalted lord of all time. He lived within her always. Even as great as he was, there was room enough for him in her little heart; it had grown to absorb the entirety of his splendid majesty ...

She forgot Sergeant-Major Sosthène very quickly, though. He sometimes resurfaced in her memory like a huge shadow emerging from a repressed dream. Anyway, it had been weeks since she had heard from him: no wonder, for the Emperor was readying a new campaign and his regiments changed their positions every week. Few soldiers wrote to their sweethearts and wives during that time.

A day arrived on which something remarkable happened to Angelina, something terrifying, upsetting, and completely incomprehensible. As she was swinging her open smoothing-iron with vigor to incite the charcoal embers, it suddenly flew from her hand, as if ripped away by some unseen force. She watched it crash against the wall, striking it with its pointed end, and then fall to the floor with the coal glowing red in its mouth. Then she felt that she herself was falling into a profound and immeasurable blackness.

She awoke in her bed. Véronique Casimir had been summoned. The kindly, trustworthy woman was now sitting beside Angelina. Angelina came to with clear memory of the iron and the strange force that had pulled it from her grip. "So it is this far along!" she heard Véronique Casimir say. These were the first words she heard upon her return to the world.

This proclamation frightened her. "What is so far along?" she asked.

And gently and calmly, Véronique replied: "You're having a baby, Angelina. I will make sure that Monsieur Levadour is notified. Have no fear. We'll fetch him for sure."

"A child?" asked Angelina. "Why?"

"It is God's will," said Véronique softly, casting her gaze to the ceiling and then crossing herself. "We'll get him," she repeated.

"We'll get who?" asked Angelina.

"Why, Sergeant-Major Sosthène Levadour, naturally!" replied Véronique.

"What do we want with him?" Angelina asked.

"We want you to have a husband," said Véronique.

"I don't need a husband," said Angelina, and she thought about the nightly attacks that she had endured on the small plush red sofa, with the hard bolster pressing into her neck.

"Certainly you need a husband!" replied Véronique. "Above all you need a man to be father to your child."

"I don't want a child," said Angelina. "I don't need a child or a husband!"

"You need them both!" Véronique insisted quietly.

Angelina shut her eyes in the hopes that it would help her avoid seeing the great terror that now seemed to be sitting on Véronique's armchair by the bedside. But under her closed eyelids, she saw it in even clearer detail. It took the colossal form of Sergeant-Major Sosthène, who had suddenly changed from a shadow into an actual being again, even though he must have by now been off in some distant garrison and perhaps—hopefully so—determined not to know Angelina anymore. What was the use? She was to have a baby, and it was the Sergeant-Major's child. The colossus was inside her and stirring within her. She was too weak to rip him from her feeble body. She decided to open her eyes again, for the danger seemed to be getting ever closer and larger. But she had no strength to accomplish even this.

This lasted only a few minutes. Véronique now bore a solemn expression, which brought Angelina even more trepidation. It felt like a dangerous yet extremely serene Sunday. She did not hear all of Véronique's words, but she was sure that what was being said with the intent to comfort was actually what she feared most. She was very tired; it felt like the events of the day and of the previous weeks were in the distant past and had been played out in another, previous life. Now a new life lay before her, totally unfamiliar and very dangerous. She closed her eyes and waited for her aunt to leave, so that sleep might come over her. But sleep did not come. Instead a great mildness filled her, a great compassion for herself, her aunt, and even for Sergeant-Major Sosthène. She dreamed with wakeful eyes of a vast battlefield, one of the Emperor's battlefields. Red hot bullets flew through the air; there was a roaring and rumbling, flaring and thundering on all sides. She could not visualize the Emperor himself, but she had a great longing to see him. She called his name: "Napoleon!" she cried. "Napoleon!" But her voice died, meek and toneless in the mighty ruckus. She found herself far away from those who were fighting and yet she was also in their midst. Suddenly she saw Sergeant-Major Sosthène beside her, wobbling on his saddle. Just then, he fell from his horse. He raised both arms to the sky and cried: "Angelina!" But she did not care about him. She felt only that in a moment he would die—and even though she was ashamed of it, she wished with all her might for his death.

She awoke, remembered the dream, and was even more ashamed. But, at the same time, an unfamiliar feeling of elation, at once warm and cool, streamed through her. She was no longer afraid.

VI

SEVEN MONTHS LATER SHE BORE A SON IN THE HOUSE of the Corsican midwife Barbara Pocci, a good friend of Véronique Casimir. Angelina rested safely, happy and without fear, in the broad, well-padded bed in which for years unmarried mothers had been bearing children. From the bed she could see many familiar things that inspired nostalgia and reminded her of Corsica and her childhood. A small, brightly colored wooden statue of Saint Christopher stood smiling and lonely on a fragile, high-legged table in the midwife's room. The same statue had been in Angelina's house in Ajaccio. On the neighboring commode shone a fat-bellied bottle, containing a miniature sailing ship carved with much detail during the leisure hours of the midwife's brother, a worthy sailor; it was one of the customary works of seafaring men. There was a similar commode in Angelina's house in Ajaccio as well and also such a ship in a bottle. Over the door, instead of a curtain, hung one of the tightly spun nets that fishermen employed to catch small creatures. Although they had probably long since left their native isle, a familiar bittersweet odor still wafted from all these pleasant objects. It was scent of algae and sea air, of mother-of-pearl shells and brownish-black sea urchins. One could practically visualize dark blue storm clouds hovering over the sullen waves of a stormy sea.

One day Véronique Casimir brought paper, quill, and ink to the bed and said: "I have his address."

Angelina understood that she meant Sergeant-Major Sosthène. She made one last meager attempt to avoid the unavoidable and asked: "Whose address?"

"Sosthène's address," answered Véronique. "Now you must write to him."

"I have nothing to say to him," Angelina insisted.

"You must! I command you!" Véronique replied. "Here, write!" She laid a sheet of paper on the bedspread, dipped the quill in the inkwell, stepped menacingly close to the bedside, and held the plume so imperiously before her niece's face that Angelina had to obey. She wrote:

"Dear Sir: My aunt, Mademoiselle Véronique Casimir, begs me to inform you that I gave birth to a child two days ago. It is a boy. I send you greetings, Angelina Pietri."

Véronique took the paper, read it, shook her head and said: "Good. I will add the rest. He won't get away from me!"

She knew where to reach him. The Emperor had just won a great battle, and the troops were still in Austria. Véronique knew not only Sergeant-Major Levadour's address but was also acquainted with the wife of the colonel who led his regiment.

Two weeks later, Sergeant-Major Sosthène Levadour actually showed up. He had been given leave, special leave, and he decided to use it in a special way. The Emperor's great victory—and the fact that he had not only taken part in a noteworthy battle but also was himself the deciding factor (he assumed) of this Imperial victory—only made him more arrogant, more colorful, and colossal. He was a giant in the low-ceilinged room where Angelina and her child were staying. He greeted her with his usual dashing but severe affection, lifting her into the air with both hands, and in this room she felt she was being dangled at an even higher altitude than on the evenings during the previous summer, that the smell of his mustache was even more potent and that it swept across her cheeks even more intensely and roughly. Then he put her down again before him, took a step back and then two large steps forward, reached the bed where his son lay, and bent over him. The little one whimpered pathetically. Sosthène lifted the wrapped bundle high. It seemed quite insignificant in his arms. He asked: "What's his name? What've you called him?"

"Antoine Pascal," said Angelina, "after my father."

"Glad to hear it, glad to hear it!" thundered Sosthène. "He'll be a soldier, he has a soldier's blood." And he laid the white bundle down diagonally on the bed.

He squeezed himself into the narrow red upholstered armchair, jerked it around the room a bit, and realized it would be difficult to free his massive figure again from the chair arms clamping him in. He felt both somewhat unsettled and a little embarrassed about it, and, because just at that moment he had something critical to say, he grew angry and his face turned purple. It looked like a colorful crown for his colorful uniform. For a time he searched for an appropriate start, thought of the amicably threatening letters that Véronique Casimir had written him and the fact that he would now, because of this pitiful little bundle, have to marry a red-haired, freckled girl. For a moment his slow and dull brain was lit by a slight spark of insight into fate, guilt, and sin. The meager stirring of his vacant heart that followed, however, only increased his wrath. At that moment he would have been willing to believe in God if only to be angry with Him and have somewhere to place all the blame. However, he did not believe in the unseen God so he doled out his wrath only upon that which he could see.

He thought with bitterness of the various and fleeting women he had possessed as a dragoon might, and it seemed to him that Angelina could not compare with a single one of them so far as beauty went. And Sergeant-Major Sosthène grew even more angry and bitter. Of the sergeant-majors in his regiment, only one was married, a certain Renard, who was over fifty years old, thus his foolish deed had occurred so long ago that it could hardly be called ridiculous anymore. He, however, Sergeant-Major Sosthène Levadour, could still advance his career and even become a colonel. A man such as he had to have money for himself, in order to live and entertain others. Besides, in Bohemia, he had just met a fine woman, a widowed mill owner who was provocatively unruly and highly sought after by men; she was obedient to love, like a dog, but also violent as a battle. What a woman! He compared her to Angelina, who was now sitting across from him on the bed, child at her side, with lowered eyes and a pale and sorrowful little face bearing freckles even more clearly evident than they had been during the summer. Oh what misery, great Sosthène!

"I will marry you!" he said finally.

"What for?" asked Angelina without lifting her eyes, as though speaking to an invisible someone at her feet.

Sergeant-Major Sosthène did not comprehend at first. He only felt vaguely that his noble intentions were being rejected and his true wishes accepted. He was somewhat insulted—and at the same time relieved.

"I won't marry you!" Angelina said.

He stared at her. She was incomprehensible, dangerous, yet seemingly offering him escape. Before he had feared the whole vile burden of this pending marriage, but now it struck him as an insult that she would not agree to go through with it. Before he had been thinking of the Bohemian widow with a lustful nostalgia, but Angelina suddenly seemed desirable. He was greatly astonished by this heretofore unknown and unprecedented complication of his emotions. A horrible suspicion awoke in him, and although this suspicion hurt him much, he held on to it with all his might, for it at least helped explain the bizarre feelings that were now stirring in him.

"So you have betrayed me?" he asked.

"I have betrayed you!" she lied. "He's not your son!" The words sounded strange to her ears, as if another woman sitting beside her had spoken them.

"Aha!" said Sosthène after a long while.

Then he pressed both of his sturdy fists on the arms of the chair that was holding him prisoner and freed himself with a powerful jerk. He retrieved his helmet, which lay next to him on the floor like a magical gleaming black-maned animal, and put it back on his head. Now he reached the ceiling. He stood there larger than ever, enlarged not only by pride but also by contempt. Angelina sat, tiny and pitiful yet bold, on the edge of the bed.

"Tell me the truth!" thundered Sosthène.

"I'm speaking the truth!" said Angelina.

She looked up at him. She covered a great distance with her eyes in order to do so, and somehow her feet were exhausted from the mountain climbing of her gaze. The thought that he would now (but never again) lift her up and kiss her made her happy.

Suddenly he turned around, reached the doorway with one of his prodigious strides, measured its height, found it too low, ducked a little, and without looking back, slammed it violently.

Angelina then heard him speak a few rancorous words to the midwife outside. She bent over the now screaming child and babbled words that were unintelligible even to her but that brightened her mood. "You are mine," she said, "he is not, be still, you are mine, you belong to me ..."

So spoke she to her child, softly and at length.

That very day, Sergeant-Major Sosthène set off to rejoin his regiment in Bohemia without even having seen his friends in Paris. When he caught up with his regiment it was already on its march back to France. He soon told his comrades that he had a fine son. He was a magnificent little fellow who, although barely three weeks old, looked and behaved like a soldier. Further, Sergeant-Major Sosthène added that thanks to his cleverness, he would not have to marry the child's mother.

VII

ANGELINA THOUGHT OF THE EMPEROR CONSTANTLY. BUT even he, unique and powerful, had ceased to be a living being whose every breath brought happiness, whose voice and glance brought joy, and whose wet footprints on bathroom tiles had inspired humble adoration. He truly had become the great Emperor of the paintings. He was now himself like a copy of his own portraits, yes, and even more remote than they. He was far from the people of France. From the battlefield he hurried to deliberations and from these back to his battles. His negotiations were as inconceivable as his victories. He had long since ceased being the hero of the common man. They no longer understood him. It was as if the power that emanated from him had enveloped him in a transparent but impregnable sphere of ice. He lived within this sphere in some kind of noble isolation, terrible and solemn. He sent away the Empress and married the daughter of a great foreign emperor in a distant country, as though there were not enough women in his own land. And just as he ordered certain wares from the countries he controlled, so had he once sent for the Pope to come from Rome; in the same way he now sent for the daughter of a foreign emperor. Just as he ordered the cannon to thunder in many parts of the world, so now he ordered the bells of Paris and all of France to toll. Just as he commanded his soldiers to fight his battles, he commanded them to celebrate his festivals. And just as he had once challenged God, so now he commanded prayer to Him. The Emperor's common subjects could feel his violent impatience, and they saw that he could act in ways both grand and small, foolish and wise, good and evil, just as they did. But so much grander were both his virtues and flaws, that they could not understand him.

Angelina alone loved him, although she numbered among the lowliest of his subjects. So much did she love him that she sometimes cherished the foolish wish to see the Great One made small and defeated, driven from all lands to a humiliating homecoming in Corsica. Then he would be almost as base as she, without the luster that he continually bestowed anew upon his own portraits.

In accordance with the rules that regulated life for those in the Imperial service, Angelina returned to work three months after her confinement. Spring was already flowing like a great strong river through the rejuvenated city. Full and proud glistened the candles of the chestnut trees along the sides of the streets. Angelina came across many mothers with children; even the poorly clothed mothers, even the pale and sickly children, smiled with illuminated faces. At each of these encounters, Angelina wished to turn back, to have just one more peek at her boy. When she stood before the gate, where barely a year earlier the multicolored mountain with the fluttering helmet plume had waited for her every evening, she stood still for a while as if contemplating a momentous decision. She could still go back and see her son and be a little later in arriving to work. In the palace garden, the thrushes were raising a joyful ruckus, and they were answered by equally overwhelming scents coming from the park—from the air itself—the voices of the acacias, lilacs, and elderberries. White as a Sunday gleamed the vests of the sentries, and the dark green of their coats was reminiscent of lush meadows. The unmoving guard looked at her. She thought she recognized the man and that he also recognized her. Within his glassy official stare gleamed a tiny spark, as if the glass were smiling, and Angelina nodded at him. This fleeting glimmer in the soldier's glassy eyes gave her courage; and she walked with swift steps toward the gate, as if afraid of losing it again.

From then on she worked only in the washroom. Loyal and industrious as always, she wielded her smoothing-iron with a powerful swing, spritzed water from her filled cheeks and pursed lips upon the silk, linen, and cambric, used the wooden stave with a learned hand and carefully pressed the shirts, collars, and pleated cuffs. When she thought about her son, she was both happy and sad. By Wednesday, no, even by Tuesday, the next Sunday already seemed almost as near as the coming evening.

Monday, however, one day after her visit to Pocci's house, was the most melancholy day of the week—and Saturday the brightest. On Saturday evenings, after inspection in the great hall, she packed everything together, both useful and useless. She packed salves and powders, serviettes, milk, cream and bread, strands of red coral beads to ward off the evil eye, buttercup root to prevent convulsions, and an herbal infusion that she was told would prevent pox.

She set out at seven o'clock in the morning. On the way she was overtaken by the fear that she would find her son ailing. She stopped for a while, powerless to put one foot before the other, shattered, as if her frightening vision were already a horrible reality. Then, confidence once more gave wings to her steps. When she finally stood in Barbara's room leaning over her child, she began to weep bitterly. Her hot tears fell rapidly upon the boy's smiling face. She lifted him up, walked with him around the room, and spoke nonsensical phrases to him. Only the measure by which her little son grew bigger and stronger and changed, made her note the unstoppable course of the months and years. It was as if previously she had lived according to the mindset that time did not advance but rolled, so to speak, in a circle.

Her hopes were fulfilled, and the little one looked not one bit like Sergeant-Major Sosthène but rather like his mother. He had reddish hair and freckles, was thin, strong, and agile. He was her son, no doubt! Yet almost from the beginning she felt he was slipping away from her and becoming more and more a stranger to her from one Sunday to the next. In fact, sometimes she believed that he allowed her affection only out of childish shyness and that he sold every kiss to her for a present. He was her son, red-haired and saturated with freckles; she had only to glance at him, and it was as if she were looking at herself in the mirror. But sometimes that reflection vanished, evaporated, or suddenly transformed. There were Sundays when she did not find the boy at home. He was off running around with his friends (whom she hated) in places unknown, and she had trouble finding him; when she did locate him, he soon escaped once more from her tenderness and care.

When he was seven, the boy was gripped by an intense passion for all things military—as was common for many children at the time. He hung around the barracks, befriended the guards, drilled with his comrades, stole and collected battle pictures and portraits of the Emperor, soon made his way to the barrack yards, ate out of the bowls of the good-humored soldiers, learned military songs, bugle-blowing, drumming, and even musket-handling. When one day he spied one of the little drummer boys, of whom there were many in the Imperial Army, he decided to become a drummer himself. He knew that he was a soldier's son and understood all that was spoken between his mother, the midwife Pocci, and Véronique Casimir on those Sunday visits. And he had a very definite and clear idea of what his unknown father was like.

So one day, the boy decided to spend the night in the barracks of the Twenty-Second Infantry Regiment, strengthened in his decision by a sympathetic but somewhat tipsy Sergeant-Major. He received many frightening caresses but thought they must be a part of the military life. He was only found two weeks later thanks to the inquiries of the influential Véronique Casimir. By now the boy was officially a soldier in the Emperor's army, and on Sundays Angelina went to the barracks of the Twenty-Second Infantry Regiment to visit him.

The first time, she came back bewildered, frightened, and affronted. Her son reminded her now (even though he still resembled her) of Sergeant-Major Sosthène. She could barely see his freckled face—the huge shako with its steep slope practically hid it; his excessively wide uniform jacket flapped about the boy's narrow hips; his pants were too long; and his boots horrendously large. She saw that her son was lost forever. At home, she looked at herself in the mirror, for the first time in many years searching for signs of time's passage and for beauty and youth, as she had done in the old days. She found the eternal and solitary comfort that Nature has granted to women; she began to wait for new miracles.

The miracle revealed itself on the next Sunday afternoon, as she was leaving the barracks of the Twenty-Second. Before her stood a man in the uniform of a Commissariat official, and this uniform seemed to block her way. When she raised her head, she saw a blond-haired, smiling, mustachioed face, which was familiar yet unpleasant. At a complete loss, she smiled at him. The man stood motionless. "Mademoiselle Angelina," he said and saluted. She recognized him at once from his voice. It was the gallant Corporal of the artillery who had attended Sergeant-Major Sosthène's farewell celebration. "Where did you come from?"

"I have been visiting my son," Angelina said.

"And your husband? My dear comrade? What is he up to?"

"I'm not married. He's not my husband. I have only my son," she replied.

"I too," began the former Corporal, as if recognizing that his fate was similar to hers, "I too have seen changes ..." and he gestured at his uniform. "I am now with the Commissariat. I've had enough of his campaigns"—and at the word "his" he pointed with his thumb over his shoulder, as if the Emperor were standing behind him. "I have a serious injury to my leg, nothing but misfortune! Nothing but misfortune! I got out at the right time. I can await the outcome in peace. Oh, I remember, Mademoiselle, your great anger that time at the party! You must now admit that you were not completely right. You certainly know what's happening."

"I don't know what's happening," whispered Angelina. "I only know that the rest of this regiment is waiting at the ready there." She pointed at the barracks. "And I'm anxious for my son," she added.

"Rightfully so," said the Commissariat official. "We're beaten! The enemy will be in Paris in two days. The Emperor comes tomorrow. I'm not worrying about that. I've served him loyally for years. Now I'm waiting to see what the great ones will decide. I'm a philosopher, Mademoiselle."

Although Angelina found the former corporal's voice, smile, and words disagreeable, she nodded when he was done speaking but she had no idea why. This encounter distressed and cheered her at the same time. Although she was looking down she could feel the man's kind and caressing gaze. That, as he had said, he was a philosopher and had been injured, that the Emperor was coming the next day, France was beaten, the enemy would be in Paris in two days, and the "great ones" were going to decide something—all this unnerved her as greatly as his kind and penetrating eyes.

He suggested that they "go somewhere." She was not surprised at his suggestion. She had in fact expected it and maybe even hoped for it. At this point she was in no mood to return to the palace and her roommates. Nor did she ask where he was taking her. Instead, she began to walk at his side. After a few steps he took her arm. A slight ripple, somewhat spine-chilling yet also somewhat soothing, came from his taut muscles. It was a compelling masculine tremor; she felt it in her arm and then through her entire body. It offended her yet also comforted her. It seemed to her that she existed in two separate parts. There were really two Angelinas: one proud and filled with disdain for the man at her side and the other helpless and grateful to him for the nameless kind of escape he offered. She was silent while he talked of politics, of the world, of the difficulties and errors of the Emperor. He led her through the city for what seemed like a very long time. Someone else was thinking for her, someone else had selected a destination for her. It was humiliating yet pleasant. She felt so alone, so betrayed. The man was a stranger, but he promised some kind of refuge, an escape at any rate. She could not go home, even though she was tired. It was a pleasurable exhaustion. The autumn day was cool. Menacing violet clouds drifted low over the rooftops and at the street corners the wind was blowing from all directions at once. Sometimes her foot landed on a crisp yellow leaf that had fluttered out of some garden. It crunched under her step with a dry and dead sound that seemed more like trampled bones than trampled leaves. Darkness fell very quickly; the Commissariat official had long since ceased speaking.

They entered a colorful, light-filled inn at Vanves, packed with non-commissioned officers, maid-servants, and accordions. It had been a long time since Angelina drank so much and so hastily. She sat on the soft red upholstered seat next to the man. The seat itself was soft, but the same-colored back was deceptively hard, a wooden board that only looked comfortable. To protect Angelina's back from this inhospitable board, the Commissariat official stretched his right arm out and laid it around her neck. With his left hand he poured more wine into their glasses. He bent his friendly pink-faced, blond-haired head toward hers. She felt it coming nearer through a thin blue-gray fog. She was shy but she did not recoil. She kissed his soft, sweet mustache. It seemed to last an eternity. She opened her eyes. It struck her that she did not even know the man's name. If only she knew his name, everything would be orderly and natural, justifiable before God and the world. So she asked: "What is your name?"

"Charles," he replied.

"Good," said Angelina. And now she felt that everything was in order and in good standing.

She spent the night with Commissariat official Charles Rouiffic. At this point she discovered, to her slight horror, that he seemed to have the ability to change himself from hour to hour—and at even shorter intervals. To start, when he removed his coat, he was a second Charles, a Charles in a vest and shirt; when he removed his vest, he was a third man, more strange than the second; and when he leaned over her and started to caress her, he was a third man who had become terrifyingly strange. After several hours he woke her, fresh, cheery, mustache brushed and pomaded, and his face looking like a little round and pink sunlit morning cloud. He was already fully dressed, and his sword hung faithfully at his hip as though it had never left his side. Now he was a fourth man, even more strange than the others.

During the day she forgot about him, and if he now and then did enter her thoughts she was soon able to chase his image out of her mind. She was ashamed—he was a stranger, and yet she needed him. That she needed a stranger only deepened her shame. But the hour was rapidly nearing when she had promised to meet him again. As she grew closer to him, he became ever clearer and more familiar, and finally he was a real person.

All this happened to Angelina in the last days before the great confusion in the land. So perhaps the state of bewilderment in which she found herself was down to the all-encompassing terror that was passing over the land like an evil, low-hanging storm cloud. Before the actual thunder of the enemy cannon was audible in Paris, it seemed to all that they could already hear the first echoes of enemy gunfire. Before it was known that the Emperor was truly defeated and was fleeing to the capital with the remnants of his army, everyone had a foreboding that he had lost and was retreating. This premonition was more terrible than the actual certainty a few days later. Evil forebodings bewilder the simple hearts of men, but evil certainty only worries and weakens them.

Angelina was no exception. She was bewildered amid the general bewilderment and terrified amid the general terror.

One day Charles, the Commissariat official, disappeared. For some days his presence at a specific place and at a definite time had been a humiliating but certain refuge. Now Angelina waited in vain. She sat in the little tavern, accordion music playing loudly, under the gaze of the staff who knew her and seemed themselves to be waiting on the appearance of Commissariat official Charles Rouiffic. All around her they were already gossiping about the misfortune of the Emperor, the misfortune of France. Angelina finally left.

VIII

MANY PEOPLE IN FRANCE AT THAT TIME IN 1814 WERE living in a state of chaos and distress. The enemy arrived. He came as enemies invariably do, with the full hellish retinue of the victor—vindictiveness, despotism, and a lust for spreading pointless misery. Numerous and very diverse were the enemies of France, but they all spread the same terror and they all promulgated sorrow and disaster through the same methods. Greater still than the confusion in the country and in the city of Paris was the confusion at the Imperial court. It was even stronger among the lower-level servants than among the high officials who were in the Emperor's service. For the simple and lowly are always the first to feel disaster's approach and also the first to suffer. The simple and the lowly are innocent of the faults and errors, the sins and fates of the great ones. Yet they suffer more than the famous ones. Storms destroy poor weak huts but they sweep past the strong stone houses.

Two days before the Emperor left the city and the country, the lesser ones began to leave him. All their simple hearts were concerned with was fear for their lives, fear of an unknown and thus terrifying danger. They fled aimlessly in all different directions. The servant men and women took refuge with friends who were also serving the Emperor, but in other palaces, as though those who had not shared a roof with the great Emperor were less exposed to danger and as though their daily proximity to him would implicate them in some type of crime for which they might have to suffer. Meanwhile, the servants in these other palaces also left, equally lost, aimless, and foolish. Véronique Casimir left as well. She who was once so magnificent could be seen packing a significant amount of luggage and driving away in a spacious coach in which even her figure, formerly so heavy with dignity, appeared at that moment to have shrunk.

Angelina took a sorrowful leave of her. She remained alone in the enemy palace. New servants appeared, dressed in unfamiliar royal uniforms. Day after day she waited for some sign from her son. There was no more work, no smoothing-iron to brandish, no cambric, no silk. There were only new and enemy faces. Perhaps her son was dead too. She recalled the hour of his birth—so long ago—the snowflakes were falling gently and pleasantly outside her window. She remembered his first smile, his first babbling, and that happy Sunday when she saw him take his first steps on his own ... and then that dreadful Sunday, much later, when she first noticed that he had become a stranger to her and was his father's son. The child she had borne and fed at her breast was long since lost. The little drummer was even more alien to her than Sergeant-Major Sosthène.

Three days after the good-natured but cold-hearted King returned, a new head of staff appeared among the court servants, Véronique Casimir's successor. Scrawny and hard, ugly and haggard, she was reminiscent of an icicle. But as she wore white lilies in her hair, upon her chest and at her waist, she was also reminiscent of a cemetery.

This new head of staff told Angelina that she must leave the King's palace.

So Angelina sought the only woman she really knew, the midwife Pocci. Her poor little woven straw box, which she had carried so cheerfully with her into Paris, grew more massive and heavy. Soon she was hardly able to drag herself along, so she put her burden down at pavement's edge and sat on it. She believed that all her distress and utter desolation was due solely to the exhaustion of her feet. As she sat there, however, she felt after a moment an uneasiness even greater than her fatigue. Strange dangers seemed to be closing in and were already lurking at the next corner. When she looked up she saw menacing clouds blowing by close over the rooftops. From a nearby street came the confused shouts of the rejoicing people who were cheering for the King and cursing the defeated Emperor. The crowd neared and she could clearly hear it cry: "Long live the King!" Tears came to her eyes. She was afraid to be seen weeping; it could put her in grave danger. The noise faded. Angelina now continued along with slow, measured, and deliberate steps. She was alone, afraid, and beaten—just like the Emperor, she thought. This thought lightened her deep despair. She believed herself to be walking so hopelessly through the streets for him, for the Emperor. He was also invisibly treading the most agonizing of paths. Who knew, maybe it was not true that he had been exiled; he could still be living in his capital, disguised as a common soldier for example, and she could encounter him and converse with him on various subjects.

Dusk was falling as she stood before the house and looked up at the familiar window. It was dark, so perhaps the midwife Pocci had also left. Angelina waited a while, afraid that she was right, but with a trembling hope that someone would emerge from the house and let her in. At the same time, however, she feared that person would be the Polish shoemaker who worked during the day in the dark passage outside his door. She had known him for two years already but was still afraid of him. She had feared him from the first moment she saw him. With his wooden leg, which made an eerie noise on the tiles of the hallway and on the cobbles in front of the house; with his ashen-colored and exotic Polish Legion lancer's mustache; with his hard, foreign accent, which ground the words instead of enunciating them; with the ill-tempered demeanor of a barbarous soldier; and with his leather-blackened hands; with all of this, he inspired Angelina with a vague but serious fear. She kept forgetting his foreign name and had reservations about pronouncing it. This made the cobbler seem even more sinister.

But she was wrong. His name was no more difficult to pronounce—for the cobbler was named Jan Wokurka, and his name was painted in clear red letters on a black board upon the front door—than his character was grim, not to mention menacing or sinister. Everything about him was quiet and gentle, except his clattering wooden leg. He was a volunteer Legionnaire, had participated in the Emperor's losing campaign, and after being injured had journeyed to Paris, where he felt he could count upon his pension and where, in addition, he would be able to work at his profession with a better prospect of earning a living than in his native village. He succeeded in obtaining both pension and profit. Still, he longed for his homeland. He was quite lonely. For although he enjoyed talking at length and in detail to all his neighbors, most of them could not understand him. He understood everything that was said to him, so he thought that the people understood him also. But as soon as the neighbors left his company, he was always struck with the bitter certainty that they found him incomprehensible. Thus it was that after each conversation all was silent and his loneliness and homesickness grew, while his left hip hurt more than before and even his leg, which was probably buried somewhere on the Oder, ached.

He was therefore determined to save money and return to Poland. He was just waiting for a "round sum," as he put it. But as soon as he secured that amount, he felt sorry and delayed his departure. In addition, despite his disability, he wished to find a wife to love him—and since he had been shy even as an unscathed man, he was now completely disheartened. His longing for a woman grew even stronger. He brushed his bold mustache, attempted to cultivate a military gleam within his light, good-humored eyes, and fell in love quickly and sincerely.

He liked Angelina because of her shy face and demeanor. But he only inspired fear in her. Even when she was standing lost and lonely, looking up at the window, she feared the cobbler more than the night that was relentlessly falling. There was still no light in the midwife Pocci's room. She went over anyway and entered the house. The cobbler was hammering away happily as usual. He soon spotted her. When he noticed her crate, he got up, his wooden leg taking astonishingly long strides, and with amazing speed he was at her side and had taken hold of the box. The full light of his three-candled lantern flashed through the large dangling cobbler's globe, casting illumination into the shadowy passageway and onto his own face. He hobbled down the three steps leading to his room, laid the box down, and was back in the hall with admirable speed. Angelina had tried to get a hold of the box but he was too quick. Wokurka took her hand

and spoke rapidly and therefore with even less clarity than usual: "They're all gone! Madame Pocci this morning. Madame Casimir was here until yesterday evening. All quite afraid. Not me. Come, Mademoiselle!" He let go of her hand but grabbed hold of her arm and pulled her toward the steps. Angelina went down. She needed to be with her box.

She sank immediately into the only armchair, next to the table. The cobbler Wokurka steered her left, right, and forward, as if he thought he could thus make her seat more comfortable. When he felt he had achieved that goal, he went to the hearth, blew on the glimmering coals, and began to heat some red wine with water. Now and again he glanced over at Angelina. When it looked as if her eyes were shut, joy swiftly filled him and he blew happily upon the glowing coals.

But Angelina's eyes were not actually closed. She was watching the cobbler's actions and taking note of all the objects in the little room. The large glass ball was swaying very gently in front of the strange lantern, whose copper decorations made it look like a glass bird cage. It was like a cage in which three flickering candle flames were imprisoned. A dark-green curtain that must have hidden Wokurka's bed awakened in Angelina a remote memory of that dream-like night ten years earlier—although it seemed more like a hundred years ago—and the heavy creases of the mighty Imperial portière. Yes, and at the moment when the cobbler placed a cup of hot fragrant red wine in front of her, she thought of the crystal decanter from long ago. The cup bore an image of the Emperor framed with a green laurel wreath, the well-known, familiar, and proud picture that reminded her of the large portrait on the wall of that mysterious room. Everything now seemed to her just as unreal as it had been then. All that she saw here, the miserable imprisoned candles, the wretched curtain, the cheap wine, the gaudy mini-portrait of the Emperor: everything seemed to be somehow connected with the expensive and exalted objects that she had found in the Imperial chamber. Perhaps they were the same objects, dilapidated and deteriorated over the course of the many, many years and through the misfortune that had befallen their lord and master.

The cobbler Wokurka stood opposite her. He was supporting himself with one hand on the edge of the table and looking at her silently. His head, with its full combed-back gray-blond hair, almost touched the dangling globe and was given a surreal glow by its odd light. "Drink!" said Wokurka finally. The gentle urging of his voice, along with the warm and seductive scent that wafted from the cup, led her to lean forward and take a gulp. It warmed her heart and she was able to look up into the cobbler's large gray eyes. They were completely different eyes from the ones she thought she had known for so long. There was no hungry lust in them after all, only a smiling light. And his prodigious mustache was no longer terrifying, but hung over the man's unseen mouth like a hairy, protective apron.

"Drink up," said the hidden mouth. "It'll do you good." She drank with delighted zeal and leaned back again.

The cobbler Wokurka turned around and pulled back the green curtain. His bed was in fact there. He sat down so that his wooden leg stuck out and almost touched the edge of the table, but even the wooden leg no longer frightened Angelina.

"Yes," began Wokurka, "they've all fled from the King as from a plague. I don't understand what they're so scared of, but I'm well aware of what terror can do. It can even confuse the minds of the normally sensible. Madame Pocci, for example, was a sensible woman. God only knows where she's gone. Mademoiselle Casimir, your aunt, whom I know well, even read the cards for some of the biggest names. She knew the future, but apparently not the present. And so you've been left alone, dear Mademoiselle."

He waited a while. As Angelina did not offer a response, he continued: "I fear that you don't understand me so well. I know I don't speak completely clearly."

This time, however, Angelina understood him perfectly. She said: "Oh yes, I do understand you completely."

"Since you're all alone now, dear Mademoiselle," he continued, "please do stay here for the time being. I won't be in your way. Don't worry about what tomorrow brings, Mademoiselle.

The world changes quickly these days. A half year ago, who would have predicted this? The Emperor was mighty and I was his soldier. I too loved him. But, as you see, we small ones pay dearly for our love of the great ones." As he spoke, a quite opportune comparison came to him, and he said: "I've lost my leg, for example, and you've lost your job. And they were futile sacrifices. We lowly ones should not allow our lives to be dictated by the great ones. When they win we suffer and when they lose we suffer still more. Right, Mademoiselle?"

"Yes," she said, "you're right."

He grabbed the wine bottle, which was on a little shelf above the head of his bed, took a generous swig, replaced the bottle, and waited a few moments. He seemed to be waiting for the courage that the gulp would arouse within his chest. As soon as he felt it, he spoke almost playfully, his bushy mustache wiggling peculiarly and divulging that his unseen mouth was bearing a smile.

"I've known you for a long time, Mademoiselle Angelina, and I know of your life." He paused briefly, breathed deeply, and continued softly: "I also know the father of your child, Monsieur Levadour. And I told your aunt that you were right not to marry him."

"Do you know if my son is still alive? Where he is?" asked Angelina.

"I don't know," said Wokurka. "But I will head out early in the morning to look for him. I have good friends in practically all the barracks of Paris." He was lying, but was glad she trusted him.

"I thank you," Angelina said. In fact she felt immeasurable gratitude mounting within her heart, as if she had returned home after wandering about for so long, home to her father's house. Her eyes closed and she fell asleep where she was. Wokurka lifted her out of the chair, laid her down on the bed, drew the curtain closed and, content for the first time since he had lost his leg and homesickness had begun to torture him, sat down in the narrow armchair next to the curtain. The candles in his lantern died out, one after another, with a peaceful flickering. From far-away streets he heard the shouts of the tireless loyalists, who were cheering the King and cursing the Emperor. The cobbler Wokurka, however, found himself on a happy island, disconnected from the changing fortunes of the world. What did the Emperor matter to him? What difference did it make to him that the King had returned? Why should he concern himself with the people causing a tumult outside? He was dreaming that he would soon be returning home, with the woman who was sleeping on the other side of the curtain. It mattered no more about round sums. Any sum was quite enough. He could hear Angelina's soft breathing from behind the curtain. She had come to him of her own volition! With that, he fell asleep where he sat, joyfully determined to find Angelina's son early the next morning.

IX

IT TOOK WOKURKA TWO WEEKS TO FIND THE BOY. DUR-
ing this time, he hobbled around the city for a few hours each
day and visited every barracks he could reach. When he at last
found the boy he limped home quickly, his wooden leg practically flying along. "We can see him tomorrow!" he said, looking
down, for he was embarrassed to see Angelina's happiness.

A long time passed before she spoke. It was already growing dark by the time she began to talk, as though she had been
ashamed to do so in full daylight.

"Where and when will we see him?"

"At seven o'clock," he said, "in the evening, after report. The
sergeant on duty happens to be my friend."

The next evening, Angelina saw her son again. His regiment
was living in different barracks now, having returned home from
the drubbing decimated, defeated, and humiliated. Two non-
commissioned officers from the old days were still there. They
recognized Angelina and she felt she was meeting familiar and
beloved ghosts. They no longer bore the Emperor's eagle, but the
King's lilies. They were no more the Emperor's soldiers, but the
King's subjects. Little Pascal too seemed to be filled with gloom
and shame. At first he stretched his arms out, but then he let
them fall again. And when Angelina began to cry, he seized her
hand and kissed it. With his shako on, he was already as tall as
she was. But then, in a sudden fit of tenderness and nostalgia, he
removed the shako and was only as high as her shoulders. She
saw his thick red hair, revealed as if to demonstrate to his mother
that he was her son and no other's. Her tears began to fall even
more intensely. She thought of her childhood, of foolishly and
senselessly giving away her body, of the odious Sosthène, of the
random meeting with the corporal, of the shameful fright of the
night in the surreal chamber, of the thick waves of the portière,
of her father's premature death, of her childless and shameless
stripping before mirrors—and everything, everything appeared

infinitely sorrowful, and worse yet, hopeless and empty. All at once she understood that all the pointless and foolish things that had happened to her had transpired, so to speak, in the Emperor's gracious shadow. His shadow had gilded her entire aimless fate; now it had gone, his merciful shadow! Only now did she recognize her foolishness as such, and her misfortune became ordinary. She was no longer weeping with emotion at having found her son again, but over an entire dead world, one that she had believed was lost forever. Since the Emperor's departure, there was nothing left. She knew at once that her love for him was greater and mightier than mere ordinary love. She was not weeping over her son, but over the King's lilies, the white Bourbon banners that hung at the barracks entrance and over the fall of the Emperor. Yet she could hear and understand what the boy was explaining: his father, Sergeant-Major Sosthène Levadour of the Thirteenth Dragoons, had come to look for his son. He had also asked about Angelina and had said he would come back soon. All this was of no interest to her. She said only: "Yes, he is your father! But I don't love him! I will visit you again. I love you, my child!" She kissed his red hair, his freckled cheeks, and his small blue eyes.

In the street she took the cobbler Wokurka's arm. She was still crying. She matched her stride with his limping steps. At times she felt like she should be ashamed at having two whole legs while he had only the one. But she also felt weaker on her healthy legs than this man at her side was on his solitary one and she clutched his arm for support. They walked in this way, arm in arm through the streets, for a very long time. Neither one spoke the whole way. Only upon reaching the door did she realize that he wanted to say something. He was holding her arm firmly. She looked at him out of the corner of her eye. The poor light of a forlorn lantern, the only one in the lane, fell on Wokurka's hollow, worried face. She felt she was seeing him for the first time. The gloomy, oily, and unsteady light of the lantern seemed to clarify his features and all the sorrow residing in his face. In a single moment it became clear to her that he was no longer a threatening stranger but rather a quiet, familiar companion; that he must love her as she had never loved anyone; and that even with his infirmity, he stayed awake long into the night for her sake in the narrow armchair. She lowered her head.

"I have something to say to you," began Wokurka softly. He waited. She said nothing. "Will you hear me out?" he asked, looking at her. She nodded. "Well," he began again, "well, I thought I could ask you—ask you—whether you wish to stay with me?"

"Yes!" she said so clearly that she surprised herself.

"Perhaps you didn't understand me," he continued, "I asked whether you wish to stay with me. With me?"

"Yes!" she repeated with the same clear voice.

They went inside the house. She lit the candles in the lantern herself, for the first time since she had been living with Wokurka. She busied herself with some pots at the hearth. She felt the man's steady gaze upon her and avoided looking his way. She thought with fear of the coming night and the love it would bring. She was gripped with sudden horror over the man's wooden leg as if the thought had just occurred to her that it was not a natural part of his body.

They ate in embarrassed silence, as on all previous evenings, the milk soup with potatoes that Wokurka loved and that eased his homesickness. Then they drank and she noticed that Wokurka poured the wine not from an ordinary bottle, as on previous evenings, but from a crystal carafe. On its front under the curved beak, in the center of its grandiose bulge, this carafe too had a small smooth oval and in this oval was the Emperor Napoleon in his traditional costume, a glass Emperor colored and infused with red wine, a crystalline Napoleon of glass and blood. As the carafe was emptied, the Emperor grew pallid and more remote, truly glass. Angelina felt she was watching his body die bit by bit, his head first, then his shoulders, his torso, legs, and finally his feet. She was transfixed by the oval. She shivered. She wanted to see the carafe filled again.

"Do you have any more wine?" she asked. "It's a pretty carafe."

"Yes, an excellent piece," said Wokurka. "Our Count Chojnicki presented it to me. He equipped us, we Legionnaires, I mean. We were in his castle and he himself drilled with us. The Emperor knew him well. He was killed the day I lost my leg. But yes, I have still got some wine left. I use this carafe only on very special occasions. And this is a special occasion for me, Angelina, isn't it?"

He was cheerful and agile, rose quickly, refilled the carafe, and poured. His cheeks were pink, his eyes bright, and his mustache seemed to be turning noticeably blonder, as though bushy new hairs were suddenly growing and overtaking the countless prematurely gray ones. He grew talkative and told stories of battles and comrades, mocking his lost leg and saying it had not been as good as the other one anyhow; but at that moment, a severe pain shot through his hip and the half of his leg that still remained. He fell silent. He did not clearly recall everything he had recounted and did not know whether or not Angelina had answered him or even if she had been listening at all, but only felt whenever he glanced at her a tremendous desire for her, a desire that the pain in no way numbed but actually seemed to heighten. He sat, as usual, on the edge of the bed, opposite Angelina. Then he rose suddenly, supporting himself with the edge of the table, and set himself in motion. Angelina rose also. She waited, trembling; she knew what must inevitably happen. It was unavoidable and she wanted only for it to be done with very quickly. She walked to him. His breath smelled of wine and lust, his shining eyes were gentle, his mustache bristled, and he awakened in her great fear, slight repugnance, but also intense compassion. Soon she was lying, eyes closed, and she heard him remove his wooden leg, the soft sound of leather being unbuckled and the faint clinking of metal clasps.

X

SHE GREW ACCUSTOMED TO THE NIGHTS AND THE DAYS
and the man. By winter's arrival, she felt at home with him, almost happy. The shorter the days, the more severe was Wokurka's homesickness. He began to repeat with greater frequency
his desire to marry and return to Poland, forget everything, and
begin a new life. At home in Poland, in his Gora Lysa, there
would be good thick snow by now and a healthy crisp frost.
There would be large round loaves of bread with brown-black
crusts and people would soon be preparing for Christmas. In
this world here it rained even in December and the damp wind
blew spitefully. The wind was in league with the restored King
and with the enemies of France and Poland; far away was the
great Emperor, who alone would have been able to quench
Wokurka's homesickness. But the Emperor himself was most
likely even more homesick now than the cobbler Wokurka. The
newspapers abused the Emperor on a daily basis, wrote of the
great congress in Vienna and lavished praise upon the traitor
Talleyrand and the good King who had returned to France and
refused to pay Wokurka's pension. All the mighty ones who had
once been Napoleon's friends betrayed and disowned the Emperor. What remained for the cobbler Wokurka from Gora Lysa
to do in this land? Here and there a couple of Poles would visit
him, former Legionnaires like himself, career soldiers with no
other occupation, who were without pension, bread, or a roof.
Although their limbs were intact they were worse off than the
cobbler. They roamed through the city as beggars. A few of them
dreamed of obtaining money enough to join the captive Emperor; and each of them was convinced that he alone was what
the Emperor lacked, that he alone could instruct the Emperor
on how to reconquer France, defeat the world anew and resur-
rect Poland. The simple Jan Wokurka, however, knew that it was
all but foolish talk; he had a simple profession, his work made
him pensive, patient, and sensible, and his injury kept him from

indulging in frivolous dreams. He prepared for his departure. He told Angelina that she must go with him. She would leave her son behind. But was he still her son? Was he not more of a stranger to her with each visit? Oh, of course he was! The boy was a soldier, he had already withstood the fire of battle. He had only one mother, and that was the army. The King of France lived in peace with all the world and there was space enough in the army for a little Pascal Pietri and also chance enough for a peaceful future for the youth.

Thus spoke Wokurka to Angelina. She was thirty years old and she felt she had aged very quickly; each year of her life was filled with so much confusion and agony. She was weary and numb. So when Wokurka spoke of his homeland, she too began to believe that his peculiar country was a safe haven for peace. Poland was far from all evils and troubles. It was as soft as the snow that covered it and was enveloped in a gentle sadness, swaddled in endless white mourning for the lost Emperor. She saw the land as a gentle, white-veiled widow grieving for the Emperor. Gradually there awakened in her also a tender and mild longing for this place. Gradually her motherly affection for her boy faded. Gradually she slipped completely into the cobbler Wokurka's world. Wokurka celebrated Christmas his way, in accordance with Polish custom. He obtained an enormous Christmas tree, which filled the entire narrow room. He put all his tools away, as well as the stool on which he normally sat in the hall, and even the globe that reminded him of his busy workdays. He gave Angelina a silk shawl, Bohemian glass earrings, and slippers that he had fashioned himself, slippers of white leather. These gifts lightened Angelina's heart. Wokurka embraced her solemnly, heartily, and thankfully. His face smelled of soap, pipe tobacco, and brandy. He swayed a little but, remarkably, he seemed to find support in his wooden leg. He had a radiant red face and festive eyes. They sat at the table, severely restrained by the branches and candles of the Christmas tree.

"Did you find your son?" asked Wokurka.

"No," said Angelina, "he was already gone."

"Pity, pity," he said. "It would have been nice to have him here." But he said it only to please Angelina. His mind was on his homeland and the journey they would soon take.

He began to serve food that he had prepared himself. They were the dishes of his native country and his youth. They had the scent of his native village, the genuine fragrance of Gora Lysa. There was a soup of beets and cream, bacon with peas, and white cheese. He had also bought brandy. Nobody drank wine in Gora Lysa. He sang with a hoarse and unsteady voice his native Christmas carols. Tears formed in his festive eyes. He had to break off and start again.

"This is the last Christmas I will celebrate in Paris," he said when he was done singing. "By this time next year, we'll be at home!" And he slapped the leather brace of his wooden leg.

As she heard him speak those words Angelina felt a sharp pain, even though she had been prepared for the journey for quite some time already. Never had she dared to set her mind upon a specific week, and a specific day, and a specific hour for their journey. It was all well and good to go with Wokurka to his native country so long as it occurred at some as-yet-undetermined time, one that would be decided by chance. When she heard now that not chance but Wokurka himself would determine the exact time, she was filled with a fear of all that awaited her in that strange, faraway land and a sadness over all that she would be leaving behind. She began to sob so passionately she had to put down the glass that she had been poised to bring to her lips in acknowledgement of his toast to a "happy journey without return."

"Without return!" This expression awoke in her a rapid string of terrifying thoughts; she would never see her son again, nor the city and street in which she had given birth to him, nor the palace in which she had been young and foolish, happy and miserable, calm and hopelessly flummoxed. She had no grasp of the true distance between France and Wokurka's homeland; thus it seemed that his homeland was a faraway and hardly reachable wilderness. She crossed her arms on the table, sunk her head into them, and wept bitterly and violently. The smoke from the dying candles on the tree branches, the brandy she had ingested, the memory of her pointless trip to her son in the barracks, a sudden apprehensive affection for the child, her remorse over having promised herself to this man without thinking it through, but also the fact that she was now saddening him with her grief and disappointing him with her fears—all this descended upon her at once, burying her under a mountain of confusion.

Wokurka stroked her brittle reddish hair. He could guess everything she was feeling and knew her despair would deafen her to all his reassurances and promises. There was nothing more he could do except continue the silent conversation between his caressing hand and her red hair. After some time she raised her pale moist face to him.

"I understand, Angelina," he said. "It'll pass, believe me, it'll pass; everything passes." She began to smile an obedient smile that made her face even sadder. It was a grateful and at the same time reproachful and resigned smile, the pained and exalted glow that lights the faces of the weak who are giving themselves up.

XI

SHE HAD ALREADY GIVEN UP. SHE HAD BEGUN TO MAKE her preparations with the conscientious determination that is equally particular to the strong as it is to those who have finally resigned themselves. It had been decided they would marry in January and set out a month later. It was thus still several weeks until their departure. To Angelina, however, it seemed that Wokurka's colossal plan decimated the laws of time. As she feared that her determination might falter, she believed there were no days left to waste.

She mulled over what she could leave her son, for she was certain she would never see him again. The cross she had brought with her from her homeland, the handkerchief she had stolen out of foolish love for the Emperor—she could give both to her little Pascal. She imagined what she would say to him: they were trivial, but for her, his mother, they were objects of importance, and she was giving them to him so he would always think of her. Of her, but also of the Emperor.

So she removed the handkerchief from her box, took down the cross she had hung over Wokurka's bed, and went to the barracks.

Wokurka escorted her. He had fashioned a pair of boots for Angelina's son, good solid boots that were fitting for a drummer.

They found the boy and went with him to the canteen. He let his mother embrace him, shook hands with Wokurka, accepted his presents, expressing delight at the handkerchief and boots, but regarding the cross, he said: "I don't need that. Nobody needs that in our regiment!" He gave it back to his mother and said: "You need it, I think!" And he had at that moment the rumbling voice of his father, Sergeant-Major Sosthène.

The canteen was filled with boisterous soldiers. Behind the buffet, on the wall over the étagère with its multicolored bottles, hung a transparent veil covering the Imperial eagle and above that an oversized and quite obvious portrait of the returned

King. His good-natured yet indifferent face, his fat droopy cheeks, and his half-shut eyelids seemed even more distant and indistinct than the veiled eagle of gleaming brass. It was as if the King's portrait were veiling itself while the veil covering the Imperial eagle was but a passing cloud.

At the tables all around soldiers were conversing. Both the sober and the tipsy were talking about the Emperor; the drunken ones even shouted now and again: "Long live the Emperor!" Little Pascal spread out the handkerchief before him and said with an affected deep voice: "Everybody says the Emperor is coming back. We don't give a damn about the Bourbons!" And he gestured with his little finger at the portrait of the returned King on the wall.

"He won't come back," said the cobbler Wokurka. "And I want to say that you, if you like, can come with us, with your mother and I, to my homeland."

"Why?" asked the boy. "The Emperor's coming back soon; everyone says so."

Angelina was silent. She heard the soldiers all around her talking about the Emperor. The Emperor was not dead and forgotten; he was alive in the hearts of the soldiers and they awaited him every day. Only she had stopped waiting for him; she alone would not be allowed to wait any longer.

And she noticed that both the man and her son became strangers as soon as she thought about the Emperor. In fact, her son only seemed close because he had spoken lovingly of the Emperor, so out of fear that she might betray her confusion and would lose her determination to follow Wokurka, she said: "Let's go," stood up, kissed her son on the cheeks, on the forehead, and on his red hair, and turned to go before Wokurka even had time to get up.

On the way home he spoke to her, gently and timidly and somewhat uncertain. He told her that the soldiers were wrong. They did not comprehend the intricacies of the political world and therefore believed the Emperor would return. But even if the soldiers were right in their prediction and the Emperor came back, this should not hinder them, Angelina and the cobbler Wokurka, from starting a new life in a distant land, far removed from the confusion caused by the great ones in the world only so that the lowly ones might suffer.

"Yes, yes," she said, but no longer believed him.

Upon arriving at the house, they saw all its residents—who were craftsmen, coachmen, and lackeys—standing at the door. Something extraordinary had happened: the midwife Pocci had returned and with her Véronique Casimir. They had both refused to give out any information, but had only asked after Angelina and proclaimed quite generally and solemnly that they came back because "a whole new era was dawning."

Véronique Casimir had not changed, nor had Barbara Pocci. Where both women had been living for so long, nobody dared ask. Both were recognizable at first glance and had returned wholly unchanged: the midwife Pocci was still trustworthy yet menacing, bony, and gaunt, and Mademoiselle Casimir was still plump yet nimble.

"You mustn't do it," she said to the shoemaker. "You'll lose your right to a pension if you go and the Emperor returns. And sure as my name is Véronique Casimir, sure as I have predicted, as all the world knows, the Emperor's battles, both victories and defeats, now I predict that he's coming back soon, and nothing can stop it."

Véronique Casimir did not say any of this lightly. She proved it too. She proved it in the presence of all the residents of the house, of neighbors in the quarter who had been either invited or compelled to come and in the presence of many strangers, all of whom had gathered—rapt, credulous, and hopeful—in the cobbler's room and even filled the passage or sometimes had to wait in the street outside. She proved it through the irrefutable cards. She repeated it every evening: "The Emperor is preparing for his departure. Eleven hundred men are accompanying him. They have anticipated many dangers, but all these dangers are dispersing and evaporating as the Emperor approaches. All doors are opened for him. The people are cheering him. He has won, he has won! He comes, he comes!"

"And then?" the cobbler Wokurka would sometimes inquire. "What will happen then?"

"That I cannot see," answered Véronique Casimir. And she collected her cards together and bustled out through a street crowded with awe-struck believers.

XII

ONE EVENING — SPRING HAD LONG SINCE ANNOUNCED its arrival, but had quickly been chased away again by winter's merciless rebirth—Angelina heard the wooden leg of the returning Wokurka rapping more hurriedly, nimbly, and loudly upon the cobbles in front of the house than ever before.

He arrived out of breath. It was hailing outside. There were wet little hailstones on his shoulders and water ran down from his single boot to form a large black puddle on the floor. He did not remove his cap. He remained standing in the doorway and said: "Angelina, things are happening! He comes tomorrow! The King is on the run!"

She stood up. She had been sitting on a stool peeling potatoes and they fell to the floor with a series of thuds. "He's coming?" she repeated. "Tomorrow? And the King flees?"

"He's coming!" Wokurka reiterated. And although at that moment he knew that he had lost Angelina, he said for a third time, with happiness gleaming on his face and joy ringing in his voice: "He's coming! It's definite!"

That evening Véronique Casimir did not come by. The residents of the house, the neighbors, and also strangers came and inquired after her. She did not come. Midwife Pocci's door also remained closed.

"Is it really true that he's coming?" Angelina asked.

"He comes tomorrow, definitely tomorrow," said Wokurka.

They ate silently. They felt both happy and unhappy at the same time, relieved and unsettled, fortunate and unfortunate. And yet neither could say why they felt these conflicting feelings.

They lay down but could not get to sleep. Each of them remained awake, hoping and believing that the other was asleep.

When dawn's light arrived, Angelina got up quietly. She thought that she had not awakened Wokurka. But he had never actually fallen asleep. He watched her get up. He saw her hastily wash and dress. She came back to bed and kissed him, but he

129

did not move. From behind his half-closed eyelids he saw her go and he knew she did not mean to come back.

He did not move. He was dead. He had once lost a leg for the Emperor; now he was losing a woman for the Emperor.

Six weeks later he learned from Barbara Pocci that Angelina was back in the Imperial palace. He immediately made his way to her. He waited outside the gate and she came to meet him. "Good day," she said. "It's nice that you want to see me again!" She was wearing the livery of the Imperial servants, the dark-blue dress, white apron, and blue cap. She looked both beautiful and foreign.

He said: "I have come, Angelina, to ask you once more whether you will go with me!"

"No!" she replied firmly, as if she had never told him she would go in the first place.

It began to rain lightly, then more heavily. It was a good, warm, almost summer-like rain. He watched as her clothes got wet, heard the rain pounding harder and harder, looked at her as she stood there, lost. He knew that they had nothing more to say to each other.

"Adieu, Angelina," he said. "If you need me—I'm not going home, I'm going to wait until you need me again."

They shook hands. Both hands were wet and there was no warmth in either. It seemed that they were not actually shaking hands but exchanging rain. Angelina watched him hobble away with concerted and cautious effort and disappear into the torrent.

XIII

A PALPABLE EXCITEMENT DESCENDED UPON THE LAND.
An even greater yet entirely different kind of excitement ruled within the palace, among both the ladies and gentlemen of the Emperor and among the servants. All the prominent events that were occurring in the world, and the even more substantial ones that were now in preparation had been caused and incited by the Emperor Napoleon himself. He was great and impetuous, but the world preferred to stay small and cautious, as it was. The Emperor's servants knew nothing of the terror that he was spreading around the world. They knew only the terror he inspired within his own house. Certainly they were of lesser importance to the Emperor than the kings, his enemies. But the servants lived near him, heard his voice on a daily basis, felt his gracious or scolding gaze upon them, heard his affectionate praise or furious curses. Thus they, in contrast to the rest of the world, felt the significance of his every occasional glance, good mood, or malicious word. The world was already arming itself for war, out of fear for his might and his rash behavior. The servants of the court, however, were preparing for the Emperor's move from the Tuileries to the Elysée. His decision to move appeared to the men and women of the court more significant than the war for which the countries of the world were already beginning to prepare. If Véronique Casimir, now restored to her old rank and former dignity, had not foretold the war's proximity with her cards, the men and women of the Imperial household would have given no thought whatsoever to the world at large, to danger, to life and death. But despite the prophecies of Véronique Casimir, and although doom was already spreading its somber wings over the Emperor's house, his servants could not feel it coming and continued to sense disaster nearing only with the Emperor's wrath or receding with his mirth. They began to prepare with genuine enthusiasm for the move. They postulated all kinds of hypothetical reasons for the Emperor's decision. The

131

evening before the move to the other palace, twelve hours before the Emperor's departure, they gathered in the hall for a detailed inspection by Véronique Casimir. Twelve coaches were already waiting below for the servants and baggage. For the last time— and they had no idea that it was the last time—they took their meal in the great dining hall. They spoke of nothing but the move. One proclaimed he knew for certain that the Emperor was moving because his wife was arriving from Vienna in two days and would not feel safe enough in the Tuileries. Another asserted that was wrong, that the Emperor was without doubt only giving the appearance of moving, with the intention of misleading the informants of the treacherous Minister of Police, whom he hated. A third insisted that he knew the truth; he had information from the Emperor's valet himself that Napoleon had no intention of living in either palace, but wanted to go to Malmaison once and for all, to ensconce himself in the memory of his first wife. Others contradicted the first, second, and third. Véronique Casimir, at the head of the long table, called for silence. She forbade everyone to indulge in such idle talk; one never knew who was safe and who was treacherous, considering the infiltration of Fouché's spies in many places.

And so it was. Long gone was that first day of spring, the day when the Emperor had returned to reign once more over his land, his palace, and his servants. Barely a week later, new and unfamiliar servants, workmen, laundry attendants, and barbers had begun to appear. Each of them bore the honest face and trustworthy eyes that are the most important qualities of a spy. Discord, mistrust, lies, and treachery soon began to take their toll. Former confidantes trusted each other no more and old friends kept a suspicious eye on each other. So it was in the palace, so it was across the whole land.

Among the Emperor's servants at the time, there were precious few who were honest and fearless. Among this number was Angelina. She was silent, for what did she have to contribute? She lived a more isolated life than before. She even felt disconnected from her aunt, recalling the months during which Véronique had been invisible and inaccessible. Angelina was both silent and aloof. Her son no longer belonged to her, she had left Wokurka, she loved only the great Emperor, she had lost herself, her sins burdened her, she had lived in confusion, weak and foolish, and had sacrificed herself unthinkingly. She was lost. She belonged to the great Emperor. He, however, knew nothing of her. She was tiny and insignificant, more insignificant then one of the flies that buzzed through the Emperor's room, a barely noticeable nuisance. A barely noticeable nuisance, but whatever the case, she loved him. Her heart was young, hot, and tender. Sometimes, when she was gazing with adoration at one of his many portraits, she felt like one of the tiny flies that crawled deliberately, even fervently, like herself but insignificant and repulsive, along the picture.

Her heart commanded her to remain close to his gracious presence, lowly and ignored as she was. To live in the golden shadow that only he of all the people in the world could cast upon his servants was bliss. To watch his every visible move with love and fervent devotion without even being noticed was pure happiness. In his presence one could be insignificant and proud. His shadow was golden and more radiant than the light of any others. One served him but he was unaware. To be in his service was pride itself.

All over people were speaking of war. They feared it. The Emperor brought war! He seemed too great for peace. He went forth not like a man but blew through the land like a mighty wind. People were now beginning to hate him. Bared swords seemed to precede him on every path he trod, while the Imperial eagle circled over his head. Whenever he celebrated a holiday his cannon boomed in the towns and villages. Angelina loved his swords, his eagle, and the booming cannons of his celebrations. And as she loved him, she also loved war. His enemies were also her enemies. She wanted his greatness to increase and her smallness to become still more insignificant. She alone longed for war, which all others feared. She had relinquished her son long ago. When she said farewell to him in the great, mercilessly shadeless barracks yard, surrounded by strange women and soldiers, her heart was enveloped in stone and iron. Her eyes were hard and dry and she saw her poor little son as though through a sheer transparent veil of frozen tears. She wept only on the evening that she watched the Emperor leave after the lackey had stamped out the torch. A sudden terror mounted in her, clamped her heart, and lodged in her throat. She fell to her knees and began praying.

A few days later, as the bells announced the Emperor's first victory, she entered a church for the first time in years. It was the little Church of Saint Julien, in which her son had been baptized. She was alone. Nobody was praying for the Emperor and his soldiers, except for the bells, high above in the belfry, but even they chimed only because they had been ordered to. It was late in the evening. Under the golden shimmer of the pleasant wax candles, kneeling before the eternal light of the cheery ruby-red lamp, with the deep boom of the golden-voiced bells causing the black pews and the bright little altar to shiver, surrounded by the breathing, holy solitude of the empty yet living space, Angelina began to recite the long-unspoken words of the "Our Father" and the "Hail Mary." She prayed, sinfully, a prisoner of her great love, for the death of all the Emperor's enemies. She imagined with a sinful blood lust thousands of mutilated bodies—the bodies of Englishmen, Prussians, and Russians; colorful uniforms riddled with bullet holes from which blood trickled; split skulls; oozing brains and glassy eyes. Over all these horrors galloped the Emperor on his snow-white horse, sword raised, and the completely unharmed Frenchmen thundered after him over endless fields strewn with enemy corpses in all directions. These images made Angelina happy and she prayed still more ardently. In a special prayer she wished the most horrible of all deaths upon the Empress Marie Louise, and she could clearly see the Empress dying, surrounded by all the terrifying monsters prematurely borne out of hell, tortured by the spectral visions that were a product of her evil conscience and cursed by Napoleon's son who stood angry and vengeful at her deathbed.

Angelina crossed herself, thanked the Lord with a full heart for all the troubles he inflicted upon the Emperor's enemies, and then left. The bells were still tolling to announce the victory. In the streets she encountered only bright and happy faces. Light and fluffy cloudlets were floating under the darkening sky like cheery and triumphant little banners. Silver shimmered the first stars, the stars of the Emperor: all the stars in the heavens were now his stars. The damp broadsides freshly pasted to the walls announced victory, the victory of the Emperor over the entire world.

Angelina ran to the palace. It was a long way from the Church of Saint Julien to the Elysée, but she made it back quickly and happily; the road itself seemed to be rising up to meet her. The frenzied cheering of the crowds that had gathered in front of the news bulletins on the walls and were greeting the Emperor's victory gave wings to her steps. She was propelled by their cheers and happy in the belief that her prayers had assisted the Emperor.

Alas! She knew not the great Emperor was at that moment wandering, defeated, dejected, and helpless yet still magnificent, among the dead remnants of his last great army. It was the very hour at which Paris was celebrating his victory. On the battlefield of Waterloo, however, the dying moaned, the wounded screamed, and the beaten were fleeing.

BOOK THREE

The Downfall

I

IN THIS HOUR THE EMPEROR KNEW THAT HE HAD LOST
the battle of Waterloo. The sun was briefly hiding behind an angry purple wall of clouds, before setting. On this evening it disappeared more quickly than usual. Nobody, however, was paying
any mind to the sun. All the men on the battlefield, both friend
and enemy, had their attention fixed on the Emperor's Guards.
Steadily and deliberately, the Emperor's Guards marched ahead
with a sublime rhythm, over ground that had been soaked by
the rain and clung tenaciously to their boots at every squishing
step they took. From the hill against which they were advancing, the enemy fired incessantly. The bullets felled the Emperor's
grenadiers, those terrors of the enemy, the chosen of the French
people, the brothers of the Emperor and his sons.

They resembled one another like brothers.

Those who saw them marching forth believed they were
watching 20,000 brothers, 20,000 brothers begotten of the same
father. They were as alike as 20,000 swords forged in the same
workshop. They had all grown up on the same battlefield, in the
golden, bloody, and deadly shadow of the Emperor. The might-
est of their brothers, however, who had breathed upon, touched,
or kissed a hundred times each one of these 20,000 foot soldiers and 4,000 horsemen, was not Napoleon but a far mightier
Emperor than he, namely the Emperor Death. They were not
afraid of his hollow eyes. They marched toward the crushing embrace of his ever-receptive bony arms with steady confidence, as
brother goes toward brother. They loved Death just as he loved

them. Their love for Death made them all alike. And because they all resembled each other so closely, the appearance was given that as soon as one fell he rose right up again, whereas in reality it was only one of his brothers who stepped into his place. The appearance was thus created that the advancing line consisted always of the same men. The enemy soldiers fired just to relieve the holy terror that awakened within them again and again as soon as the smoke had cleared and they saw the unwavering steps of the very same men. Soon, however, one could notice that their square was growing ever smaller. And briefly the enemy was struck with an even greater dread, for the Emperor's grenadiers thus accomplished a greater miracle than the typical one of legends and fairytales, in which one is immortal. The grenadiers of the Emperor were not immune to death, rather they were consecrated to death. And since they had realized now that they were hopelessly outnumbered by the enemy, they were no longer marching toward the enemy but toward their familiar brother, Death. But to show their other great brother, their earthly brother, that they loved him even in their last hour, they shouted with roaring voices, from mighty throats, which were stronger than the jaws of the cannon because it was loyalty itself that issued from their throats: "Long live the Emperor!" And so powerful was this cry that it drowned out the foolish and senseless rumble of the cannon. The loudest cries came from those who had just been struck. They shouted not only out of loyalty but also Death: "Long live the Emperor!"

Thus it was Death himself who spoke louder than the cannon.

When the Emperor heard the cries and saw that all of his 20,000 brothers on foot and his 4,000 brothers on horseback—even the horses themselves were his siblings at that moment—were lost, he too was gripped by an irresistible longing for death. He mingled with them, was now at their head, now on one of their flanks, then at their rear, then again at their head, and finally back in their midst. His back ached, his face was jaundiced and he was panting. When he heard his Guards shouting, "Long live the Emperor!" he drew his sword, lifted it toward the sky like a steely, imploring sixth finger, and cried through the tumult in a hoarse voice: "Death to the Emperor! Death to the Emperor!" But Death heeded neither his imploring sword nor his cry. For the first time in his proud life the Emperor began to pray, breathlessly, with a wide-open mouth and throat from which no sound would issue, as he galloped back and forth. He prayed and not to God, whom he knew not, but to Death, his brother; for of all otherworldly powers, this was the only one he had seen and often felt. "Oh Death! Sweet kindly Death!" he prayed breathlessly and soundlessly. "I await thee, come! My days are fulfilled, as are the days of my brothers. Come soon, while the Sun is still in the heavens! I too was once a sun. It must not sink before me! Forgive me this foolish vanity! I have displayed much vanity, but I have had wisdom and virtues too. I have known it all: power and superiority, virtue, goodness, sin, arrogance, and error! I have lived, Brother Death! I have lived and had enough! Come and get me before our sister, the Sun, sets!"

But Death did not come for the Emperor. He watched the sun set. He heard his wounded soldiers groaning. The enemy granted him a brief respite, time enough for him to walk helpless, ailing, and at odds with treacherous Death among the deceased and wounded. A soldier led his horse by the bridle and his adjutant hobbled along behind it. He could not yet grasp that all was lost, everything was destroyed, and he alone still lived. Only two days ago one of his generals had betrayed him. Another had acted foolishly and a third carelessly. But the Emperor quarreled only with the greatest of all generals, the greatest of his brothers—with Death. At the same time, in a strange voice that may once—so long ago!—have been his but that now did not seem to be his, he cried out to the soldiers who were retreating all around him and fleeing past him like so many flitting ghosts: "Halt! Halt! Wait! Wait!" But they did not listen. They continued along on their way and disappeared into the night. Maybe they had not even heard him. Maybe he had only imagined shouting and had in reality said nothing.

A soldier accompanied him with a lantern, and the Emperor

signaled to him to bring it ever closer. For over and over he believed that he could recognize this dead man or that wounded
one at his feet. Ah, he knew them all better at this hour than the
living, scattering soldiers knew him! He gestured once again
to the man with the lamp and bent over a tiny, remarkably tiny
corpse. It was one of the little drummers of the Imperial Army.
Blood was still trickling slowly from the corners of his childish
mouth and congealing before the Emperor's eyes. The Emperor
bent lower and then kneeled down. The soldier lowered the lamp
to give the Emperor some light. Upon the poor scrawny body
of the dead boy lay his instrument, the drum. He still clutched
a drumstick in his right hand, but the other hand had fallen
into the black muck in which his body lay half-immersed. His
uniform was spattered with long-since dried mud. His shako
had rolled away from his head. The dead little boy had a pale
and thin face saturated with freckles. The hair above the boyish forehead was reddish, like a glowing little flame. His small
bright blue eyes were open and glassy. He had no visible wounds
on his body. Only out of his mouth did blood ooze, slowly but
steadily. The hooves of a horse must have knocked him over and
killed him. The Emperor examined the little body very closely.
He pulled a handkerchief out of his pocket and wiped the trickling blood from the corners of the corpse's mouth. He opened
the boy's vest. A red and blue handkerchief, folded four times,
laid upon the little one's breast. The Emperor unfolded it. Ah, he
knew it well! It was one of the hundreds of thousands of handkerchiefs that he had once ordered manufactured for his soldiers
when he was General Bonaparte, along with the pocket knives
and the drinking cups. Ah, he knew it well, this handkerchief!
On a blue background within red borders, it contained a map
with blue, white, and red circles to denote the places where he
had fought his battles.

This boy—who could hardly have been fourteen years old—
was thus probably the son of one of his oldest soldiers. The Emperor spread the handkerchief across his knees. Half of Europe,
the Mediterranean, and Egypt were shown on it. How many

battles had followed these! Never again, thought the Emperor, will French soldiers receive such handkerchiefs! Never again will I be able to mark new battles! Let then this last one be included here! He demanded writing implements. They were handed to him. Then he dipped the quill into the silver inkwell, stretched the handkerchiefs across his knees and drew a firm line toward the north, to the point at which the red border already began. On this spot he drew in a large black cross. Then he carefully placed the handkerchief over the boy's drum, looked into his face once more and suddenly remembered a radiant, sunny morning on which he had spoken to this youth, imagining the bright ring of that boyish voice in his ears and ordered that the pockets of the dead be searched. They found a crumpled note signed "Your mother, Angelina." In this note, the mother had told him he should definitely expect her in his barracks on the following Sunday at four o'clock in the afternoon. The Emperor carefully folded the note and gave it to the adjutant. "Inquire!" he said, "and give me your report!" Then he rose. "Quickly," he ordered, "bury the boy!"

Two soldiers hurriedly shoveled out a shallow grave. The boy was quickly lowered in, for isolated random shots could again be heard. The lantern flickered and the wind gusted from time to time. The clouds dispersed, the moon rose, and the night was clear, cold, and cruel. Small as the little corpse was, it did not fit properly into the hastily prepared grave. The Emperor stood there, silent and livid, while behind his back his white horse whinnied inconsolably. It was like a deep sigh, sounding a bit like a human lament and a bit like a human curse. The Emperor remained still. Dirt was heaved back in over the tiny corpse. The soldier raised his lantern. He presented it like a gun.

Then the Emperor drew his sword and lowered it over the fresh, shallow grave. "For all of them," he was heard to murmur. "For all." His adjutant, the General who was standing behind the Emperor, had no weapon. He instead raised his hat. Suddenly other generals of the Emperor's—Gourgaud, la Bédoyère, and Drouot—were there. They had been watching him from a distance, and they now approached, respectfully but embarrassed and confused.

"The horse!" ordered the Emperor.

They rode in silence, the Emperor leading. At five o'clock in the morning, when it was already quite light and a delicate blue-tinged fog was rising slowly from the lush dark-green grass, he ordered a halt. He was shivering. "Fire!" he ordered, and a pitiful little fire was kindled. It burned, yellow and weak in the silvery-blue glimmer of the early dawn. The Emperor tirelessly fanned the weak yellow flames. He looked at the soldiers, his soldiers. They fled on all sides, passing the little fire—infantry, artillery, and horsemen. Now and then, the Emperor lifted his head. Some of the passing soldiers recognized him. They saluted silently. They no longer cried "Long live the Emperor!" Ever paler was the fire and ever stronger the morning light. A formidable silence enveloped the Emperor. The silence seemed to burn stronger than the fire. It seemed to the Emperor that the retreating soldiers of his army were making ever-larger detours around him. A great stillness descended upon the meadow. And the soldiers who went past and saluted him so silently—the officers with their sabres, the men with their fixed gaze—seemed no longer to be living soldiers. They were the fallen and the dead. That was why they were silent. That was why they were voiceless.

The little fire went out. The day broke triumphantly. The Emperor sat down on a stone at the roadside. They brought him ham and goat cheese. He ate hastily and mindlessly, as was his way. More and more fleeing soldiers passed by. The Emperor stood. "Onward!" he commanded.

He mounted his steed. Behind him he heard the galloping of his generals' horses and from a distance the occasional sound of his coach's rolling wheels, following further back. And he closed his eyes.

He fell asleep in the saddle.

II

TO PARIS! THIS WAS THE ONLY CLEAR GOAL FOR THE EM-
peror. One of the generals was riding close behind him. Although
his entire retinue already knew that he had decided to return to
Paris, the Emperor said once again: "On to Paris, General!"

"As you wish, Your Majesty!" said the officer.

The Emperor was silent for a while. The young morning foretold a glorious, triumphant day to come. Out of the blue heavens
came the carefree jubilation of unseen larks and from a distance
the faint muffled echo of marching soldiers. There was a melancholy clanking of weapons, a yearning weary neighing of horses,
the rising and then dying murmur of human voices, and here
and there a loud and quickly subsiding shout or rather curse. To
the left and right, and through field and meadow the disorderly
troops stomped along. The Emperor lowered his head. He forced
himself to see only the undulating silvery mane of his animal and
the yellowish-gray strip of road along which he rode. He became
engrossed in them. But against his will all the miserable sounds
forced themselves upon him from both sides, and it was as if his
army's weapons were whimpering pitifully, as if the fine, strong,
defeated, ashamed, and humiliated weapons were weeping. He
knew that even if he had a hundred more years to live he would
never forget this sobbing of the weapons and horses or the whin-
ing and moaning of the wagons. He could avert his gaze from the
retreating soldiers. The clinking whimper of the weapons, however, pierced his heart. In order to fool himself and the others into
believing that he was nevertheless planning some further under-
taking, he ordered that guards be posted to look for deserters and
arrest and punish anyone who strayed from the road, yet even as
he was so busy issuing them his mind was not on the superfluous
orders. He thought of Paris, of his Minister of Police, of the deputies, of all his true enemies who at this point seem to him more
dangerous even than the Prussians or the English. Twice he ordered a halt for he had decided to arrive at night.

In Laon, before the tiny post office, stood a crowd—officials, officers of the Garde Nationale, and curious villagers with their good-tempered peasant faces. It was quite still and the sky was becoming noticeably darker. The hitched horses before the station neighed, happy about the oats they were being fed, a flock of geese honked busily home to their pen and in the distance could be heard the peaceful lowing of cows, the cheerful crackle of a herdsman's whip and a sweet fragrance of lilac and chestnut mixed in with the acrid odor of dung, hay, and manure. In the low room of the post office it was already getting dark. Someone lit the solitary three-candled lantern. It seemed to the Emperor only to intensify the darkness in the room. Four additional lanterns with protective glass were brought inside. Four soldiers positioned themselves in the corners of the room and held the lanterns steady. The wide double door was fully open and directly opposite sat the Emperor on the smooth-planed bench that was intended for travelers awaiting the next arriving coach. So there he sat, legs spread, in his dirty and stained white breeches and mud-spattered boots, hands pressed down on his chubby thighs, and head lowered. The light fell on him from all four sides and from the lantern in the center. He was sitting directly opposite the open door and all the inhabitants of Laon stood outside and were watching him with an unwavering gaze. He felt like he was sitting on the defendant's bench and they stood in silent, terrifying judgment over him. They would soon deliver their verdict, an unnervingly quiet one, and they were already deliberating silent and voiceless over this deaf, dumb, and awful verdict. He stared for some time at the strip of floor between his boots, at the two narrow planks of wood. He thought of Paris and his Police Minister and suddenly recalled the broken crucifix that he had brushed to the ground in his palace. The two dirty gray planks at his feet transformed themselves into the narrow golden-brown strip of inlaid flooring in his room, the Minister Fouché was announced, and a boot hid the fragments of the ivory cross. The Emperor stood up, for he could sit no longer. He began to walk back and forth, back and forth, back and forth across the small low room of the station. No sound issued from the throng of people outside the open door, yet he waited to hear some human voice. This silence was frightful; he waited for a single word, not a shout, not a cheer, but only a word, just a single human word. But nothing came. He walked up and down, acting like he did not know that the people at the door were watching him, yet it hurt him to know that they were staring. The deadly silence that these people emitted, their immobility, their undying and unwavering patience, their quiet eyes, and their immeasurable sorrow filled him with a previously unknown horror. The silent, limping general, his adjutant, his shadow, had risen with him. The adjutant hobbled exactly three steps behind. Suddenly the Emperor turned to the open door. He stood for a brief moment as if awaiting the customary cry of "Long live the Emperor!"—the cry that his ear so loved, the cry that so softly caressed his heart. The Emperor stepped to the threshold. The lanterns in the room illuminated his back, so the crowd outside could not make out his face. The people outside saw only the light behind his back. He was facing them and his countenance was lost within the blue-black darkness of the quickly descending summer night. The already silent people seemed to become even more still. The nocturnal crickets cheeped at full volume in the surrounding fields. Already had the stars begun to twinkle in the sky, kindly and silver. The Emperor stood in the open double doorway. He waited. He waited for some word. He was used to shouts, to cries of "Long live the Emperor!" Now the black dumbness of these people and the night washed over him and even the pleasant silver stars seemed sullen and hostile. Directly in front of him, in the first row, a bareheaded peasant spoke. His simple face was made clearly visible by the bright night as he said aloud to his neighbor: "That's not the Emperor Napoleon! He's Job. He isn't the Emperor!" Immediately, the Emperor turned. "Onward! Forward!" he said to General Gourgaud.

He entered his carriage. "He's Job! He's Job!" rang in his ears.

"He's the Emperor Job!" the wheels repeated.

The Emperor Job continued toward Paris.

III

HE SAT ALONE IN THE CARRIAGE. HIS BACK HURT HOR-
ribly. The carriage sped along the smooth highway. It cut through
the night, whose silvery blue luster and sweet summer scents of
grass and dew were wafted in on both sides through the open
carriage windows. The Emperor had long since overtaken his
retreating soldiers. The pathetic clink of the defeated weapons
could no longer be heard far and wide. All that was audible was
the steady rapid hoof beats of the horses on stones, dirt, and
wooden bridges, and the dreary rumbling of the wheels. Occasionally they seemed to speak. They repeated now and then:
"He's Job! He's Job! He's Job!" Then they fell silent once more,
as if they remembered that they were mere carriage wheels and
had no right to take on a human voice. Because of his severe
back pain the Emperor reclined. But as he lay practically pros-
trate upon the cushions a new and different pain suddenly awakened, stabbing like a dagger through his heart, lasting only a
second before darting from his chest and transforming into a
delicate saw that began slowly and finely to slice through his in-
testines. The Emperor sat upright again. He looked through the
windows of his carriage, left and right. This summer night was
endless. Paris seemed further away than ever. As quickly as they
were moving, it seemed to the Emperor that the horses were
gradually slowing and he leaned out the window and shouted:
"Faster, faster!" Down came the whip like the crack of a shot
awakening a long, solemn sharp echo in the still of the night. The
wheels began anew their rumbling chant: "He's Job!" And the
old familiar pain returned to the Emperor's back.

He thought of old Job. He no longer had any clear idea of
those biblical stories. He had never wished to conjure one of the
downtrodden servants of God in his imagination. If ever he had
made a fleeting attempt to conceive a vague notion of one of
them, he saw him basically in the form and effeminate costume
of a priest. Yes, a priest! And at that moment, for the first time,

he could see old Job quite clearly; he even recalled having once met him, immeasurably long years ago. Years that were as wide as oceans. And they were red, like oceans of blood. The Emperor had once seen old Job himself; he was the kind and fragile poor old man whom people called "the holy father" and whom he, the Emperor, had once brought from the Holy City of Rome so the old man could anoint him. The Emperor now saw the pathetic old man again. Job seemed to be sitting opposite him in the back seat, just as humbly as once he had sat in one of the armchairs at the Imperial palace. With his patient old eyes he stared into the bold impatient ones of the Emperor. And sharp and clear-sighted as were the Emperor's eyes, he knew that the humble and frail old man could see more than he himself, the Emperor. Yes this old man was Job, thought Napoleon. And for a moment he was comforted by that thought. Then it seemed that the old man was trying to whisper something, leaning over so as to be better understood, and repeating: "You too are Job! One day we will all be Job!" Yes, so it is. The Emperor nodded.

Just then the rapid hoof beats drummed loudly upon a wooden bridge and the Emperor awoke. He looked out the window. The horizon seemed to be brightened by the lights of the nearby great city, his city of Paris, where his throne stood, and he thought no more of old Job. The wheels also seemed to have forgotten him for they now sang a different tune—"On to Paris! On to Paris! On to Paris!" Now everything will be fine again, thought the Emperor. Now I will reveal and punish the traitors. Now I will discipline the lawyers, gather my soldiers, and defeat my enemies. I am still the Emperor Napoleon! My throne still stands! My eagle still circles! A few minutes later, however, as they got closer and closer to the capital, he grew anxious again. He could still see his soaring eagle, but it was being chased and was soon overtaken by numerous black ravens that flew more swiftly than he. Surrounded by crows the Imperial eagle hovered.

What was a throne? Indeed, he the Emperor, who had erected so many and demolished so many, knew very well that it was just a piece of furniture, fragile enough to be smashed by accident.

What was an empty throne, a throne without an heir? What was an Emperor without a son? Oh, if only his son still lived in this city! For whom else except his son should he reveal the traitors, scold the lawyers, round up his soldiers, and crush his enemies? For his vain and foolish brothers? For the lowly family from which he had sprung but that in reality sprang from him, as though he were the begetter and not the begotten? For his weak and traitorous friends? For the women who had succumbed to him, as was their nature, and who might just as easily have offered themselves to his fine grenadiers? For those children whom he had perhaps fathered with careless passion? For the army? Yes, perhaps for it alone! Yet he himself had allowed its destruction only a few hours ago! There was no army! His son and heir was far away and powerless! Only the throne remained in the city of Paris, an empty throne, nothing but an armchair of wood and velvet and gold! Worms were already eating through the wood. Moths were already gnawing holes in the velvet. Only the gold survived, the most permanent and deceptive of all materials, the devil's confidante!

All at once the horses' pace seemed too swift, the rolling of the wheels too hurried, and he wanted to order that the carriage be driven more slowly. He was suddenly overcome by a fear of Paris and of the empty throne, of the traitors and the lawyers. He needed a little more time to think things over but the city was nearing rapidly, increasingly fast as though it were approaching him so as to meet him halfway, with its teary face and its spectral throne. He wanted to shout: "Slow down! Go slowly!" But they had already reached the first lanes; he could already sense the proximity of the Rue du Faubourg Saint-Honoré. He wanted to ask what time it was, for he was puzzled at the darkness of the streets; it seemed to be well past midnight. According to his calculations, however, it could hardly be so late. All the shops were already closed. All the houses were lifeless. Their windows grinned with an empty darkness. He leaned out of the carriage window but could not tell who was now riding alongside. He had wished to ask what time it was, but it came out as: "What day is it?"

"The 20th of June, Your Majesty," cried an officer next to the carriage.

The nagging pain in the small of his back grew stronger and the Emperor leaned back. He did not know whether he had asked incorrectly or whether the man outside had misunderstood him. "The 20th of June!" It was on the 20th of March that he had come to this capital, just like his pain and related to it, his old superstition returned and terrified him. On the 20th! What a date! His son had been born on the 20th, the Duke of Enghien had been executed at his order on the 20th, and he had returned home for the first time on the 20th! Yes, today was the 20th of June! It was three months, exactly three months! Then— Oh, he remembered very clearly—it was an ominous evening, a cold and spiteful drizzle fell from the heavens, but the people of France, the people of the Emperor, warmed the city with their very breath. They cried: "Long live the Emperor!" Torches and lanterns seemed to be as bright and eternal as the stars that were stubbornly denied by the heavens and the melody of the "Marseillaise" that rose up to him seemed powerful enough to send the clouds fleeing from the sky. A thousand pale bare hands reached out for the Emperor and each hand was like a face; it had been necessary for him to shut his eyes at such sheer triumph, light, and devotion. Now even the windows were black in Paris; it was a fine summer night, calm and silvery blue. The acacias' scent was overpoweringly strong. The stars glittered doubly bright since the streets were unlit. Pleasant was the night now that he, the Emperor, was defeated! It had been grim then, on the night of his triumph! Cruel was the inscrutable God who so spitefully mocked the Emperor Napoleon!

When the coach stopped, there were no cheering cries—only a hatefully peaceful, a terrifyingly peaceful summer night. The Emperor heard the shriek of a screech owl coming from deep within the palace park. So great was his back pain, it was almost as if he himself had howled as the steps were let down and he prepared to descend. He noticed his old friend, the Minister Caulaincourt. The good man was waiting alone on the white

151

stone steps under the silver-blue glow of the night sky. Behind him was the golden reflection of the light that streamed out of the windows of the Elysée. The Emperor recognized him immediately. He embraced him. It seemed that the Minister had been waiting an eternity there on the steps, waiting alone for the unhappy and pitifully defeated Emperor. The Minister had decided to receive the returning Emperor with one clearly consoling phrase: "Your Majesty," he had wanted to say, "it is not over yet!" But as the Emperor stepped out of the coach this oft-practiced phrase died upon Caulaincourt's tongue. When the Emperor embraced him, Caulaincourt began to weep hard and fast, tears that fell audibly upon the thick dust that had collected for days on the shoulders of the Emperor's cloak. His tears were like candle wax dripping on the Emperor's shoulders. The Emperor released himself quickly from the embrace, hurried through the door and to the stairs. As if to reward the loyalty of this Minister, whom at this moment he loved more than any of those who had been with him on the battlefield, he explained rapidly and humbly why the battle had been lost. Yet at the same time, he realized what a miserable and melancholy favor he was granting his friend—and he suddenly fell silent.

"What do you say?" he asked when they were in his room.

"I say, Your Majesty," replied the Minister, and he tried to make his voice loud and clear, and to halt the tears that were already mounting in his eyes and choking his throat, "that it would have been better if you had not returned."

"I have no soldiers," said the Emperor. "I have no guns. I offered myself to Death. It rejected me." He was lying on the sofa. He raised himself suddenly, sat up with a foolish deceptive hope that seemed to promise deliverance. "A bath!" he ordered. "A hot bath!" He stretched his arms. "A bath! And hurry!" he repeated. Water, he thought, boiling hot water!—he could think of nothing else. All at once he believed that hot steaming water had the ability to solve all puzzles, to purify the mind, and to cleanse the heart.

As he entered the bathroom, followed by his Minister Caulaincourt, the first sight that met his eyes was his loyal servant standing at attention beside the steaming water, as if on guard over the treacherous element that might perhaps betray the Emperor—as a general and his own wife had betrayed him. Through the second door, which led from the bathroom to the servants' corridor, he saw one of the female attendants leaving at that very moment. He suddenly felt an obligation to say a kind word to her, probably one of the lowest members of his household, a word of farewell perhaps. He gave his servant the signal to bring her back. She turned and stood before him. Then she fell down and began to sob loudly. She did not even cover her face. She remained on her knees and lifted her face up toward him, tears streaming down from her eyes, creating a hot wet veil. The Emperor bent down slightly toward her. He recognized her. He looked at her meager freckled face and remembered her from the evening in the park, and at the same time he could see once again the visage of her son, the little drummer boy.

"Stand up!" he ordered. She rose obediently. He ran his hand quickly and gently over her cap. "You have a little son, right? Where is he?" asked the Emperor.

"He was with you in the field," said Angelina. Through the warm wet veil of her tears she looked at him with fearless clear eyes, and her voice was equally clear and ringing.

"Go now, my child," said the Emperor. As she remained motionless, he repeated: "Go! Just go!" Gripping her gently by the shoulders, he spun her around. She went.

"She will be told," the Emperor ordered, "that her son has fallen and that I myself have buried him. Tomorrow she will be paid five thousand." Turning to his servant, he added: "You'll take care of it personally!" He allowed himself to be undressed and stepped into the bath. He had thought he would be able to remain alone in the hot water that he so loved and in which he felt cozily at home, but then his brother Joseph and the War Minister entered. He let them approach the bath and told them about the battle, becoming foolishly agitated, which he realized was pointless but could not control, and making accusations against Marshal Ney. Arrogance and shame filled him as he sat there naked in the water. Through the steam he could perceive their faces growing hazy, and he gestured with his bare arms, slapping at the water with his hand so it sprayed out of the tub high and wide and sprinkled the uniforms of the nearby men. The men did not move. Suddenly he once again had the feeling that all was lost and his excitement evaporated. He stopped speaking, leaned back, and from the midst of the hot water felt a great chill. He asked, so as not to reveal that he had suddenly become weak and helpless and yet admitting it after all: What should he do?

He knew at that moment, however, that his future depended not upon himself or on others but had been dictated long before by some terrifyingly unknowable, all-powerful decree. Oh! He had believed that as usual the bath would bring him strength and comfort. For the first time, however, he found himself helpless. Weary as he was from misfortune and numerous sleepless nights, his large eyes, which remained open and awake only on account of his immeasurable sorrow, saw clearly for the first time—despite the steam wafting through the room from the hot water—signs of weakness in the faces of his brother and his friend. Whatever they tell me, he thought, will be utter nonsense. They can only advise someone of their own kind. I obeyed special laws when I was great and strong; I must also obey special laws now that I am helpless and defeated. What do they know of me? They don't understand me! They don't! They understand me as little as the planets understand the sun that grants them life and around which they orbit! For the first time in his life the ever-alert Emperor had tired eyes; and for the first time he felt that one could see further and more clearly with tired unhappy eyes than with fresh sharp ones. Once again he thought of old Job and the Holy Father and the friends who had come to console him over his defeat, and like Job he rose and stepped naked before his friends. Only for a moment did they glimpse the naked Emperor, with his sallow, creased belly, the chubby thighs that always seemed so powerful and muscular in those snow-white Imperial breeches, the short strong neck, the rounded back, the small feet and dainty toes. This lasted for just a moment before the servant came and wrapped the short body in a great wide white flannel towel. The Emperor's bare feet left distinct wet marks on the floor with each step.

A few minutes later Angelina returned as her duties prescribed. She saw the tracks of the Imperial feet and as she scrubbed the floor she felt she was defiling and insulting the Emperor's footprints because she was forced to erase them. The servant, who was still organizing the bottles, soaps, and towels, approached her and said very gently: "I have something bad to tell you. Do you hear me? Something very bad!"

"Tell me," she replied.

"Your son—" he began ...

"He's dead," she said quite calmly.

"Yes. And the Emperor himself buried him."

Angelina leaned against the wall. She was silent for a moment and then she said: "He was my son. He loved the Emperor. Just as I love him."

"You will be given five thousand gold pieces," said the servant.

"I don't need them. Keep them," replied Angelina. "Go!" she said "Don't disturb me! I must work!"

Once she was alone she fell down to her knees, made the sign of the cross, and tried unsuccessfully to pray. She remained for a long time like this, on her knees, brush in hand. She looked as if she were attending to the floor but her mind was on Heaven, her dead child, and the Emperor.

Her heart was heavy; her eyes remained dry. She mourned her son, but also envied him. He was dead, dead! But he was buried by the Emperor's hand.

IV

THE NEXT MORNING AT TEN O'CLOCK THE MINISTERS
assembled in the Emperor's palace. The generals and the high
officials of the Empire awaited him in the corridor. They stood
motionless, arranged in two rows looking respectful and reverent, anxious and sorrowful. In reality, however, most of them
were more fearful for their own fates than the fate of the country
and the Emperor; and some were even inspired more by curiosity than by sorrow. Still others were concerned for the effects
that all of this would have upon their reputations and the living
they had earned since the Emperor's return. They stood there
solemnly, convinced that they alone were the critically important, the agents of destiny itself. Fouché was already waiting
in the chamber. His face was even more pale and sallow than
usual. He bowed his long gaunt head very low as the Emperor
entered. But the Emperor did not look. He felt nonetheless both
the veiled glance of his Minister of Police and the frank, ruthless
eyes of old Carnot. The Emperor had no need to look at them
all; he had known each one for years. He already knew what they
were thinking and what they would say. He sat down.

"The meeting is now open," he began with a calm voice. "I have
returned," he continued, "so as to halt the calamity that is about
to overtake us. But for some time I will need absolute powers."

They all lowered their gaze. Fouché alone fixed his light eyes
unwaveringly on the Emperor. The whole time he was writing,
note after little note, one after another without stopping, God
only knew to whom, in plain sight of the Emperor. The Minister
of Police wrote without even looking at the paper. He kept his
gaze focused on the Emperor as if his untiringly scribbling hand
had its own eyes. Now the Emperor stood. "I see," he said, "that
you want me to abdicate?"

"It is so, Your Majesty," replied one of the ministers.

The Emperor had known it. He posed each question so as to
confirm the answers he had long expected. Nonetheless he said—

and it was as if a stranger were speaking through him: "The enemy is in our country. Come what may, I am a man of the people and of the soldiers. One word from me and all the representatives are done. I can still arm one hundred and thirty thousand men. The English and Prussians are weary. They may have won, but they are depleted. And the Austrians and Russians are far off!" All the ministers were silent. Once more, for the last time, they all perceived the sublime tone of the Imperial voice. They listened to him, but only to his voice itself, to the ring of his words, not to their meaning. The Emperor himself was well aware that he was speaking in vain. He broke off suddenly. Every word was useless. He was no longer interested in fighting for his throne. For the first time in his life since he had become powerful, he felt the bliss that renunciation brings. In the midst of his speech he was overcome by the grace of humility. He suddenly felt the blessing of defeat and a very, very secret satisfaction that he could on a whim order the dismissal or imprisonment—even the beheading or shooting—of these very ministers to whom he was speaking, these parliamentarians who were poised to overthrow him. If he wanted ...!

But he did not want. It was a blissful feeling, one he was experiencing for the first time, to be capable of something and not wish to do it. Throughout his entire endlessly rich and full life he had always desired and wished for more than any earthly inhabitant could be granted. Now, for the first time and in his very hour of disgrace and defeat, he had great power but did not want it. It was a euphoric feeling. It was as if he held a sharpened sword in his hand, one that made him happy precisely because it remained unused. He who had always believed that one must strike, and with precision, was now experiencing his first foreboding of the happiness that comes from weakness and is a gift of humility. For the first time in his strong and proud life, he knew of the nobility of the weak, the defeated, and the abdicated. For the first time in his life he felt the desire to be a servant not a master. For the first time in his life he felt he had much to atone for because he had sinned so greatly. And it seemed to him that to save his soul he had to open the hand holding the honed sword, so it would fall harmless and humble as he himself was at this moment.

Yet there still breathed another within him, namely the old Emperor Napoleon, and it was he who now began to speak to the ministers again. He could have a new army in two weeks; he could certainly defeat the enemy, so said the Napoleon of old. But he already knew that he would not be able to convince the deputies as he might the ministers. He hated the lawyers, and he well knew he could oust them, but he hated them too much to use force against them. In any event he who had always been violent no longer desired violence. He had used enough force! He wanted to abdicate. He no longer wanted to be Emperor. Occasionally out of the distance yet ever clearer he believed he could hear a call, sorrow's seductive call. The voice became gradually louder and even more distinct than the shouts of "Long live the Emperor!" from the people outside the palace. For they were still shouting before the windows: "Long live the Emperor!" Poor friends, he thought, they love me, and I love them as well; they have died for me and they live for me, but I was unable to die for them. They want to see me mighty, so great is their love for me! I, however, I now love powerlessness. It is impotence that I love! I was for so long miserable in my might: I will be insignificant and happy!

But the people still continued to cry: "Long live the Emperor!" as if they knew what he was thinking and wanted not so much to pay him tribute as to remind him that he was their Emperor and that he must remain their Emperor. There were moments when these cries reached the very core of his being, and thus he knew that his old arrogance still lived within his heart. This old Imperial arrogance answered the cries, unheard by the crowd but strong within the Emperor's breast: "They call to me, so I am still their Emperor," said that old arrogance within his chest. But then another voice spoke from within: "I am more than an Emperor. I am an Emperor who abdicates. I hold a sword in my hand and I let it drop. I sit on a throne and I hear the woodworms gnawing away. I sit on a throne but already see myself lying in a coffin. I hold a scepter but I wish for a cross. Yes, I wish for a cross!"

V

THAT NIGHT FOUND HIM SLEEPLESS. IT WAS SOMBER and sultry. All the millions of stars were up in the silvery blue heavens, but when the Emperor gazed at them, they seemed not to be real stars, just the pale, distant images of genuine stars. That night he once again felt he could see right through the seemingly sublime intentions of the Ruler of the Universe. He had yet to really know God but he now believed he could see right through Him. The Emperor believed that God too was an Emperor but a wiser, more cautious and therefore more lasting one. He, however, the Emperor Napoleon, had been foolish through arrogance; he had lost power through arrogance. Without that arrogance, he too could have been God, created the blue dome of the heavens, regulated the brilliance and position of the stars, and orchestrated the direction of the wind, the drifting of the clouds, the passage of the birds, and the destiny of man. But he, the Emperor, was more modest than God, carelessly generous and thoughtlessly magnanimous.

He opened the wide windows. He could hear the cheerful monotonous song of the crickets in the park. He detected the rich peaceful fragrance of the summer night, the overpowering lilac and the cloying acacias. All of it made him furious.

No longer did he want a throne or a crown, a palace or a scepter. He wanted to be as simple as one of the thousands of soldiers who had died for him and for the country of France. He hated the people who tomorrow or the following day would force him to abdicate; but he was also thankful to them for forcing him to resign. He despised his power but also his lack of power. No longer did he want to be Emperor, yet he wanted to remain Emperor. Now at this very hour they were debating in the House of Deputies whether he should remain Emperor or not.

Restless and lost, he paced, stopped a moment at the open window, turned around again, sat at the table, opened its hidden drawer, and attempted to organize his papers into three piles.

Some were harmless and could stay; others were sensitive and had to be destroyed; still others he wished to keep and even take with him. He held a few of the letters to the golden flame of the wax candles. He mindlessly allowed the ash to scatter on to the table and the rug. Suddenly he stopped, gently replaced the condemned papers, and began anew his pacing. It had occurred to him that it was perhaps too soon to destroy these letters and he was gripped by a fear, his old superstitious fear that he might have carelessly given Fate a hint, a sign. This thought wearied him, and he tried to stretch out on the sofa. But as soon as he lay down, he felt more helpless than ever. Black worries seemed to be swooping down upon him like sinister crows on a corpse. He needed to get up. He looked again at the sky and then checked the time. This night was endless. Confused visions ran across his mind; meaningless images with no temporal reference rose up as if from totally different and newly unlocked compartments of his memory. Meekly he gave in to them, sat down, supported his head with his hands, and fell asleep in his chair.

The first hesitating call of a newly risen bird woke him. Day was dawning and a gentle wind softly swayed the crowns of the trees and blew the high casement windows. They creaked a bit on their hinges, startling the Emperor. He left the room. His servant, who was nestled on a chair outside the door, sprang up and made ready to follow him. But the guard at the gate, although standing fully upright with weapon shouldered, was in a deep sleep. He was quite a young lad, and a soft and delicate little black mustache grew above his lips, which opened and closed with every breath, while his chubby peasant cheeks were as pink as if he had not fallen asleep erect, weapon on shoulder, but rather at home at his girl's side. Perhaps one day my son will look like that, thought the Emperor. "And I won't see him. Such a mustache will sprout on his upper lip, and he too will be able to sleep standing, but I will not live to see it." He put out his hand and tugged the young man's earlobe. The soldier jerked awake and forced his round golden-brown eyes wide open, looking like a startled, uniformed fawn. It took him a few seconds to recognize the Emperor, at which point he mechanically presented arms, still half asleep yet already anxious and frightened. The Emperor left him standing there and continued on.

All the birds were celebrating the jubilant morning. The wind had subsided and the trees stood motionless in a still, light-blue splendor as if rooted for all eternity. This is the last day, thought the Emperor, that I will still be the Emperor of France. Yes, that was already definite. The morning itself seemed to say so; the birds were celebrating in all too spiteful and shrill voices and even the sun, which had now emerged above the thick and lush greenery, bore a malevolent yellowish-red face. The Emperor did not feel the summer calm of the morning, nor did he wish to. Nevertheless, while he walked for a few seconds with his eyes closed, he felt that God and His world had good intentions for him and that other men in his place, in this very garden at this very hour, in the blue-green-golden shimmer of the rising day, would have been thankful, humble, and happy. But the morning seemed to be mocking him. God's eternal sun was rising, rising as it had done from the beginning of time, as if nothing had happened, on the very day his, the Emperor's, own sun was setting. Night! It still should be night! And to avoid seeing the day grow any brighter, the Emperor suddenly turned around. He ordered the curtains drawn. He wanted to have a few more hours of night.

He fell asleep in his uniform, in his boots. He had forbidden anyone to wake him, yet they dared disobey, and his first thought upon waking was that even his lackeys no longer followed his orders. But it was his brother Jerome, his youngest and most beloved brother. Jerome stood there, before the sofa, and despite the already rich golden sunlight seeping in through the drawn curtains his brother looked pale white and bleary-eyed—a souvenir of his sleepless night.

"They refuse," was all he said.

"I knew it!" replied the Emperor. He rose.

The familiar daily cries of "Long live the Emperor!" could already be heard before the palace. He sat down and said to his brother: "You hear that? The people want me to live but their representatives want my death. I don't believe the people, and I don't believe their representatives, either. I have only believed in my star. And that is now setting."

His brother was silent. He lowered his head. He was young and he felt even younger and more foolish during this unfortunate time, yet at the same time he felt even now that it was his duty to invigorate and rescue the Emperor, his brother, who was like a father to him. And thus he said hesitatingly: "You're still Emperor! You're still Emperor! You mustn't abdicate!"

"I will abdicate," answered Napoleon. "I am not tired, but I, my dear brother, dearest of my brothers, I am changed. You see I no longer believe in all those things in which I used to have faith—in force, might, and success. That's why I will abdicate. It's true that I still cannot believe in that other thing, the Power that we cannot know. But you see, my brother, I stand today between two faiths! I no longer believe in humanity and I don't yet believe in God. Yet I can already feel Him, I am already beginning to feel Him."

He was speaking to himself; he was well aware that his brother did not understand. And it was true, his brother Jerome did not in fact understand and thought the Emperor was tired and babbling.

He was kind and honest and loyal, and he had no idea of the Emperor's confusion, of his meaning or his sorrow. The Emperor knew it well. He continued to speak, anyhow, because he had been silent for the whole endlessly long night and because he knew that Jerome, the simplest and most dear of his brothers, did not understand him.

Jerome kept his head bowed. It was true that he grasped nothing. One thought alone filled him with terror: Soon they will come! Soon they will come!

VI

THEY CAME AT TEN O'CLOCK IN THE MORNING. THEY
wore solemn, sorrowful, and despairing faces. The Emperor
studied them with keen attention, one after another—old Caulaincourt, his brother Joseph, the beloved Regnault. Others were
waiting next door in the ministerial chamber. Fouché, the Minister of Police, was announced. "Send him in," said the Emperor,
"and immediately!"

He came in. His head was lowered and remained in this position so long that it almost seemed he actually had trouble
straightening his back again and lifting his head. In his right
hand he carried a thin portfolio of dark green Moroccan leather
and in his left his ministerial hat. With even greater attention and
scrutiny than he had viewed the others, the Emperor studied the
most hateful of his enemies. It was as if he wanted to create a
lifelong mental impression of all the minute details of this man's
figure; as if he had summoned him solely for that purpose. His
eyes were feasting upon the appearance of this ugliest of ministers with the bliss of an artist who has found the perfect subject.
He is still afraid of me, thought the Emperor. I can still disrupt
him, disrupt first and then perhaps destroy. In that green portfolio he carries my death warrant, but only I have the authority to sign it, and he fears I still don't want to. He doesn't know
me, and how could he? So little does the devil know the Lord!
I'll make him wait a bit longer! What a perfect specimen! What
harmony between face, hands, manner, and soul! I have let him
live and have not interfered, as God lets the devil live and doesn't
stop him. But now that I'm no longer a god, he lives by his own
grace; by tomorrow he will live by the grace of the English, the
Austrians, the Prussians, and the King.

"Look at me!" said the Emperor.

Fouché lifted his head. He wanted to speak but could not get
the words out once he met the Emperor's gaze. He had often
merely shivered under this look. But now for the first time this

regard also rendered him paralyzed. He suddenly had dry, rough lips, through which not a word could pass so that he involuntarily moistened them with the narrow and pale tip of his tongue. What harmony! thought the Emperor. His every little movement gives the impression of a snake. So true it is, this symbolism!

"Write to the gentlemen who await some word, that they shall have it soon. They can rest easy."

Fouché approached the Emperor's table. He laid his hat on a chair but retained the portfolio, gingerly took an empty sheet of paper from the table, placed it atop the portfolio, and wrote while standing.

The Emperor looked at him no more. He turned to his brother and ordered: "Write!" And he began to dictate: "... I offer myself as a sacrifice to the hatred that the enemies of France harbor against me. May their word prove sincere that they have only pursued me and me alone ... All of you should unite for the general good, so that you may remain an independent nation ..."

He got that far. Around him stood his old friends and servants. Through the open windows the dazzling summer heat poured into the room in heavy, oppressive, and stultifying waves. Nothing moved. People and things were petrified; even the delicate yellowish muslin curtain before the window hung there in motionless, stony folds. One could believe that the world outside had also been petrified. Paris no longer breathed under the burden of this golden heat that was heavier than lead. All of France dozed in the brilliant sunshine, dozed and waited; the towns and villages slept as the enemy approached from the north; the sleepy grass in the meadows waited to be crushed and the grain in the field already realized it was growing in vain; no more corn would be ground or baked that year; and one could see still and dead mills scattered throughout the entire land. Only the dead stones in the street and lanes still breathed, but even their breath was no more than murderous heat ...

All of a sudden the shrill scream of a woman in the street came through the window, "Long live the Emperor!" This scream cut into the sweltering summer silence like a blinding spark in dead, dried-out timber. The men in the Emperor's chamber began to breathe audibly. Their eyes came alive and opened wide focusing on the Emperor. Someone moved delicately, as if to test whether his stiffness had truly abated and others shifted in the same way. The woman's shrill shriek had not yet faded when it was followed by the muffled thunder of a thousand male throats outside, "Long live the Emperor!" One of the men in the room opened his lips as if wishing to join in the cry; the Emperor saw him and his eyes commanded the man so threateningly to be silent that his friend's mouth remained open for a while and everyone practically believed they could see the man's tribute dying between his tongue and teeth. Once more, a third and a tenth time the people outside boomed: "Long live the Emperor!"

The Emperor had stopped dictating. He did not turn around. He sat with his back to the windows through which the cries came, as though he were intentionally and indignantly turning his back on them. But in truth they made him both sad and proud. He was still thinking of the last sentence that he had just dictated: "All of you should unite for the general good, so that you may remain an independent nation." He had formulated this sentence the previous day and the day before that; but it had already been alive in his heart for a long time. Now that he had spoken it and given it life, it was as though the woman outside, this woman of the people, had heard it—along with the rest of the people. Yes, they were his people, they were his Frenchmen and women! He always said the right word to them at the right time, and even if he hadn't said it, they would have sensed and noted just as they did now. He knew all the people outside, the men and women from the outskirts, both low-ranking and high-ranking officers, the women with their red scarves, many adorned with violets, all of them children of France; and the sweet melody of the "Marseillaise" as could be heard trembling through the great thundering timpani that were beating outside. There was suddenly an old, familiar, and beloved odor in the Emperor's room, entering through the windows like an endearing guest—the smell of soldiers, the smell of the people, of gunpowder, of steaming soup in bivouacs, of burning, crackling sticks, and also the smell of warm human blood; yes, the breeze even contained warm human blood.

The Emperor felt an unknown pride rise up within, an entirely different one from the pride he had felt the evening after a victorious battle or after meeting with an arrogant and defeated enemy who was begging for peace. It was a new pride, a distant and much more noble brother of the pride that he had known so well. In the hour when he was humbly extinguishing his light, the people of France themselves lifted and supported him. He was laying down the crown that he had bestowed upon himself; and now the people were giving him a new crown, invisible but real, one he had always longed for but never understood how to attain. The entire time he had ruled the French people they had seemed uncertain and fickle. Now that he was smashing his scepter, he had become the true Emperor of France. Outside they continued to cry: "Long live the Emperor!" The expressions of those gathered in the room betrayed their growing uneasiness. "Shut the windows!" the Emperor ordered. They were closed, but the cries could still be heard, though muffled and distant.

At that moment one of the men sobbed aloud, a violent sound, immediately curbed and cut short, but so intense and upsetting that tears began to well up in the eyes of the others. "I can write no more," the Emperor's brother said very softly. He was practically whispering, but in the stillness all could hear it clearly.

They don't know me, even now, thought the Emperor. I am proud and indifferent, I have just learned the meaning of sorrow, sadness makes me feel good. I could even say that I am happy. And my friends are weeping! Any of my grenadiers would have understood me ... And indignantly, he ordered: "Fleury de Chaboulon, sit down and start writing: 'My political life is over. I nominate my son, under the name Napoleon the Second, as Emperor of the French.'"

Everyone was silent. The quill scratched hurriedly and brusquely. Suddenly they heard a loud drip fall upon the paper. In the stillness it sounded hard, as when a drop of candle wax falls on paper. But it was not dead wax, it was a living tear. It fell from the writer's eye on to the paper. He stopped the next tear quickly with his left sleeve, without interrupting his writing.

The Emperor snatched the paper out of his hand. He signed it in flowing script as was his custom. And during the brief moment that his signature required there was a fierce and noble gleam in his lowered eyes that nobody saw, and his lips were somewhat crooked. They saw his mouth and thought the Emperor was suffering. But he suffered not; he only scorned.

He stood up, embraced the writer, and dismissed everyone. He had abdicated. And he felt as though he had just been crowned for the first time.

VII

HE REMAINED ALONE UNTIL THE EVENING. ONLY A SER-
vant came, the young man whom he liked. He brought the type
of meal the Emperor enjoyed when alone: one that could be
eaten quickly and impatiently. The young man's kind eyes were
concealed by his half-closed eyelids while his normally tanned,
smooth face was jaundiced and suddenly marked by numerous lines. He looked as though he were recovering from some
horrid fright or a long and difficult journey, or perhaps a wild
dream. "Stay here!" said the Emperor. "Sit down and get that
book over there"—he pointed to the little table on which lay a
stack of books and maps. "Read to me, beginning or middle, it
doesn't matter."

The servant obeyed. He sat down and began to read. It was a
book about America, and he began to read from the first page,
out of respect for the book and also the Emperor. He read deliberately and attentively in a monotonous drone, as he had read
when he was a schoolboy, impressing everything on his mind—
the nature of the soil, the plants, the people; he read many pages
without daring to lift his eyes from the book, sensing only that
the Emperor was not listening anymore, but had stood up and
gone to the window, then returned again to the table. He guessed
that the Emperor would soon begin to speak and became unsettled and read ever faster. "Enough!" The Emperor said. "Look
at me!" The servant stopped in mid-sentence. He looked at the
Emperor. "Have you been crying, my son?" asked the Emperor.

"Yes, Your Majesty,"—and he felt the tears welling up again.

"Look here, you are young," began the Emperor. "You don't
yet understand the ways of the world and the laws of life. Heed
what I'm about to tell you, but don't repeat it to the whole
world—and, above all, never write it down. For one day, I know,
you too will wish to pen your memoirs. We all do, we who have
really lived. So keep it to yourself, what I'm about to say: everything obeys incomprehensible but very definite laws—the stars,

the wind, migratory birds, emperors, soldiers, all men, all plants. The law to which I am subject has been fulfilled. Now I will finally try to live. Understand?" The servant nodded. "Tell me," asked the Emperor, "are you weeping over my misery? Do you take me for unhappy?"

The servant rose, but could not answer. He opened his mouth, hesitated, lowered his gaze, and said: "Your Majesty, I know only that I myself am very unhappy."

"Very well, go!" the Emperor ordered. "I must be alone!"

Now that there was no more noise, he heard once more the untiring cries of the people in front of the palace. Evening was already nearing and only the people, his people, the people of France, remained so persistent in their love. They already knew that he was Emperor no more but they paid no mind to his abdication and cried longingly, as on the evening of his homecoming: "Long live the Emperor!"—as if he had not lost the greatest of all battles and the lives of all his soldiers. Not of all! he thought suddenly. His military mind began immediately, almost against his will, to calculate—as it had done so many times before—that he still had 5,300 guards, 6,000 infantry, 700 gendarmes, and eight companies of veterans: the army of General Grouchy was still available. In a flash the Emperor had forgotten the entire day gone by, his resignation, his plans; he heard only the cries of "Long live the Emperor!" in the persistent appeals of the people. Once again the Emperor Napoleon, he walked briskly to the table and unfolded his maps; never—so he believed—had his mind worked with such speed and certainty; errors he had committed appeared to him now as childish, ridiculous aberrations; he could not fathom why he had been so blind. All at once he felt eliminated as if Grace had come over him and he believed he could guess, better yet know, the plans of his enemies; he lured, outwitted, trapped, entangled, beat, and destroyed them; the country was finally free, but he continued to drub the enemy, far beyond the frontiers; he had already reached the coast, the English were escaping in their ships to the safe shores of their island—how long would England herself be safe from the

Emperor? One day he would even cross the sea, usually hostile but occasionally merciful, and take revenge, revenge! Oh, sweet revenge!

It was already dark, but the Emperor was so engrossed in his maps that he hardly noticed. He was not actually reading the maps. He was instead visualizing the actual villages, the hamlets, the roads, the hills, the battlefields, all potential and future battlefields, so many battlefields, thousands of battlefields, and suddenly all the beloved comrades of his youth rose up again; his fallen brothers, the generals and the grenadiers; Death returned them all to him and he needed no others. He would achieve victory with the resurrected dead alone. It would be the greatest battle of his life, the most wonderful, the most brilliant; victory was a game, practically enjoyable in all its awesome destruction.

There was a knock and he awoke. The Minister Carnot was announced. Two candelabra with lit candles were brought in. The chandelier was lit. The Minister was then let in.

"You have disturbed me!" said the Emperor.

"I beg forgiveness, your Majesty."

"I forgive you. But you have wrecked the most beautiful battle. I can win. I can chase them to the borders. I need no more soldiers than are available to me now. I can win!"

"It is too late, your Majesty. You will be forbidden from remaining here. You will be in danger when the enemy arrives. The ministers cannot safeguard your life. You must leave!"

It was suddenly very hot in the room so the Emperor himself opened one of the windows, and with boundless force came the people's thundering cry: "Long live the Emperor!"

He did not turn. With his back toward the Minister, as his ears inhaled the loving, beloved, boisterous cry of the crowd, he said aloud: "So I must go! In spite of everything, I must go!"

VIII

IT WAS A WARM, GOLDEN SUMMER. IT SEEMED TO BE THE
last, radiant tribute of the country, of the French soil and the
French sky. The French soil and the French sky were saying: "You
will never again see a French summer, Emperor Napoleon! Take
the memory of this one, the most beautiful we can offer you."

He was no longer an Emperor, he was a prisoner in the chateau
of his first wife, the dead Empress Josephine. Her daughter
Hortense lived there. She frequently reminded him of her dead,
beloved, now doubly beloved mother. The way she tilted her
neck, cut her food, or leaned back, the very distinct way she had
of smiling when one said something she did not understand and
did not care to understand—she had learned all these manner-
isms from her mother and that was why the Emperor loved her.
At the same time he was actually a little, just a tiny bit jealous of
himself; he wanted his wife, the Empress Josephine, to remain
the sole woman he had ever loved, just as he had been the sole
Emperor of the French people.

Ah, but there was nothing left for him to do but give in to
his memories of this woman. "I used to walk here with her," he
would say in this or that avenue, as if it were the only avenue
along which he had walked with her. "Look here," he gestured to
Minister Carnot, not realizing that he had now passed the spot
and was heading in a different direction, "here, as I have been
wanting to tell you, was where my son visited her. She kissed
him. What a woman. She embraced the child, the child of another woman, and it was really on account of this child that she
had ceased to be Empress. Listen to me, Carnot!"

"Yes, your Majesty," said the Minister.

This Minister had been a lifelong enemy of the Emperor. He
had called the Emperor a betrayer of freedom; yes, a hardened,
blunt heart was Carnot's distinguishing feature. Now, however,
on this golden evening, while they walked along, as he listened

171

to the Emperor confiding his reminiscences with their fond distortion of the truth, confessing his errors and concerns, Carnot began for the first time slowly but surely to recognize that there were other laws governing the world, other laws than those to which he himself subscribed, other laws than those of strong conviction and conscience, loyalty and treason. "Your Majesty," he said with the blunt candor of an old Jacobin, "when I hear you speak in this way, I ask myself why I had convinced myself for so long that I must consider you a traitor. Today, although sadly it is too late, I take you for the most loyal man in the world!"

"For that it is never too late," said the Emperor softly.

A servant approached. He announced the Countess Walewska. It seemed so long since the Emperor had last seen her. She stood there holding her child—his child—by the hand. She wore a black dress and her face was partly veiled. He was startled by this sight for a second and hesitated, having the impression she had come to his funeral, that he was already a corpse. Perhaps she noticed his alarm, for she came toward him and bent over his hand. He took her arm and led her to the room that he had once furnished for himself for the sole purpose of consoling the Empress Josephine and making her believe he would be staying there often. He gave the boy his hand, smiled, and stood silently for some time facing the woman. He pointed at the sofa a couple of times but she remained standing. "I wanted to see you again," she said. Not long ago her face had been just as sleek and delicate as when they had first met. Now it appeared gaunt and haggard. How quickly women changed, especially lovers and the afflicted! Her white, narrow cheeks had once been covered with a delicate silvery blonde fuzz—sweet moss in which his lips had delighted. Now those same cheeks were naked, bare, and sunken. Her lips were but a thin, severe slit.

"I have to beg your forgiveness, Your Majesty," said this sparse mouth.

"Not at all, not at all; why, what for?" cried the Emperor.

"Well," said the Countess, "that is why I have come. I must tell you. I must tell you," she continued.

"Please do so!" said the Emperor almost impatiently. He already knew everything she wanted to tell him.

She was silent, startled at his impatience. She had already thought everything out carefully, but now all the words had vanished completely from her mind. She could not even bring herself to cry.

The Emperor approached her, gently laid his hands upon her arms, brought his wide, light eyes close to her face, and said: "You wanted to confess that you have not always loved me. I have known it for a long time already. You had love only for Poland, your homeland. You accepted my love to make Poland free. Only then did you learn to love the Emperor a little bit. Am I right? Is this what you wanted to tell me?"

"That is not all," she said.

"What else?"

"I love you now, Your Majesty!" She replied and raised her face, almost defiantly. "I love you now, you alone, not Poland, not the Emperor. And wherever you go, I will follow."

The Emperor stepped back. He was silent for some time, then spoke in the clear, hard voice with which he normally addressed his soldiers: "Go, Countess! There is little room by my side. Please go. I still love you. I will never forget you. I still love you."

He watched her walk out proudly and firmly, the sleek, vigorous, strong legs he had loved, with their sturdy step that swayed her whole body and made her delicate, frail shoulders look strong, erect, and royal.

He realized that he had been hard on her. But she was the only woman he knew who understood him and loved his hardness. And she probably also understood that he could not remain with her any longer. He listened for a while. He heard her sobbing outside, behind the door. He heard the consoling voice of his daughter Hortense.

A great impatience gripped him. He did not want to stay any longer. His law had been fulfilled, and he was already hurrying toward new horizons. He sent for his brother and his friends—Bassano, Flahaut, and La Valette. "I wish to go!" he cried.

"Where is the ship waiting? Where are the passports? Where am I going? I want to go, I want to leave!"

"The enemy is here," General Lavalette answered quite calmly. "The Prussians are in Bourget."

"And the English?"

"None have been seen," replied the General.

The Emperor suddenly left the room. The four men looked at one another in silent consternation. Before any of them could speak, he had returned with his sword, booted and spurred, in the uniform of the gardes-chasseurs.

"I will stop them!" he cried so loudly that the chandelier clinked. "Get the horses saddled! I will stop them! I can; the French soldiers can! Go and tell the gentlemen that I want the authority to stop the Prussians. I no longer need a crown. I am no longer Emperor. All I need is one division! I am a division commander!"

Then he was silent. They all stood stiff and dumb. Only the chandelier trembled and clinked. From outside came strains of the tune being sung by marching soldiers. They heard clearly the officer's command to halt and the abrupt side of boots. The soldiers faced the palace and cried: "Long live the Emperor!"

"So we ride tomorrow!" the Emperor ordered.

IX

But no! They did not ride on the next day. Barely had the men left the room, before the Emperor realized that he would not be permitted to have even one division. He unfastened his sword and flung it onto the table. He called for his servant. He asked that his boots and uniform be taken off. He felt ridiculous. He had displayed the élan of a little boy. Alas, it had been no more than a dream, an old and vain dream; no, he who had lost a great battle as Emperor could not win a small one as a colonel or general. He realized this and was silent as he was told that he was forbidden to defend the city. Paris awaited the enemy—he had known it for a long time, although they continued to shout outside: "Long live the Emperor!" Paris was already waiting for them—the enemy and the King. The shouts outside no longer had a true ring, but rather a historical one. They were like shouts in a theatre. They were no longer meant for him, the living Napoleon, but rather for the dead, the immortal one.

All that remained was to say farewell and then go far away, wherever the wind might blow, whether that wind was merciful or spiteful. He was prepared to let himself be carried forth and was even awaiting it with longing. He offered no more than a quick farewell to his brother, Josephine's daughter, and his friends. Now all that was left was the most difficult farewell, taking leave of his mother!

For this last farewell he selected the darkest room in the house, the library. His mother's eyes had long been weak and light-sensitive. She arrived, supported by two ladies in waiting and followed by the Emperor's servant. She was wearing a black dress and wore no jewelry. As she entered, the room seemed to grow even darker. Even though she was walking with support, she seemed so tall and strong. She appeared to be so powerful, even though her face was thin, pale, and drawn, that the entire room was saturated with the somber breath of her gloomy dignity. Everything fell under her shadow. It looked as if she had

175

come not to take leave of a living son but to bury a dead one. The room was already darkened on account of the dark-green curtains having been drawn, but now the room grew even more noticeably dark. Even the delicate golden brown of the book spines along the walls was muted. Only the pale face of his mother glimmered, only her large dark short-sighted eyes glowed. She motioned and the servant disappeared. The ladies in waiting followed. The Emperor himself supported his mother. It was hardly five steps to the wide dark armchair, but he wished that distance would grow ever greater. He hesitated at every step; he was even weaker than his mother, his knees wobbled and his arm trembled. She clung to his right arm and he felt for her left hand and kissed it with each stride. It was a large strong hand with long firm fingers bearing tiny wrinkles at their tips and shockingly white nails, and it sprang from a bony yet muscular wrist with thick blue veins on the bottom. How often had this hand scolded or caressed, even caressing as it scolded? He was a small child once again; gone were the stormy, bloody, terror-inspiring years of his fame. The sight of this motherly hand alone made him young and small. It was only now that he was truly abdicating, every time, every single time he brought his lips to his mother's hand once again. As he gently set her down into the armchair, his elbow briefly touched her full breast and a pleasant shiver ran up his arms and to his heart; he quivered slightly. It was a blissful tremble, equally as delightful as those he had experienced as a child of his mother's breast.

She seemed to tower above him and he felt quite small as he pushed a chair near her armchair. He would rather have been perched on a stool at her kind feet. He was now sitting opposite her, their knees practically touching, and she seemed to grow ever taller, prouder, and more noble in her armchair, while the Emperor made himself ever smaller, sinking lower into his chair until his head touched his breast. "Look at me," his mother said in her strong, deep voice and she stretched out her hand and placed her fingers under her son's chin as a signal for him to lift it. He obeyed and raised his head for a second, but let it drop down again at once, his shoulders trembling. His mother opened her arms and he fell forward, his head landing in her lap. Her fingers began to stroke his smooth hair, slowly at first, then ever quicker and more vigorously. Her fingers combed his hair, feeling with maternal delight as she tousled it and then smoothed it down again, stroked his hair, bent over, and kissed her son's head. The whole time, she grasped him firmly by the shoulders, as if worried he would escape from her. He had no desire to leave, he only wanted to lay forever in his mother's kindly lap, upon her black dress. Her hands roamed over his head, ten kind motherly fingers, while from above, her mouth spoke some words in the native tongue of his homeland. He did not catch their meaning clearly, and neither did he want to, for it was enough just to hear the old familiar sound of her voice, the language of his mother, his mother tongue. Often, so very often, he mused, I should have lain like this, with my head in my mother's lap. Why had he sat in so many saddles, why had he ridden through so many lands? His mother's lap was welcoming, so welcoming was his mother's lap; saddles and battlefields were evil, so evil—and so were thrones. Crowns hurt; for a son's head was meant to be in his mother's lap. Out of this lap he had emerged, so long ago, forty-six years ago. He had ruled the world; if only he could die now just as he lay at that very moment, ending in his mother's lap what had begun there. On his account, on the Emperor's account, many thousands had died, many thousands of sons who otherwise would have been able, as he did now, to rest their heads in their mothers' laps. He did not move. He lay there very still. His mother was startled. Suddenly she said: "Get up, get up, Nabulio!" "Nabulio," she said, as she had called him when he was a boy. He obeyed and rose quickly. His eyes were quite dry and glistened brightly as though filled with frozen tears.

"I will go," his mother said. "But I will not leave you, my child! I will follow you all over, most handsome and beloved of my children!"

"I go alone, Mother," said the Emperor, firm and loud. Then, fearing he had been too harsh, he added: "You may be certain, mother, I'll be back, we will see each other again." He was lying and they both knew it, mother and son.

She rose, went to the door, looked around once more, put her arms around the Emperor's neck, and kissed him on the forehead. The door opened, she went out and the Emperor followed her to the staircase but she did not turn around once the ladies in waiting met her. As he watched her going down the stairs, with her strong, erect posture, grand shoulders, and deliberate steps, he cried out: "Adieu, Mother!"

She paused, turned at the penultimate step, and said: "Adieu, my son!"

He turned quickly and entered the dead Empress's room, the room with the sky-blue ceiling and stood in front of the wide bed for a long time. It was nearly as comforting as his mother's lap. Only these two things could bring him joy: his mother's lap and his beloved's bed—and perhaps a third thing that he had not yet experienced, but would one day know, the embrace of Death, his good old brother. Night was ending and the morning was already dawning when he went to his room, removed his uniform, donned a brown coat, a round hat, and blue breeches, fastened his sword and exited the palace through a rear door. There were people waiting outside before the main gate, crying relentlessly, untiringly: "Long live the Emperor!" He stood there for a moment. The crowd thundered, the insistent cry of a persistent people. A barouche was waiting at the main gate so the people believed that the Emperor was coming out that way. The chirping of the nocturnal crickets grew ever weaker as the day broke with triumphant power. The first birds were already chirping. As if fleeing the sun, the Emperor hastily entered his coach. He did not look out. He drew the curtains and cried: "Forward!" in a firm voice. And they departed.

The wheels crunched with a soft melancholy and the axles moaned with human-like voices.

X

HE FELL ASLEEP IN THE CARRIAGE. THE SUN ROSE, JUST
as it always had, mighty and golden. The morning was already
as hot as midday. The carriage wheels crunched along as the axles groaned. The Emperor's three companions were silent. They
studied his sleeping face. He was pale yellow, and every so often
his mouth fell open, revealing his even, gleaming white teeth,
before he sighed gently and closed his mouth again. They gingerly lowered the windows, on account of the untenable heat in
the carriage. The fresh breeze awoke the Emperor. He forced
his great, pale eyes open, ran his hand over his brow, and for
a moment looked at his companions as if they were strangers
he did not recognize. Then he smiled at them, as if to appease
them, and asked if he had slept long and where they were. "Near
Poitiers," said General Bekker. Poitiers!—It was still far from the
coast! The Emperor was very impatient. He wished to get to the
coast quickly.

"Let's hurry, gentlemen," he said. "I long for the sea. I want
to see the water, I want to see the water!"

They remained silent. They were astonished and a little startled. The Emperor's words seemed bizarre to them and they
exchanged uneasy looks. The Emperor noticed his companions
were uncomfortable. He smiled. "Don't be surprised," he began,
"that I long for the sea. I've had enough of the land. Fate truly
has middling notions, like a middling poet. I was born amid the
sea and I must see it again. I'd like to see Corsica too, but that
is not to be. But the sea, gentlemen, every sea reminds me of
Corsica."

None of his companions knew exactly what he meant, but
they all maintained solemn and attentive expressions. Still, he
could tell that they understood nothing of what he said. How
wide a gap already separates me from the common people! he
thought. Only a week ago they understood a wave of my finger,
a passing glance, every nuance of my lips, but now they do not

even understand my clearly spoken words. One must, he thought further, speak very plainly to them. And although at that moment he had no desire for it, he said, just to be friendly: "May I have some snuff?"

He was given an open snuff box, took a pinch, inhaled slowly with pretended pleasure, then closed the lid. He was about to give back the little box when his gaze fell upon the lid. It featured a miniature portrait of the Empress Josephine—that endearing, smiling face, the wide tan cheeks, and the great noble red curve of her mouth. Her strong, slender neck gleamed white, and her enticing breasts peeked, dainty and inquisitive, from her neckline. The Emperor examined the box, closed it, ran his hand over the lid, brought it near his eyes and then his lips, and said: "May I keep it, General?" The General bowed silently. The Emperor held the box in his folded hands. He closed his eyes. He fell asleep again.

It was early evening when they reached Niort. He climbed out of the carriage at the Golden Ball Inn. Nobody recognized him. The innkeeper came along, thick, pudgy, and noiseless—himself a ball, a soft red rubber ball that moved as if some unseen player had pushed him, sending him rolling toward his destination. He even rolled up the stairs. He opened up the room and attempted a bow, but was wholly unsuccessful. As a desperate attempt to demonstrate respect and out of confusion over the gleaming carriage and the distinguished gentlemen, he said to the Emperor: "Your Reverence, here is the room."

"You might have addressed Monsieur Talleyrand by that title," murmured the Emperor. As the innkeeper was preparing to roll back down the stairs again, the Emperor grabbed his coat and ordered: "Stay here!"

The Emperor tossed his round hat on to the bed, and the innkeeper noticed his forehead with the black lock of hair and light eyes—and gave a terrific start. Downstairs in the breakfast room hung a portrait of the Emperor bareheaded. This same face was painted on all the plates, engraved on all the knife handles, and permanently imprinted in people's minds. The gentleman looked like the Emperor, and the innkeeper rolled a step backward to the door. He wavered for some time between the impulse to drop to his knees and the fear that told him to flee the room as quickly as possible. But the Emperor, who could see the man's misery, smiled and said once again: "Stay here! Have no fear!"

Yes, now the innkeeper was certain of the identity of his guest. He wished to kneel but because of his rotund body he could only fall down and thus he lay at the Emperor's feet, stammering incomprehensibly. "Stand up!" the Emperor ordered, and the man rose surprisingly quickly and stood with his fat rounded back touching the door and his large black bulging eyes rolling (also like balls) pitifully and helplessly in all directions.

Just then there was a commotion outside; through the window came the joyful and melancholy whinnying of horses and the loud voices and coarse laughter of men. The Emperor went immediately to the window. Below in the plaza before the inn he saw soldiers, his soldiers and his horses. In the blink of an eye he forgot everything—his abdication and the sea for which he longed—only the soldiers registered in his brain. He forgot even the innkeeper, who was still leaning against the door, now resembling a neglected ball. One of the soldiers suddenly lifted his head toward the window and saw and recognized the Emperor. Within seconds all the soldiers were crowded beneath the window, longing faces raised upward, giving voice to that old cry through their wide open mouths: "Long live the Emperor! Long live the Emperor!"

He turned around. There stood the innkeeper at the door; he too was shouting: "Long live the Emperor!"—with such a resoundingly loud voice he could have been shouting in the open air and not a few steps away from the Emperor. Someone knocked, bringing news to the Emperor that the enemy was just outside Paris and that the artillery fire had begun.

"Write immediately to Paris!" the Emperor ordered. The General sat down, and the Emperor dictated: "We hope that Paris will defend herself and that the enemy will allow you ample time to await the outcome of the negotiations that are being conducted by your ambassadors …You may now look upon your Emperor as your General and call upon my services as someone inspired solely by a desire to be useful to his motherland …" But hardly had the General left the room with this message when the Emperor was again overcome by that already familiar feeling of unhappiness—by sorrow, by uncertainty, and by regret over the letter he had just dispatched. He was no longer Emperor. He had abdicated. How could he have believed, even for a moment, that he could still be a general? The country did not need him! It was exiling him too. He had come from the coast to conquer it. Now it was returning him back to the coast! He knew this. "Onward, onward," he ordered. And: "The sea! The sea!"

XI

THERE IT WAS, THE SEA THAT HE HAD SO CRAVED, THE eternal sea. He sat in a cramped room on the ground floor of a little house on the Île d'Aix. The bed, table, and wardrobe were all black, like ebony coffins. The Emperor woke several times during the night. The sea did not let him sleep. Long gone were the days when he was able to sleep in happy unison with the song of the sea. He had been a young man and it was his native sea, the sea that surrounded Corsica. Even when it was rebellious, its frothy waves betrayed a kind of tender joy amid the anger, and its crests of spray were not storming the shore but caressing it with stormy passion. That was what he hoped to hear now when, unable to sleep, he opened the window and listened to the regular, excessively violent crashing of the waves against the beach. Oh, how amicable it had been, his native Corsican sea! But this was no French sea; its waves seemed to speak English, the language of the enemy, the eternal enemy. From his window, he could see lights a few miles out to sea. The English ship *Bellerophon* was waiting. Its captain's name was Maitland. These names, thought the Emperor, will become immortal through me, an honor they don't merit! *Bellerophon* and Maitland! Hundreds of years from now people will still talk of them. By then the ship will have sunk or its parts been salvaged to build another; the captain will be lying on the ocean floor or in an English graveyard. I myself will be dead, although probably lying in a more solid coffin! But even that too will one day be gnawed at by worms. It will be a coffin like this black ebony dresser, like this black bed on which I'm about to lie and which already looks like a catafalque. But their names will be remembered—Maitland and *Bellerophon*, *Bellerophon* and Maitland.

The Emperor's brother Joseph came to see him. The Emperor had been awaiting him for some time. When he entered, Napoleon thought: You should have come sooner. But he said, "Good that you're here." They embraced briefly and coldly.

"Well?" asked his brother. It was as if he were there to demand payment.

"I know what's on your mind," said the Emperor. "You're wondering whether I've decided to escape from the English. No! I've decided to surrender to the English!"

"Have you thought this all out?"

"No. I haven't. I stopped pondering once I realized that my poor brain refuses to think. I surrender to my heart. I know, I know, this makes me seem ungrateful. I know it. A few noble friends have concrete plans to whisk me away and maybe they would be successful. But I won't go through with it, do you hear? I refuse! Sometimes when I can't sleep—and I don't usually sleep very well—I see corpses, corpses; all the corpses that lie behind me. If they were stacked upon each other, they would create a mountain, my brother; if they were spread out, it would be a sea of bodies. I cannot! How many cannon have been fired on my behalf? Can you count the shots, or even the guns? Going forward I will not have even a single shot fired on my account. Do you understand?"

"You're in grave danger," said his brother. "They could kill you."

"Then it will be one more life lost," replied the Emperor. "I have already lost so many!"

He lay upon the high black bed, next to which was a small ebony table with a three-armed candlestick, and closed his eyes, the flickering candles casting eerie, wavering swaths of light over his face. It gave his brother the impression that the Emperor was dead and lying on his bier.

My brother should go off someplace alone, thought the Emperor, with the money he has acquired and saved. What do they want with me?

"Leave me alone, all of you!" he said. "Don't worry about me, my destiny will be fulfilled. Go away, to the New World, start a new life!" Once again, the Emperor felt that vague suspicion that had troubled him previously—that they all wanted to save him and they did love him, but they also wanted to tie their names to his misfortune just as they had formerly clung to him when he was successful.

"Leave me be!" he repeated. "I share the fate of Themistocles. He too was alone. I go to the enemy. I've written the English Prince Regent. I'm placing myself in his hands."

"I must warn you once more," said his brother. "They will take you prisoner. They will keep you caged like a vicious animal. I have confidential reports to this effect. Captain Maitland has secret orders from the admiral to get you on that ship by any means necessary, with subterfuge or force."

"He will not need to employ either one. Tomorrow or the day after I will go to him freely."

"Then let us say farewell," said his brother in a cold, practically hostile voice and rose. The Emperor sprang up. He opened his arms. They exchanged two kisses, one upon the cheek and one upon the forehead.

"We shall see each other again," said the Emperor. He waited. He hoped that his brother might still say: "Take me with you! I shan't leave you!"

But all his brother said was: "You'll be back. We'll work toward it and fight for it."

"Poor fighters," murmured the Emperor. And then: "Farewell!" he added in a loud firm voice. He turned to the window and listened to the roaring measured crash of the waves to which he would surrender himself the next day or the day after; to an enemy ship and to enemy waves.

XII

HE WENT TO BED IN HIS CLOTHES. IT WAS STILL EARLY. The summer sun, large and hot, sank slowly into the sea, casting a warm red reflection on the windows that was mirrored in the glossy black furniture. The white cushions on which the Emperor was resting were tinged with a kind of golden blood. The reddish shimmer fell upon the Emperor's sleeping countenance for a long time and transformed it into a bronze face. A few steps away from the bed, stiffly perched upon one of the stiff-backed chairs, sat the Emperor's servant. The Emperor wished to be awakened punctually at midnight.

The red reflection faded, replaced by a silver-gray glow. A lighthouse blinked in the distance and sent a fleeting intermittent glimmer through the windows. The only sounds were the quiet breathing of the sleeping Emperor and the roar of the eternally wakeful sea. The servant did not move. It grew dark but he left the candles unlit. Every so often he glanced at the little clock on the mantelpiece. The time passed slowly; the hours did not fly by as usual, even though the clock was ticking with its normal, everyday, diligent regularity. He could also hear a bell tolling from the church tower. But between one peal and the next lay eternities filled with stillness, deep black eternities.

The servant sat there stiffly. He feared he would fall asleep, so finally he rose cautiously and tiptoed across the room. Even as softly as he tread, the Emperor woke immediately, sat up and asked:

"How late is it?"

"Not yet midnight, your Majesty," replied the servant.

"Will everything be ready?" asked the Emperor.

"By eleven o'clock everything will be loaded, your Majesty."

"That's good," said the Emperor. He lay down again, eyes open.

The door seemed to suddenly open. He wanted to call out but was unable to speak. He well knew that he was lying there half-asleep and powerless, but at the same time he pictured himself fully dressed walking across the great red room in the Tuileries. The door closed again but it was no longer the door of the shabby little room where he lay sprawled and helpless, but the great gilt-decorated double door in the Tuileries. Into the room came an old man wearing a long red soutane that failed completely to cover his polished buckled shoes. He walked hesitatingly and bowed numerous times. The Emperor got up from the bed, suddenly wide awake and young again, booted and spurred. As he crossed the room to greet the old man, his spurs clinked loudly, too loudly, although the thick carpet should have dulled the sound, and his sword smacked against the hard lacquer of his boot with an unseemly noise.

"Have a seat, Holy Father," he said and pointed to a wide red plush armchair and was surprised to find himself speaking so informally to the old man.

The old man sat down and carefully arranged the pleats of his cassock over his knees. Out of modesty he tried to hide his shoes. He folded his hands in his lap, and the Emperor saw that they were the thin pale hands of an ancient man with a thousand intertwining little blue veins.

"Your Majesty," said the old man, his bluish lips quivering, "why have you sent for me?"

The Emperor remained at his side and replied: "Because I am the Emperor Napoleon! I need the crown and the blessing of Heaven. It is beneath me to make a pilgrimage to Rome. I have conquered Heaven itself. I have brought Heaven down to earth. I should not have to make a pilgrimage to Rome! What is Rome compared with Heaven? The stars are my friends! What is the See of Rome compared with the stars? I want the Imperial Crown. I want to be anointed. The stars themselves have blessed me. The divine stars. I have sent for you, Holy Father, so that mankind will believe in me!"

"You are only an emperor," said the old man. "You know nothing about the stars! You have displayed violence toward me. You are violent with everyone! And they obey you, but obedience of men of violence is different from mine. For I am not a violent man! I am the only man of peace who obeys you—and that will be your undoing. Thus far you have conquered only men of violence. I alone, I have no weapons or soldiers, and I obey you because I am powerless. Nothing is as dangerous to the powerful as the obedience of the powerless. The weak defeat the mighty!"

"I will," proclaimed the Emperor, "make the Church of Christ great and mighty!"

"The greatness and might of the church cannot be guaranteed by the Emperor Napoleon," replied the old man. "The church has no use for violent emperors. You sent for me, not the other way around! The church is eternal, emperors are ephemeral."

"I am eternal!" cried the Emperor.

"You are transitory," said the old man, "like a comet. You shine too brilliantly! Your light consumes itself as it shines! You were born from an earthly mother's womb!"

Then the old man appeared to morph into his mother. The Emperor fell to his knees and buried his head in her lap. "Nabulio!" she said to him. She wore the flowing red vestments of the Holy Father, and she murmured: "I forgive you everything! I forgive you everything! Nabulio, most beloved of my children!"

He rose, for it was striking midnight from the towers of the sleeping city.

The tower struck midnight with deep, reverberating tones. They were answered by the delicate silver bell of the little mantelpiece clock. "Light!" the Emperor ordered. He rose quickly. He stood before the mirror, fixed his hair and called: "My uniform! My sword! My hat!"

The servant dressed him. The Emperor stood there before the mirror, staring intently at his face, lifting his feet and legs out of habit, almost involuntarily and watching as he was transformed. The reflection of his white breeches, which had been freshly chalked, was quite dazzling, and his boots gleamed, themselves black mirrors. His sash shimmered. The handle of his sword glistened. "Is this coat really blue?" he asked. He had always had difficulty in distinguishing one color from another and at that moment he was not actually talking of the coat or its color but of the fact that he was often incapable of distinguishing red from green. One day in a meadow, and he could no longer remember exactly when or where, he had seen blood flowing from a dead man's wound on to the green grass, and it had looked like the blood had assumed the color of the grass. It startled him. He had long since forgotten this trivial incident, which only now came back to him as he was putting on the coat.

"Blue?" he asked.

"Your Majesty's coat is green," the servant said.

The Emperor looked closely in the mirror. For a few seconds, as he studied himself, he had the feeling he was not actually alive, that everything was make believe, now and always. Often had he watched his friend, the actor Talma, looking in the mirror before one of his great scenes. The real Emperor Napoleon was hidden deep within the most remote corner of his heart. The real Emperor never saw the light of day. Everything in the world was no more than a game. It was meaningless theatre and he himself, the Emperor Napoleon, was now performing the role of the Emperor Napoleon giving himself up to enemy hands. That was why he had rejected his civilian clothes and official uniform: so he could surrender to the enemy looking just like the hundreds of thousands of portraits by which he was known throughout the entire world. "Between green and blue," said the Emperor, as if speaking to his reflection, "I have never been able to make a precise distinction." The servant shuddered. He had never heard the Emperor speak in such a manner. "And once," continued the Emperor, "I even believed that human blood was not actually red."

"Yes, your Majesty," said the servant, trembling with embarrassment.

There were loud voices outside, under the window. The baggage of the Emperor and his retinue was being loaded down below. He went to the window and stood motionless, as he looked out. "My friend," he said after a long while, finally turning around, "this is my last night in France."

"If that is the case, then it will be my last night too," stammered the servant.

"Come here!" said the Emperor. "Have a good look at it!" The servant went up to him. They stood next to each other at the window for a long time, silent and still.

The sky grew lighter and a silver haze hovered over the sea. The wind picked up and the windows rattled faintly.

"It's time!" said the Emperor. "Let's go!"

They went. The Emperor led the way with a firm stride, head held high, in his dazzling white breeches and bright, shiny boots, his spurs clinking faintly with each step. The island fishermen were already awake, standing quietly in front of their huts, heads bare. The gravel crunched under the steps of the Emperor and his companions. All was still except for the sound of the men's feet, the answer of the gravel, and the occasional shriek of a gull. The boat was already waiting with swelling sails. The Emperor climbed aboard. He didn't look back.

There was a light breeze. Up ahead was the *Bellerophon*.

When the sloop arrived for the Emperor, the sun was emerging from the sea at his right, red and mighty, rising slowly above the clouds. The dense flock of white gulls rose from the jetty and fluttered in squawking, energetic swarms over the boat.

Nothing could be heard save for the shrieking of the seagulls and the faint splash of water upon the hull. Suddenly the sailors cried: "Long live the Emperor!" They tossed their caps into the air and shouted: "Long live the Emperor!" The startled gulls scattered.

This is the last time, thought the Emperor, that I will hear that cry. Until that moment he had still been hoping that he was only acting, as during the night before the mirror; that he was not really the Emperor Napoleon but rather an actor playing him. The sailors, however, who had shouted: "Long live the Emperor!"— they had not been acting. No, this was not a scene! He was the Emperor going to his actual death, and the sailors were truly shouting with full force: "Long live the Emperor!"

As he boarded the *Bellerophon* he felt that tears were coming.

But he had to keep them from being seen. The Emperor Napoleon must not cry. "My field glasses!" he commanded. They were handed to him. Through these glasses he had observed many battlefields, spotted many an enemy, and determined their plans. He brought them quickly to his eyes. His hot tears ran down into the black cavities, instantly clouding the glass, while he pretended to be searching the sea. He turned to the right and the left and all who saw him believed he was scanning the sea or studying the coast. But he could see nothing through the glass, nothing at all—he only felt his hot tears, each of which seemed to him as vast as an ocean. He pressed the glasses tightly against his eye sockets and lowered his head so that his hat shaded his face. He strained mightily to hold back tears. He lowered the glasses. Now he could see the coast of France, which appeared bold and serene in outline, so pleasant and delightful. "Back," he said very softly—and realized that he could no longer give orders to anyone. The sun's silver gleam played upon the millions of tiny ripples on the calm surface of the sea. The ocean was wide, wider than all his battlefields. It was even wider than the battlefield at Waterloo. He now envisioned all his battlefields stretching out, one next to another, over the endless mirror of the sea—and many dead also, with blood flowing from their open wounds. The sea was green, like a meadow, a meadow strewn with dead, including a little drummer in the foreground, a boy whose face was covered with a red handkerchief, the same one the Emperor had once given out to all soldiers in his army and on which all his battlefields were noted.

The ship's captain approached. When he was three steps away from the Emperor, he stopped and saluted.

"I place myself under the protection of your Prince and your laws," said Napoleon. But as he spoke these words he was thinking of other words:

"I surrender as your prisoner!"

XIII

THE SAILORS PRESENTED THEIR WEAPONS. OH! THEIR manner was so different from that of the French soldiers, the men of France! They were English soldiers, and they had defeated the Emperor, but they did not know their exercises! And there suddenly stirred within the Emperor the old, basic, childlike soldier's desire to show these men how to present a weapon. At that moment he forgot that he was a great, a great and defeated, the greatest of all defeated Emperors; he became a petty drill sergeant instructing the men in French exercises. Taking a gun from one of the sailors in the perfectly aligned row, he showed him how one presented weapons in the French Army. "Like so, my son!" he said. "This is how we present arms!" As he demonstrated the simple motion, he was thinking of one, of any, of the nameless soldiers of his great army, and he could hear the immortal tune of the "Marseillaise," which his military bands used to play as arms were presented.

He gave the sailor's weapon back and let the captain lead him to the cabin that they had prepared for him. As he entered, he said: "Leave me be!" in such a loud and severe voice that the astonished captain and his retinue froze up for a moment before heading back to the door. The Emperor remained alone and studied his cabin. It was spacious with two round windows, a room with two eyes, the two eyes of a sentry. Through these eyes, the Emperor thought, I shall be watched for days, for weeks, by the sea, by the enemy sea. It has forever been my enemy! What an enemy! It will not bury me or consume me! It will transport me to a shore even more hostile than itself!

At that moment the little clock on the table began to strike eight o'clock, and hardly had its eight melancholy tones faded when from within came the tune of the "Marseillaise," a very thin, very faint, practically trembling version of the "Marseillaise." It was as if the little clock were whispering the mightiest and manliest of all the world's melodies. Thin and faltering, it came from deep within the instrument, as if the melody were mourning itself, as if it were coming from the hereafter, a dead "Marseillaise" that kept on playing. Nonetheless, as he listened, the Emperor could hear a mighty chorus of hundreds of thousands of throats mixed with cries of "Long live the Emperor!"—the mighty cry of hundreds of thousands of living hearts, the song of the French, the song of battle, and the song of freedom. Whoever sang it alone became a comrade to millions, and whoever sang it with others became like them, a brother to millions. It was the song of the humble and the proud. It was the song of life and death. The people of France, the Emperor's people, sang it on their way to his battles, during his battles, and while returning home from his battles. Even defeats were transformed into victories by the song. It also conquered the dead and invigorated the living. It was the song of the Emperor, as the violet was his flower and the bee was his creature.

When he heard the thin, timid tones coming from the clock, he was startled at first and froze in place. Finally he brought his hands to his face and wanted to weep, but the tears would not come. Long after the music box had stopped playing, he remained in the middle of the cabin, watched by the two round dead window-eyes. With a choked-up voice, he called to his servant, whom he knew was just outside the door. "Marchand," he cried, "Stop the clock! I cannot listen to the 'Marseillaise' any longer."

"Your Majesty," said the servant, "I don't hear the Marseillaise.'"

"But I hear it," said the Emperor in a low voice, "I hear it. Be still, Marchand! Listen! Then you will hear it!"

And although the clock has long been silent and although nothing could be heard save the gentle splashing of the waves against the sides of the *Bellerophon*, Marchand pretended to listen and after a while, he said:

"Yes, sir, Your Majesty, that's the "Marseillaise.'"

And he went to the little clock, fiddled with it a little and then reported:

"Your Majesty, it plays no more!"

At that moment a seagull flapped against the window. "Open!" the Emperor ordered.

The servant opened one of the round windows. The Emperor stood before it, looking out. He saw only a narrow silver strip of the French coast.

BOOK FOUR

The End of Little Angelina

I

MANY PEOPLE VISITED JAN WOKURKA DURING THOSE days. His old comrades, the Polish Legionnaires, kept bringing new men with them, homeless friends, Imperial soldiers who were left even more helpless by the Emperor's great new misfortune. Before, they had only been unhappy; now they were completely lost. The ground quaked beneath their feet and they could not understand why, for it was their native ground. It was Paris, the capital of their country! Yet their native Earth was collapsing under the feet of its own sons. The soldiers of the enemy armies were marching fully armed through the streets of Paris. One could hear the enemy's marches played and trumpeted by the enemy's military bands. All the armies of Europe, or so it seemed to the old Imperial soldiers, had arranged to meet in Paris. They drilled every morning. After that they marched, well fed and flawlessly uniformed, through the streets of the city. Meanwhile, the soldiers of the Imperial Army crawled along the edge of the pavement, ragged and starving. They were like masterless dogs. The Emperor was far away! He was sailing around somewhere upon unknown seas toward an unknown but certainly horrible fate. A new leader, a former leader, sat upon the throne of France—a fat, jovial king. They did not hate him, but the enemy had arrived with him, the well-fed troops with their hostile march music. The Imperial soldiers gossiped about the fact that the King's carriage, in which he had returned to his capital, had been preceded by English cannon, Prussian cavalry, and Austrian hussars. The rest of the people had the very same thought. Since the enemy had brought the King, the King was also an enemy. Was he even the ruler of France at all, this man through whose capital the foreign soldiers were marching? Did France still have a leader? Was it not already the prey of the whole world?

Once upon a time, the whole world had been the great Emperor's prey. Every soldier of the Imperial Army had been at home in each country of the whole great, colorful world. Now they were all strangers and vagrants, shuffling through the streets of their own capital. And that was why they gathered, as evening fell and dusk made them seem even more homeless, in the apartments of old friends. For they were hungry, and they wished longingly for a tobacco pipe and a glass of wine. And people such as the cobbler Wokurka were hospitable.

They were clear, cloudless summer days. The old soldiers felt that the summer was mocking them; that the sky was demonstrating quite clearly that it did not care about the misfortunes of France or her Emperor. In a steady serene blue it arched over the sorrowful earth. Distant and aloof, the sun cast its rays upon the enemy's hated banners. Summer itself was celebrating the victory of the enemy.

II

ONE HOT DAY THE COBBLER WENT TO THE PALACE TO look for Angelina. He had already been there a few times before. He loved her with all the might of his simple soul. He worried about her these days. What if she said something rash and put herself in danger? She could potentially get herself killed. She had not sought him out yet, even though he had told her he would be waiting for her if there were trouble. She was certainly in distress by now, and yet she had not come. So he set out on his way to win her back.

He stepped out blithely into the scorching sun. The sweat ran down his face, made his bushy mustache tacky, soaked his shirt, and made the poor stump of his leg, packed in leather padding, sting with the ferocity of an open wound. It was just after noon when he reached the Elysée. He asked to speak to Véronique Casimir. One of the soldiers on duty went to find her but it took a long time for her to come. The burning sun was unrelenting but Wokurka was not allowed even to wait in the narrow strip of shade just past the gate. Véronique finally arrived, embraced him emotionally, with sadness, but also with a somewhat duplicitous warmth. She actually needed him now; what a miracle that he had come! She and Angelina had a handcart and were just packing their things. All the palace servants had to take an oath to the returned King, and whoever refused was released. Naturally, she and Angelina were among those leaving. How good it was to have a man's help, she said—and then looked at Wokurka's wooden leg. He saw her staring, knocked on the wood with the knuckle of his forefinger, and said: "It's good and strong, Mademoiselle Casimir. Better than my old one!"

She left. He had to wait half the afternoon, but despite the heat he was not one bit tired. He hobbled back and forth, up and down, back and forth, eventually awakening the suspicion of the secret police on patrol around the palace. He was well aware of them but was not afraid. He had already prepared an answer in case one of them questioned him. He had worked hard on his response, and he thought to say something like: "Ask your Minister Fouché, what he's doing with the King!" He thought it was a perfect reply; ambiguous yet meaningful, witty yet non-contradictory.

Finally, as the shadows were getting longer and the guard was being changed, Véronique Casimir and Angelina arrived. They were pushing a small two-wheeled cart before them. Piled upon it and tied down with ropes were their belongings. Each of the women was holding one of the cart handles. They were held up at the gate by the guard and then by a policeman in civilian clothes. Véronique talked her way past them, waving her papers. They would be back in an hour, she said.

Wokurka had not seen Angelina for quite a while. Yet as he looked at her now, it hardly seemed a day had passed since they parted. Her face was so familiar and endearing to his enamored eyes. The Emperor had come and then gone, the King had returned, thousands of soldiers had fallen, Angelina's son was also dead—but the cobbler Wokurka felt that it was just yesterday, or the day before, that Angelina had left him. Great and important events had transpired during their separation, but those months were obliterated in one moment. He offered Angelina his hand, but said nothing. Then he took both handles of the cart in his callused fists and asked, with an anxious heart: "So, where to?"

"To Pocci's, naturally," said Véronique.

He limped along between the two women, rolling the heavy cart along like a toy. He was cheerful and spoke loudly so as to be heard over the stamping of his crutch and the rumbling of the cart on the bumpy stones. What did he, Jan Wokurka, care that afternoon about all the miseries of Paris, France, of the world? For all I care one hundred great Emperors could leave and one hundred fat old Kings come back, he thought, what did it matter? And he expressed his thoughts: "You see, Angelina, I told you so! Why should we care about the fate of the great ones? If only we had gone to my village in Poland back then! By now you would be quite at home and would have forgotten everything!"

He was not exactly certain what it was that Angelina was supposed to have forgotten, but he became emotional as he spoke those two words "forgotten everything" and was filled with an overwhelming feeling of compassion for Angelina. "One should not," he went on, "give one's heart to the great and mighty when one is as small and insignificant as we are. I've been saying this for a long time and lately I've been repeating it to my unfortunate friends. You see, Angelina! You see, Mademoiselle Casimir! What did it get me? I hung my heart on a great ideal and a great Emperor. I wanted to free my fatherland. Yet here I am, still a shoemaker, I've lost a leg, my country has not been liberated, and the Emperor is defeated! Nobody should ever tell me again to concern myself over the great advance of the world! The little things, the little things are what I love. I care about you alone, Angelina! Tell me now, after all this, are you coming? With me?"

"I thank you," she said simply. "We shall speak of this later." She could not possibly have explained what was running through her mind, for she lacked not only the courage to voice her thoughts but also the ability to choose the right words and express herself properly. In her opinion what Wokurka said was not false, but the great ideal for which she had sacrificed her heart happened also to be her own personal little ideal, and it was all the same whether God intended one to fall in love with a great Emperor or with some ordinary fellow. Ideals were both great and small at the same time, she believed. But could she explain it? And even if she could, would anyone understand? For all the confusion, agony, and shame that she had experienced since arriving in this city, she knew that nothing was more powerful than her precipitous love, which encompassed everything else—longing and homesickness, pride and shame, desire and sorrow, life and death. Now that the Emperor was lost forever—oh, how well she knew this!—even though she was far removed from him, in the distant reaches of the lengthy shadow he cast, she felt certain that she drew life from him alone; from his Imperial existence alone. Her son was dead and the Emperor was a prisoner. How could she feel anything except numb? Wokurka was good to her. But was kindness alone great and strong enough to revive a heart, a dead little heart? If only I were a man! she thought. She accidentally said it aloud: "If only I were a man!"

"What would you have done?" Wokurka asked.

"I would not have let him go. I would have gone with him!"

"The great events of the world," said Wokurka, "do not depend on men, either. One would have to be just as great a man as he to affect anything. When one is a nobody, it's all the same, man or woman!"

It was already full in Wokurka's workshop, as it was every day at that time, when they arrived. He typically left his door open so that his friends could come and go as they pleased. Some of them were standing outside talking to the neighbors. Dusk was falling, the fearsome dusk of the lonely and unfortunate. They helped to bring the luggage up to the midwife Pocci's room. How did things look in the palace, and had she seen the King? they asked Véronique Casimir. One of them asked the women if they knew where the Emperor was being taken. Another interrupted and said he knew for certain—to London, where they would behead him. Angelina trembled. It was as if her own death sentence had just been pronounced.

"Who says so? Who says so?" she cried through the chaos of voices.

"It can't be helped," one man said. "The great ones have made their decision."

The little room was jammed. They stood crowded together or crouched on crates they had brought, or on chairs, stools, and Wokurka's bed, as thick gray clouds of smoke wafted from their pipes; it looked as if there were even more guests than there actually were, all with the same faces. One of them—an old Polish legionnaire, with the Legion of Honor upon his tattered, heavily stained uniform, a gray black beard, and bright red cheeks—took a bottle from his coat pocket, raised it, took a big gulp and said: "*Ah!*" so loudly and so severely that it could not be mistaken for satisfaction but sounded like resentment and annoyance; and it was true that resentment and ill humor has long been smoldering within his heart and the drink was stoking the flames. He took another swig, for he felt he would very soon need to say something extraordinary. Quite simply his honor demanded it. He was good-hearted, excitable, and boisterous. Wokurka knew him well. Together they had marched, together they had fought, together they had drunk and eaten— even sharing the same plate and the same pipe. Although amid the thick smoke all the faces were cloudy and distorted, Wokurka could recognize in the eyes of his friend—Jan Zyzurak was his name and he had once been a blacksmith—that old flickering flame that meant this Zyzurak was in a state of extreme agitation. Wokurka was afraid of what Zyzurak would do; there were women present. The midwife Pocci, Angelina, and Véronique Casimir sat silently on the bed where a spot had been cleared for them. They were scared, uncertain what would happen next. The men and the spirits they were consuming—each of them carried a flask in his threadbare pocket—their desperate faces and their grim talk instilled a great fear in the women. Yet they did not dare get up.

As for Zyzurak, his second long gulp made him see the guests not double but tenfold. He believed himself to be standing outside before a vast crowd of people, and spirits came over him, the spirit of his ill-fated Polish fatherland, and also the spirit of the Emperor. Both of these spirits commanded him to speak and he felt he had numerous and important things to say. He raised both hands imploringly and in a loud voice requested silence and light ("for it is already evening," he said, "and I need to see you when I speak to you"). Someone lit the three candles in the lantern. The light was immediately lost within the grayish-blue smoke, not bright enough for the blacksmith to see his friends. Nevertheless, he believed he could see his audience of thousands perfectly. He was standing under open sky on a warm summer's night, and eight lanterns were shining as brightly as eight moons. "People of Paris!" he began. "Yes, people of France! I have received a secret message that right now the Emperor Napoleon is being dragged to England, to the Prince Regent's fortress in

London. They are already sharpening the hatchet that will be-head him. Can you hear the blade being honed? Are we girls or men? The Emperor did not leave the country willingly, as the newspapers would have us believe. Those whom he thought were his closest friends betrayed him and forced him onto a ship. A general—you all know who, and I would be ashamed to speak his name—betrayed his plans to the enemy three hours before the battle. Treachery! Betrayal! Everywhere treachery!" He paused and stretched out his hand.

"Treachery! Treachery!" cried the others. "He's right! He's right!"

The blacksmith continued on in this vein for some time, but the others were no longer listening. They were only a small group of twelve men, but each of them had drunk too much and eaten too little. They were all seeing double and triple, and Zyzurak's salutation still rang in their ears—"People of Paris!"—and every one of them felt the words were addressed to him specifically. They did not even notice when eventually their comrade stopped speaking. He had broken off in the midst of his speech. One of them, a sergeant of the Thirteenth Chasseurs, was convinced that the only thing left to do was raise a cheer, the old cheer that he had so often voiced. "Long live the Emperor!" All answered with the same cry. They removed their pipes from their mouths and set their bottles upon their lips once again. Suddenly someone began to sing that old tune whose melody had been ever present as they were transformed into men and soldiers. They sang, hoarsely and with drunken hearts, the "Marseillaise," the song of the French people, the song of the Emperor and his battles. The lantern rocked violently over Zyzurak's head and the windows rattled. Those who were seated stood up and sang. They kept the beat by tapping their feet. Although they remained in their seats they all felt they were marching along the great roads of the world, roads along which the Emperor had once led them. Only when the song was over did they look upon each other helplessly and foolishly. The magic had vanished. Gone were the broad highways of their army days. They realized they were still in Wokurka's room.

It was quiet for some time. The men all stood there, with numb arms, while the women looked on, faces hot, red, and embarrassed. "Let's go!" cried someone amid the silence. "Let's go!" others repeated. "Where to?" asked Wokurka.

"Where? Don't listen to him!" cried the chasseur. "I'll lead you! What is life to us? Who among you is afraid to lose it?"

They were inspired by the sound of their own voices, weak from the hunger raging within them for days, intoxicated by the liquor that had alone fueled them, light-headed from the smoke, and crushed by their misfortune. They saw their potential actions not as futile but easy and natural; not as foolish but useful. Yet still they hesitated, indecisive and tentative. Suddenly Angelina shouted, as if someone else were speaking through her, some unknown being crying out of her—"Let's go!" She yelled it with such a piercing voice she shocked herself, and she actually looked around trying to determine from whom the cry had actually issued. She stepped forward, toward the door, and the astonished men made way almost as if her sharp cry had forged ahead and cleared a path for her. She was bareheaded, her red hair flamed and her poor little freckled face was hard, spiteful, grief-stricken, and suddenly quite old. She had no idea what was motivating her but after standing at the door briefly she went out and the men followed her. Into the street and under the silvery blue evening sky this ragtag little group marched, silent at first except for the sound of Wokurka's wooden leg pounding against the stones. Suddenly, the chasseur began to sing the "Marseillaise." The rest of them sang along. They filled the lane with their hoarse singing. Windows flew open. People looked out. Some waved. Others cried: "Long live the Emperor!" They were not far from the royal palace, and this realization awoke within them a fervent but senseless desire to head there. They were a small party, a ridiculously tiny party! But as they howled so loudly, cheers flying at them from numerous windows, it seemed to them they numbered in the hundreds, in the thousands, the entire population of France. A moment later, however, they heard from the bank of the Seine, the direction in which they were heading, a hostile song and an empowering cry from a thousand actual throats, a cry of: "Long live the King!"

So the ragged little band headed straight into the midst of a tremendous parade of royalists. At this point they stopped for a moment, but then turned around and scattered. Only Wokurka, who was at the tail end, tried to reach Angelina. He saw as she too hesitated at first. But then she ran forward straight into the flank of the crowd. Her red hair looked to be ablaze, truly on fire. She had raised her arms, her dress fluttered, and she seemed to be flying, her head crowned by a flaming torch. With a shrill scream, which to Wokurka sounded inhuman, savagely animal, and yet at the same time boomed with heavenly authority, she launched herself straight into the dense, dark throng. "Long live the Emperor!" she screeched. And once more: "Long live the Emperor!" Wokurka watched as they seized her. Part of the surging crowd paused for a second—no longer than that. Then Angelina was whirling about in the air above their heads. Her dark chest puffed out and hands were raised to catch. Once more she was tossed up high but this time she was not caught. She fell to the ground somewhere and the crowd marched endlessly onward.

In the midst of this royalist crowd someone was holding up an absurd effigy high above their heads, a doll patched together out of rags, out of colorful tattered comical rags. It represented the Emperor Napoleon, the Emperor in the uniform in which the people had known and honored him, the Emperor in his gray cloak and with the little black hat upon his head.

Upon the breast of this doll, hanging from a piece of coarse string, was a heavy white cardboard upon which was written in large black lettering, easily legible from a distance, the first verses of the "Marseillaise," the song of France—"*Allons enfants de la patrie!*" The poor head of the Emperor, fashioned from miserable scraps, was attached to a piece of flexible material and drooped pitifully from one side to the other, or flopped backward and forward; he was like an already decapitated Emperor whose head still hung by a thread. The effigy of the Emperor Napoleon waved and swayed among countless royal banners, among the white banners of the Bourbons. The doll itself was a mockery, but the presence of the many banners increased the derision hundredfold.

When the royalists saw that little Angelina, even as she was being tossed into the air like a ball, was still attempting to sing the "Marseillaise" with a closing throat and a heart that sensed imminent death, one of them thought it amusing to throw the effigy of the Emperor Napoleon along after her. So it was that when Angelina, after being spun about in mid-air, finally fell upon the rocky bank of the Seine, the miserable doll landed just beside her smashed body. She could not tell that it was a doll, a mockery of the Emperor, just an effigy of pathetic scraps. She could not distinguish fake from genuine and her eyes perceived the real Emperor next to her, lying close to her battered body. And she could read, very clearly, the opening words of the "Marseillaise," "*Allons enfants de la patrie!*" As she read the first line of the great anthem, she began to sing the song that she could never quite get enough of, despite having heard it so frequently. With the song on her lips she fell asleep beside the figure of the Emperor, an Emperor of rags and scraps. Before her fading eyes lay the first verse of the "Marseillaise" and Napoleon's little black hat, the comically fashioned, tattered, Imperial hat.

After the procession finally passed, which took an eternity, Wokurka hobbled over. He found Angelina lying on the embankment. Her blood reddened the pebbles. It trickled slowly and steadily from her mouth.

He sat at her side the whole night. But he dared not look at her face. Instead, he tirelessly stroked her hair, which still offered a gentle rustle. The Seine gurgled busily past him as he sat there stunned, staring vacantly at the water rushing by. It was a mirror to the heavens. It carried the sky along with it and all the silvery stars too.

Translator's Afterword

Joseph Roth's (1894–1939) prodigious output included numerous novels, novellas, short stories, and newspaper articles in the space of only sixteen years (between 1923 and 1939). While much of his fascinating œuvre has been made available to the English-speaking world in recent times, *The Hundred Days* has remained out of print in English for seventy years. With the publication of *The Hundred Days*, all of Roth's completed novels are now available in English.

Born Moses Joseph Roth of Jewish parentage in the town of Brody, Galicia (present-day Ukraine), about fifty-four miles north-east of present-day Lviv (then called Lemberg), Roth was a product of the Austro-Hungarian Empire. After service in the Austrian Army during the First World War he moved to Berlin in 1920. After Hitler came to power in early 1933, Roth fled Germany permanently, spending the rest of his life living in hotels in France and other parts of Western Europe.

The setting for the majority of Roth's novels is Eastern Europe from the turn of the twentieth century to the 1920s, and so *The Hundred Days* (*Die Hundert Tage*, 1935) is a departure from the usual Roth formula, in both its time period and setting. Written immediately after *The Antichrist* (*Der Antichrist*, 1934, Roth's journalistic and autobiographical novel about the dangers of modern civilization in the early 1930s), *The Hundred Days* takes place in a much earlier era (1815) and much further west (France) than the rest of his works. The novel is divided into four books, two told from Napoleon's perspective and two from the vantage point of the diminutive, freckled Imperial laundress Angelina Pietri, who happens to be utterly smitten with the Emperor.

So why did this Austrian writer, who was clearly fascinated by the dynamics surrounding the events leading up to and immediately following the First World War—including the collapse of the Austrian Empire, the rise of communism, the Weimar Republic, and Nazism—choose to write about Napoleon? In a letter to his French translator, Blanche Gidon (whose translation of this book was published as *Le Roman des Cent-Jours* in 1937 by Éditions Bernard Grasset in Paris), Roth explained the motivation behind writing the novel. He told her, with some degree of excitement, that he wished to chronicle the transformation of Napoleon from a god to man over the course of the hundred-day period of his return to power from exile on Elba in the spring of 1815. "I would like to make a humble man out of a grand one," he wrote in November 1934. He was interested in the idea of the great Napoleon as someone who has, for the first time in his life, become truly small: "This is what attracts me."

Besides the attraction of the topic itself, Roth was likely happy for the chance to set one of his novels in Paris. His love affair with the city began in 1925, when he was assigned to Paris as a foreign correspondent for the *Frankfurter Zeitung*. *Flight Without End* (1927) is partly set in Paris, and the city also plays a role in the book that followed *The Hundred Days, Confession of a Murderer*. The essays Roth wrote while in France have been published as *Report from a Parisian Paradise*. Roth said in a mid-1930s interview: "The only thing I love after my 'lost Vienna' is Paris. I love my Latin Quarter, my Hotel Foyot ..."

At the time of its first English-language publication, the critics' reception of *The Hundred Days* was lukewarm. The *Daily Independent* called Roth's Napoleon "much too benevolent," but in the end proclaimed the book still "a fine piece of work." The *New Statesman and Nation* cited "long passages of literary dithyramb" and opined that *The Hundred Days* was a "prose-poem dressed as a novel." The *Sunday Times* said it lacked realism, while the *Observer* called Roth's attempt at dealing with the subject matter "an impossible task" and "an inevitable failure." On the other hand, the *Gloucester Journal* called it "enlightening" and "moving." Across the Atlantic, while acknowledging Roth's fine abilities as a writer, the *New York Times* stated that the story lacked reality, charm, passion, and warmth. Evidence indicates that Roth himself may have been somewhat disappointed in the way his book turned out. In any case, its initial reception may in part have been the reason why *The Hundred Days* remained unavailable in English for so long.

But, like *The Antichrist*, the other Roth work that had until recently remained out of print in English and had had mixed reviews at the time of its debut, *The Hundred Days* comes across differently today than it would have in the mid-1930s, that turbulent time when Hitler rose to power and readers may not have been very receptive to a pathos-filled story about a dictator's fall.

As is usual in his work, Roth expertly employs atmospheric details to convey mood. The somber and stultifying library where the Emperor says farewell to his mother; the Imperial room where Angelina waits, with its heavy green curtain; the cramped flat of the cobbler Jan Wokurka; the many shimmering dawns and starlit evenings—these are practically characters in themselves, invested with personality and emotional weight. Roth remarked that he was often "haunted by a place, by an atmosphere."

Roth expends great effort trying to convince the reader of Napoleon's constantly fluctuating mental state over the course of his final days in power. In the two sections of *The Hundred Days* told from the Emperor's perspective, Napoleon at turns loves and despises the French people, and throughout the book has similar and frequent changes of attitude toward his family, his ministers, power, war, God and the Church, and life in general. "I no longer believe in all those things in which I used to have faith—in force, might, and success," he tells his brother when he is ready to abdicate. Yet, once he discovers that the enemy has arrived at Paris he dictates a letter to his adjutant, to be dispatched at once: "You may now look upon your Emperor as your General and call upon my services as someone inspired solely by a desire to be useful to his country." Moments later, however, the Emperor is filled with unhappiness and regret at the letter he has just dispatched.

Both Napoleon and Angelina struggle to find religion, with limited success. They, like Roth characters in other novels, are prone to believe more generally in fate (in this case represented by the stars in the heavens and the fortune-telling cards of Angelina's aunt) than they are in God and the Church specifically.

The one being worshipped in *The Hundred Days* is not God but Napoleon himself. The Emperor is buffeted by cries of "Long live the Emperor!" throughout the book (in fact, fifty-two times), cries which vary in their veracity and meaning.

Despite the frenzied noise of devotion, it is often the moments of silence that carry the most emotional weight. One of the most poignant scenes in *The Hundred Days* takes place on the battlefield at Waterloo, when the Emperor's soldiers are flying silently past him in retreat, no longer offering any cries of solidarity, passing like the scattering ghosts of the dead soldiers.

Had Roth's novel been told strictly from Napoleon's viewpoint, it would have been a far less interesting book. Remaining inside the Emperor's head for the entire book would perhaps have been overwhelming, and the introduction of Angelina Pietri into the story provides a welcome, rich, and multi-dimensional fullness to the tale. Young Angelina comes to France from her native Corsica and immediately goes to stay with her aunt, who is the First Laundress (and occasional fortune-telling card-reader for the Emperor) at the imperial palace. Over the course of several years and a few brief moments with the Emperor, Angelina's devotion to him does not waver: "Her heart commanded her to remain close to his gracious presence, lowly and ignored as she was." She eventually comes to realize that much of her life has been lived within the Emperor's great shadow, and all the major events—including her unpleasant relationship with a colossal sergeant-major, the birth of a son and his eventual death on the Emperor's battlefield—have in one way or another stemmed from Napoleon. It seems the powerful Emperor and the powerless Angelina are both caught up in their own misfortune by relentless fate.

The most sympathetic character in *The Hundred Days* is neither Napoleon nor Angelina, but the kindly and patient one-legged Polish cobbler Anton Wokurka, with whom Angelina takes up residence once the Emperor is exiled in 1814 and her aunt flees the palace. Wokurka (who is referred to as both Jan and Anton in the German version) was originally slated to play a much more central role in the book; among Roth's manuscripts was a typed, seven-page unpublished preface to *The Hundred Days* in which Roth introduces the Anton Wokurka character as a friend of his grandfather's. Roth explains that he met this cobbler, a good twenty years older than Roth's grandfather (himself seventy-three years old), as a young boy. The white-bearded, bald-headed, pipe-smoking Wokurka, a veteran of Napoleon's great campaigns who lost a leg in his service, lived in a room decorated with pictures of the Emperor and his battles and palaces as well as a framed commendation from days of yore. Every year young Roth was sure to spend time with this interesting old man while visiting his grandfather's village. When the Roths' vacation was over, Wokurka would say: "Good-bye. See you in a year, punctually!" On one particular visit Wokurka asks Joseph if he has learned much about Napoleon. Joseph answers that he has and that the storybooks he has read either depict Napoleon as very evil or very noble: "I think they are all lies," he says. Wokurka says that Joseph is right and that if the boy is patient he will recount for the him the true story of Napoleon's one hundred days. "I knew the Emperor ... and if you are curious, I can tell you an instructive story ... but I will need a long time." So Joseph visits Wokurka every morning at 9 a.m. over the course of four days. Thus Wokurka tells Joseph the tale of the Emperor's last days in power, as the boy listens, entranced: "There sat Wokurka, a soldier of the Emperor, and it was as if he was already speaking from the grave. It was as if I myself sat in the crypt in which Wokurka lay buried ..." Years later the sound of Wokurka's voice still rings in Roth's head, and he realizes he should share the Emperor's tale with the world, despite feeling woefully inadequate to recapture the great storytelling of the "splendid" Wokurka.

In 1934 and 1935, as he was writing *The Hundred Days*, Roth was consumed by work, sometimes even writing for twelve or fourteen hours a day. "It [writing] is truly my Waterloo," he explained in February 1935, referring to himself as "old and miserable Joseph Roth." He worried constantly about his precarious finances— when he would be paid and how much he was owed. Although several of his books met with substantial critical and commercial success, he was always in need of money. He complained that the Nazis, after he left in 1933, had confiscated 30,000 marks of his. Whatever level of comfort and success he had achieved during the German years, by 1934 Roth was desperate for money. He described himself in one letter as depressed, buried under "mountains of chagrin," and in another letter said: "I work in a great anguish, a true panic." Sick and full of misery over everything from financial troubles to the decline of civilization, the Roth of *The Hundred Days*—this fascinating book so unlike any of his other novels—was just forty years old, only four years away from his very premature, alcohol-induced death.

* * *

In an interview for a French newspaper, Joseph Roth admitted that while writing his novels he was "always haunted by a musical theme." His writing style was all about rhythm. "For me," he claimed, "a good translation is that which renders the rhythm of my language. For me, a good translation is neither about the anecdotal contents nor the sentimental contents, it is about the rhythm." I have tried my best to preserve the rhythm of Roth's writing, being mindful of how the differences between German and English syntax occasionally make it a challenge to achieve the precise effect toward which Roth was striving. Roth's manuscript featured heavy usage of exclamation marks. I have eliminated some of the most flagrantly unnecessary, but kept the great majority to be true to the spirit of the original, which is quite emphatic by virtue of Napoleon's larger-than-life personality.

I would like to thank Barbara Epler, Peter Owen, Antonia Owen, and Simon Smith for their belief in this project. Thanks also to the Leo Baeck Institute—the Joseph Roth Collection there is invaluable to scholars—and in particular the resources pertaining to *Die Hundert Tage*, the typescript manuscript (AR 1764; series 2, subseries 1, box 1, folder 36) and contemporaneous reviews (AR 1764; series 2, subseries 4, box 2, folder 82).

RICHARD PANCHYK
2014